DATE DUE

Rainbow Range

OTHER FIVE STAR WESTERN TITLES BY ROBERT J. HORTON:

The Hanging X (2003)
Guns of Jeopardy (2005)
Riders of Paradise (2006)
Forgotten Range (2007)
Ryder of the Hills (2008)
Man of the Desert (2009)
Marble Range (2010)
Bullets in the Sun (2011)

Rainbow Range

A Western Story

Robert J. Horton

FIVE STAR

A part of Gale, Cengage Learning

Detroit • New York • San Francisco • New Haven, Conn • Waterville, Maine • London

Five Star Publishing, a part of Gale, Cengage Learning.

Set in 11 pt. Plantin.

LIBRARY OF CONGRESS CATALOGING-IN-PUBLICATION DATA

Horton, Robert J., 1881–1934.
Rainbow range : a western story / by Robert J. Horton. — 1st ed.
p. cm.
ISBN 978-1-4328-2560-7 (hardcover) — ISBN 1-4328-2560-7 (hardcover)
I. Title.
PS3515.O745R35 2012
813′.52—dc23 2011047018

Published in 2012 in conjunction with Golden West Literary Agency.

Printed in Mexico
1 2 3 4 5 6 7 16 15 14 13 12

ADDITIONAL COPYRIGHT INFORMATION

Chapter One

They were looking down the street, five of them, standing on the steps of Riverdale's one hotel. Everyone was looking down the street, for that matter, except those who were running to join the throng down there where the dust was flying in the hot July sun.

Among those on the steps was Polly Arnold, daughter of Pete Arnold, owner of the big Bar A Ranch. She was by far the prettiest of the five girls. Her hazel eyes were aglow with commingled excitement and concern.

"It's Ted Wayne!" she exclaimed to her companions. "I just know it's him! He didn't go home after the Fourth and now he's in another fracas. If it comes to guns. . . ." She bit her lip and ceased speaking while the others sought to allay her fears.

And it was indeed Ted Wayne. In the center of a ring of spectators he stood, tall and capable, a young man of magnificent build, wavy chestnut hair, cool gray eyes, clear-cut features—son of Ed Wayne, owner of the Whippoorwill, as the great WP Ranch was called.

On the ground, covered with dust, his jaw clamped shut and his eyes blazing, was another youth, heavier than Wayne, red-haired, with bulldog features. He was leaning on his left elbow in the dust of the cow-town street.

"Now, listen, Jake," Wayne was saying sternly, "before you get up, tell me if this fight is ended or not. If it isn't ended, you'll have to throw away that gun. No . . . don't make a move to touch it. If you want to go on with this, somebody else will take your gun and I'll hand mine over to somebody."

Jake Barry's lower lip drew back against his teeth. "Come and get it, some of you," he snarled.

A man came forward and took the weapon from its holster while Wayne tossed his aside to whomever might catch it. Then Barry got to his feet. He towered a full three inches above Wayne's six feet of height. His big hands were covered with a thick reddish growth of hair, his big arms were long, his legs were stocky, his chin square. Never did a pair seem more unevenly matched.

He crouched and in another instant sprang like a tiger at the man before him. It was tactics such as this that were losing the fight for him. He sought to overwhelm Wayne with his strength. He was a wrestler, rather than a boxer. And Ted Wayne knew that, if his opponent ever got him down, he was lost.

But Wayne had been in fights before—too many of them, almost everyone agreed, including his father and Polly Arnold. These lunges on the part of Jake and his wild, vicious swings were his meat. He had succeeded in knocking Jake down, but it had taken a terrific blow to turn the trick, a blow with every ounce of muscle that Wayne possessed behind it, and it had landed fully on Barry's jaw. Wayne knew in his heart that he could not knock Barry out. This knowledge made him a more dangerous opponent for the larger man than otherwise would have been the case.

As Jake hurled his huge bulk at him, Wayne side-stepped and got in a hard left to Jake's left eye. So great was the force of Jake's lunge that he staggered forward and fell to his knees.

Wayne was there when he got up, and no sooner was Barry on his feet than Wayne whipped a hard blow to his opponent's right eye. These were not taps. They carried everything Wayne could put into a short blow and that was plenty, as the spectators agreed.

Again Jake charged. His eyes were blazing fire. He was literally insane with rage for the time being. What the fight had started over none knew, but it wasn't long before the onlookers were aware of Wayne's strategy. He met this second rush of Jake's in the same manner as before—leaping lightly aside and driving another blow to Jake's left eye. He was like a cat on his feet, dancing about the bigger man, taunting him and urging him on, luring him into those wild rushes and planting blows on either eye. It was cruel, but Wayne knew, if Jake ever got him down, he would break his back, or an arm at least, before anyone could interfere.

Jake's eyes were swelling terribly. Blood was flowing from cuts on his face. He kept spitting into the dust that swirled about them. But he was game to the core. And his great strength would enable him to keep up his aggressive tactics for some time. The fact that he couldn't get to Wayne, who was a boxer above the average, maddened him and robbed him of all judgment.

Time and again Wayne drew him about in a circle and got in a blow as the giant crouched for another spring. Once he clipped the bigger man behind the left ear with such force that he spun him around. Then came his chance. Once again he drove his right to that protruding, square jaw. Behind that blow was everything that Wayne ever could hope to have.

Barry staggered back, unsteady on his feet, then braced himself and looked out of his fast-closing eyes for his opponent. At that moment Wayne could probably have driven another terrific blow for a knockout. The crowd expected it and waited breathlessly. Wayne expected it himself, but for some inexplicable reason he could not bring himself to plant the blow.

His indecision nearly cost him the fight. Jake had recovered more quickly than anyone could have suspected. He dived suddenly at Wayne, striking out at the same time, and Wayne took a glancing blow on the jaw that nearly sent him to the ground.

This blow made Wayne a charging demon. Heretofore he had been cool, his face frozen in stern lines, his eyes hard and calculating. Now his eyes flashed and narrowed and he renewed the battle with such fury that it seemed to those looking on that he would tear Jake's face to pieces.

In his attacks he was inexorable. It was he who now was on the aggressive. Barry was merely staggering about in the choking dust. It was brutal—a fearful thing to look upon. There were murmurs among the spectators. It ought to be stopped. But none made a move to stop it. It was whispered about that Jake had brought it upon himself. He had called Wayne a forbidden name in the Blue Grouse resort and had invited him into the street. Wayne had followed him out to what everyone thought would be a massacre. It was going the other way. It was Jake's own fault. Thus none moved forward to interfere.

Back and forth and around the contestants battled. But now it really wasn't a battle. It was the massacre that many had expected, but it was ending as they had not expected. Blow after blow—on the eyes, the nose, the jaw, in the midriff—and then the crowd suddenly cried out and Wayne stepped back.

Big Jake Barry stood helpless, his eyes so swollen they were completely closed. He was shaking and choking in the dust. One fierce blow to the proper spot would put him down and out for a long, long count.

"I guess we're through, eh, Barry?" said Wayne.

"Go ahead and finish it," said Barry thickly.

"I wouldn't hit you again for love or money," said Wayne. "You started it and I've finished it. I'm satisfied. I'm not even going to ask you to take back what you said . . . which I expect you wouldn't do. I don't care about it. I'm satisfied, as I said. And I know just what's in your head. You're thinking that, if there's a next time, it'll be gun play. Just remember, I'll be expecting that."

He turned away and retrieved his weapon from a spectator. Several advanced to help Barry. The fight was over, but the memory of it would live in Riverdale and the Teton range for many years to come.

Wayne slapped the dust from his hat that someone had handed to him, and brushed his clothes as best he could. Then he pushed his way through the crowd and came face to face with Polly Arnold. For half a minute they stood there, looking into each other's eyes. Polly's were cool and accusing; Wayne's were surprised and a bit bewildered.

"Why . . . hello, Polly," he stammered. "I thought you'd gone home."

"Ted Wayne, you're a brute!" exclaimed the girl.

"We've discussed that before, Polly," said Wayne. "This had to be. If you knew what had started it, or, if I could tell you, you wouldn't be so hard on me."

"That's what you always say," returned Polly with a toss of her head. "You've always got an excuse."

"Have you ever investigated any of them?" Wayne inquired.

"Of course not," she said indignantly. "Why should I?"

"Well . . . well, come to think of it, why should you?" said Wayne, remembering to take off his hat. "It's tough, Polly, that you should be around so many times when I . . . when there's trouble."

"It isn't that, Ted. It doesn't make any difference when I'm around. It seems there's always trouble."

"It's my bad luck," he said, frowning. "I've got to blame it on something and I'll blame it on that."

"You're always seeking a way out," said Polly seriously. "What will your father think? You know he has threatened more than once that if you got in another fight. . . ."

"I know, I know," Wayne broke in. "I'll blame that on my bad luck, too. No, I won't. I'll take the blame for everything without a word and face the music."

Polly was nonplussed at this. She looked up at Wayne, but he was looking away from her as if he were seeing something at a great distance. Her thoughts began to jump about. Then: "Ted . . . do you . . . remember what you asked me not so long ago?"

"How could I forget it?" he said quickly, looking at her in surprise.

"Well . . . if I did marry you, would it help any?" she asked seriously.

His eyes lighted. "You mean . . . ?" His eyes clouded. "It wouldn't be fair, Polly, honestly. It wouldn't be fair to you. I just don't know. Maybe the devil is in me to stay. That's a hard question, because I love you."

"Well," said the girl softly, "you think it over, Ted."

He watched her as she walked rapidly up the street to rejoin her companions at the hotel. She had had to find out what the trouble was about. Wayne's brain was whirling. A word and he could have Polly! It was incredible, unreal, but it made his heart leap with joy and then with pain. He could have Polly if. . . . *The thing for you to do is get something to eat, go back to the ranch, and face the music,* he told himself.

He started for a restaurant, knowing full well that the news of the fight would beat him to the ranch. Such had always been the case, and he saw no reason for an exception now. Suddenly he realized that he didn't care.

Chapter Two

Wayne scarcely remembered riding back to the ranch that afternoon. He had not come out of the fight with Jake Barry unscathed. The cuts on his face smarted and his knuckles were nearly raw. It was of Polly Arnold that he thought as he rode in the hot sun across the golden expanse of plain. Polly was so utterly desirable, such a sweet girl, a good rider, fun-loving, full of life, glowing with health, and he loved her. Such was the trend of his thoughts as he covered the miles homeward.

He arrived at the ranch at sunset. Almost the first man he met after he had put up his horse was Jack McCurdy, the foreman.

" 'Lo, Mac," he greeted. "Anybody been along this afternoon?"

"Not a soul," replied the foreman, looking at Ted's face and hands. "Who was it this time, Ted?"

"Well, I'm in luck for once," said Wayne with relief. "For once I'll be able to break the news to the Old Man without his having heard about things beforehand. I'll have to wash up and sort of patch my face and hands. C'mon to the bunkhouse, Mac."

They went on to the bunkhouse where McCurdy, who was an expert in such emergencies, began to cleanse Wayne's cuts and make him presentable before he went into the ranch house.

"It was Jake Barry," said Wayne simply.

McCurdy whistled softly. "You didn't pick out any soft spot," he said. "How'd you make out with that big bruiser?"

"Gave him everything I had in the right place and couldn't knock him out. He's heavy on his feet, though, and I closed both his eyes. I could have knocked him cold then but didn't. Last I saw of him they were leading him away."

"How'd it start?" McCurdy asked.

"He picked it," replied Wayne with a frown. "Picked it out of thin air. You know I never had anything to do with him. Made out like he was soused and bumped into me. Then he said things, called me a few choice names, and invited me outside. Reckon he figured I would come."

"That was a frame-up," McCurdy decided.

"Looks that way to me, Mac. But I can't see why he would want to do it to me. I hardly know him except by sight. Never even had a drink with him or sat in on a game where he was playing."

"That's just it. Some reason for it, unless he really was drunk."

"Drunk your eye," scoffed Wayne. "He was no more drunk than you are. There must be something behind it."

"You know the gang he travels with, I suppose," said McCurdy casually.

"Worst set of bums in Riverdale and you can't call 'em anything else," Wayne answered in contempt.

"But he don't stay long in Riverdale and he isn't there often, Ted. His range is over east in the Rainbow Butte country. Rainbow is his headquarters. He'd be sure to pick the toughest town on the range. He runs with the Darling outfit."

"No!" Wayne exploded. "Is he in with that bunch of cutthroats?"

"He sure is," McCurdy affirmed. "And that's why I don't like the looks of this lay. You've got to step easy, Ted. Jake won't forget this . . . not in a million years."

"I made him throw away his gun in the fight," Wayne mused.

"And when it was over, and he was standing there like a store dummy, I told him I knew what he was thinking about. He was thinking the next time, if there was a next time, it would be with guns. I told him that and said I'd be expecting it."

McCurdy stood back, surveying his handiwork with approval. "You can do it, Ted. You can get in more messes quicker and easier than any man I ever saw. But I'm with you thick or thin."

"I know that, Mac," said Wayne. "Do I look pretty enough to go into the house?"

"You'll pass." McCurdy nodded. "But don't get in a strong light."

Ed Wayne was a big man, not merely in a physical sense, but from the standpoint of influence in the vast domain of range that he dominated. Probably the only person in the Teton country who did not fear him was his son Ted. As an only son—Ed Wayne had no other children and had lost his wife when Ted was ten years old—it could be assumed that Ed thought a great deal of Ted, which was true. If Ted had been more or less of a mystery to his father when a boy, he was many times more a mystery as a man. Ed Wayne knew nothing of the handling of children. He had allowed his son to have his own way and to do as he pleased. Despite this lax attitude on the part of his parent, Ted had mixed with the men, worked cattle, tamed broncos, until he possessed all the knowledge and skill of a first-class cowpuncher. Also, he tolerated many of the vices. If he was wild, it could not be said that he was bad, intentionally or otherwise.

Conflicting emotions assailed Ted as he entered the house. It was not trepidation in expectation of having to explain to his father what had taken place in town, for he knew he would have to do that, and his explanation would be terse but thorough, but for once, having to do the explaining himself, he was curious as to the result. Moreover, it wasn't going to be so easy on his part, for it would be the first time he had played the rôle. A vague uncertainty made him uneasy. For once in his tempestuous life he confessed to himself that he didn't know where he stood. It was a feeling he didn't relish. Anyway, he wanted it over with as soon as possible.

He strode through the kitchen with a nod at Mary, the colored cook and housekeeper. But Mary called him back.

"Your father said when you come and had your supper to go out on the porch." She nodded. "He wants to see you. I got your supper all ready. It won't take a minute."

"Oh, all right," said Ted in a tone of relief, hanging up his hat and dropping into a chair in the dining room. "Sling it on, Mary, and I'll do what I can to it."

His father was waiting for him on the porch and wanted to see him. Then somebody had been along with the news. Fair enough. He could acknowledge what he wished of the story and supply any details his father required. He could answer questions better than he could make explanations. It would be the same as it had always been before. Give and take, and damn the consequences.

When Mary had his supper on the table, he did full justice to it. Trouble never affected his appetite. If his father threw him out, he would take the long trail of adventure. He had long nourished a wish to do this. Yet, the Whippoorwill was his home, and. . . . He put down his coffee cup with a bang. Was he getting sentimental? But there was Polly Arnold to be considered. He rose and walked rapidly to the porch, his lips firm, his eyes slightly narrowed. It still was light enough for his features to be clearly distinguished.

He found his father sitting in the big, green wicker rocking chair, as he knew he would find him. " 'Lo, Dad," he greeted.

"Sit down," said Ed Wayne, indicating a chair to one side and slightly ahead of his own where he could see his son to good advantage. "Why didn't you come back with the rest of the boys?" he demanded as Ted took the chair.

Ted's brows went up in surprise. "Why, I've always stayed in town a day or two longer than the rest of the bunch," he answered. "You've never objected."

"You don't feel that you're a part of this outfit, do you?" said his father in that cool, smooth voice he always used on such occasions, a voice that Ted didn't like.

"I don't see why you should ask me that," Ted returned a bit sharply. "I've rode with 'em, worked with 'em, gambled with 'em, and fought with 'em. I wouldn't do that with an outfit if I didn't think I belonged." His father had been looking at him intently and he expected the explosion to come with his next remark. But it didn't.

"Very well," said Ed Wayne in a voice that lost some of its stern fiber. "But it might have pleased me if you'd come along with the outfit just once. But I couldn't expect you to think of that. After all, I'm seeing that I can't expect very much from you. It looks like. . . ."

"Now listen, Dad," Ted broke in, "you can expect just what you ask for. I can't remember more'n a dozen times that you've given me a definite order on this ranch. I've worked with Mac and taken his orders, and carried 'em out, as he'll tell you, but you didn't seem to care whether I took orders from anybody or not."

Ed Wayne leaned forward in his chair. "Are you throwing that up to me?" His eyes were flashing angrily because he knew his son was speaking the truth. "I've given you one order . . . not given, but begged. I've asked you to keep out of brawls . . . now deny that."

"So somebody's beat me to it again," said Ted with a trace of bitterness. "Well, let's have it. I've stood it before and I can stand it again. But I'm thinking that these pony express riders who go racing around the range could find business of their own to attend to if they looked for it."

"And just what do you mean by that?" said the stockman.

"Exactly what I said," Ted snapped back in a tone he never before had used in speaking to his father. "I had thought that for once I would be able to tell you about a fracas before somebody else got to you. And this time I won't try to explain anything or answer any questions. Whatever you've heard goes as you heard it." Ted was angry.

"You've been in another fight?" his father asked quietly.

"And well you know it," Ted snapped out.

"And you think somebody's beat you here with the news?"

"I can read sign," said Ted.

Ed Wayne rocked silent in his chair for a space. "I knew you had been in a fight," he said finally. "I'm not blind yet, if I am old. I knew you'd been in a scrap soon as I put eyes on you. But no one has been here ahead of you, if that's what's in your head. There hasn't been a soul on this ranch today that didn't belong here. I'll expect you to take my word for what I've said."

Ted was staring at his father. No messenger! His father never lied. Then what was it all about? "All right," he said grimly. "I'll tell you about it myself, and I won't leave out anything because I have the privilege. It was. . . ."

"Just a minute." His father held up his hand. "I don't want to hear a word about it. Not a word. And if anybody else tries to tell me about it, I'll close his trap as soon as he opens it, if I have to knock all his teeth out."

Ted's eyes now were wide with astonishment. It was some little time before he could find his tongue. "Whatever you've got on your mind, Dad," he said, "you should hear about this mix-up. It's . . . it's important."

"I don't care how important it is," his father said coolly. "I don't want to hear about it. I'm no longer interested in your fights. If you want to go about the country getting into brawls that reflect on the ranch and on me, and make people think I brought you up to do this sort of thing, and that I'm agreeable, go right ahead. I've threatened to throw you off the ranch, but it was only a threat. I couldn't throw you out if I wanted to, because you're my son. That may mean something to you, but it probably won't. I wanted you back a couple of days earlier because I have something for you to do . . . an order to give, for once."

Ted was flushing through his tan. "I . . . didn't know," he stammered lamely. This was far worse than if his father had upbraided him and then ordered him to get out. For the second time since he had returned to the ranch he was at a loss to know what to think or do or say.

"We'll go inside," said Ed Wayne. "It's getting dark out here."

Ted followed his father into the big, comfortable living room where a large lamp shed its rays on the big center table from under an ornate shade. Ed Wayne sat down with an arm on the table and Ted took a place across from him. The stockman was drumming on the table with his fingers, a sure sign he had something weighty on his mind, as Ted well knew.

"Do you know, or have you ever heard of a man called Jim Hunter?" Ed Wayne asked.

Ted racked his brains. "Not that I can remember," he answered at last.

"I expected that would be the case," said his father. "Anyway, I want to see this Jim Hunter. I want to see him here in this very room as soon as I can. He'll come if I can get the word to him. I'm going to send you out to look for him. I think you're just smart enough to turn the trick." He looked across at Ted for the first time and found his son's eyes alive with interest.

Ted merely nodded.

"The last I heard of him," Ed Wayne went on, "he was over in the Rainbow Butte country. Maybe he's in Rainbow, and, if he isn't there, you might get word of him there. I'm going to give you letters to two men over there who may be of use to you, and I'm going to describe him to you so well that you'll know him on sight anywhere. There might be a little danger mixed up in this, but I don't want you to take any chances. You must not take any chances, whether you get the word to Hunter or not. That's an order. You understand?"

Ted's eyes were flashing with excitement. Rainbow. The town where Jake Barry of the Darling gang was supposed to make his headquarters. He was glad now that his father hadn't heard about the fight.

"I understand." He nodded briefly.

"Don't forget that particular order," his father said sternly. "Here are the letters." He drew two envelopes from his inside coat pocket and passed them over to Ted. "It won't be hard to find those men, but don't find 'em when they're with anybody, and don't tell anybody anything about your business. If you find Hunter, he'll come back with you. You can tell him the second you see him. He's a big fellow, yellowish sort of eyes . . . well, not yellowish, maybe, but queer-looking . . . dangedest light eyes you ever saw. You can't miss him, because the end of his nose is shot off. You could tell him by his nose in any crowd. He isn't what you'd call snub-nosed. And if any man called him Snub Nose, that man would never have use for any more words. I've never known him to be without a corduroy coat. If he's changed any, one or both of those men you have the letters to will be able to tell you. Now . . . do you think you want to take on the job?" He looked again at his son, quizzically this time.

"I'm not only going to take on the job," replied Ted, "but I'm going to find Jim Hunter and bring him back."

Chapter Three

As Ted was leaving the room, his father called him back. He glanced at Ted's empty holster—for Ted had merely discarded his gun in the kitchen and still wore his belt—and then looked his son squarely in the eyes. "Was there any shooting?" he asked succinctly.

"No," replied Ted readily. "I saw to that."

Ed Wayne nodded and satisfaction shone in his eyes. "That's good, Ted. It's dangerous for a man to be as fast and sure with a shooting iron as you are, and you can make your gun your worst enemy." He nodded absently. In his day, Ed Wayne had been listed with the best of them. He had several notches to his credit. Secretly he was proud of Ted's prowess, but he dared not flaunt this pride openly. "You want to be right careful on this trip, Ted."

"Is this Jim Hunter a gunfighter?" Ted asked curiously.

"When he has to be," Ed Wayne returned.

"Will he know who I am? Maybe I ought to have some kind of identification, if he never has seen me."

The stockman thought a moment. "I hadn't thought of that," he confessed. "But I would have thought of it before you left in the morning. Come in the office . . . no, go get your hat and bring it in with you."

When Ted returned with the hat, his father sat at his desk in the little office off the living room. Before him was pen and ink. He took the hat, turned out the sweat band, and on its inside on the right inked his brand, *WP,* and after it he fashioned a crude wing.

"There," he said, handing Ted his hat, "if he wants identification, show him that. I don't have to tell you not to show it to anyone else, I reckon."

Ted grinned. "I'd be likely to cut it out and wear it for a badge," he said. For the first time that night Ed Wayne smiled.

The stockman sat at his desk, fingering the pen absently, staring straight ahead, thinking, and remained thus for a long time after Ted had left. He was sending Ted on an errand of much greater importance than the youth could realize. Several times he was tempted to change his mind and try to get word to Hunter in some other way. Had he listened to Ted and learned of the trouble his son had had with Jake Barry in town, Ted never would have been entrusted with the mission assigned him. He might change his mind yet, he thought, not knowing that Ted would not give him a chance to change it, that he would be on his way in the morning with the first faint glimmer of the dawn.

When Ted left the house, he hunted up Jack McCurdy and they sought seclusion in a corner of the nearly deserted bunkhouse.

"Listen, Mac, I'm not supposed to tell a soul a thing about this, but I know I can trust you, and maybe you can give me some information of the right brand," said Ted. "You've had more than one confidence from me before and I reckon you can handle another. Am I right?"

"Right as rain," said McCurdy with a nod.

"Don't breathe a word of this, Mac," said Ted earnestly. "Dad is sending me to find a man in the Rainbow Butte country and the first place I hit is the town of Rainbow itself. I've only been there once, and that was when I was a kid. But I know how to get there and I've been within a few miles of the town several times."

"Why, you can't miss it," said McCurdy. "It's just south of the butte, about halfway between the butte and the river on Rainbow Creek. Any trail out there will take you to town so long as you keep south of the butte. But holy smoke!" He paused and looked at Ted curiously.

"Yes, holy smoke." Ted nodded. "Now where does this Darling gang hang out over there?"

"Isn't that a question," snorted McCurdy. "If they're not working some job, they're in town or in their hang-out in the butte breaks. You know there's a swamp east of the butte where the creek goes to pieces and runs everywhere before it gathers itself together again in the south. Tumbled country, willows and trees, and some soap holes, too, where the quicksand is fine as salt. Be careful about how you wander about there, boy, and, if you meet up with Jake, there's goin' to be fireworks. Funny to me the Old Man should send you over there after what happened in town." He shook his head in perplexity.

"He doesn't know a thing about what happened in town, Mac. Nobody has been along to tell him and he wouldn't let me tell him, and, when I found out he wanted me to go over there, I wouldn't have told him on a bet. Just asked me if there had been any shooting."

"I see," said McCurdy. "Who you goin' over there to find?"

Ted hesitated, and then shook his head. "I can't answer that, Mac," he said slowly. "I expect you'll understand. Maybe you'll know the man I'm going for, and maybe you won't . . . but I can't tell you. But there's one thing I want to ask you. Just how fast is this Jake Barry with his gun?"

"I thought it would come to that," drawled McCurdy. "He's fast, Ted, but he's tricky. He's awful tricky. After what you told him, he'll be on the look-out. If you meet up with him, you must draw on sight. And make your draw good. Say, Ted"—he put an arm about the younger man's shoulders—"I'm just in for a day or two and I'm supposed to go right back on the range. But I can sneak a day or two or three. Won't you let me go with you, buddy?"

Ted shook his head. "It isn't in the cards, Mac, old boy. I've got to do this alone. But you know how I appreciate it. And if I need you, I'll send for you some way, don't worry. One thing more, Mac. Are they antagonistic out there toward the WP?"

"They're nothing else but!" exclaimed McCurdy. "That's why I hate to see you go alone. But the whole outfit is ready and at your disposal. All we need is the word, and, if you're not back in three days, out we come, whether you like it or not. Paste that in your hat!"

Ted put a hand on McCurdy's knee. "You're several kinds of a brick, Mac . . . but use your own judgment. Remember, we . . . I don't want any gun play, but if it has to come. . . ."

"I hope you'll be first," interrupted McCurdy grimly, "and I have a hunch you will."

It was not yet daylight when Ted Wayne had his breakfast in the cook house and rode away on his charging gray—the best saddle horse on the ranch. McCurdy watched him go, and, if he harbored any misgivings, he kept them to himself. When old Ed Wayne rose an hour later, his son had gone.

"How long has he been gone?" the stockman asked McCurdy.

"Since about daylight," replied the foreman. "Maybe an hour, maybe. . . ."

"Look here, McCurdy," Ed Wayne interrupted sternly. "Don't be beating around any bushes with me, understand?" It was the harshest tone he ever used in speaking to his chief aide. But the rancher was annoyed this morning to the point of anger. He had wanted to see Ted before he started. He hadn't been altogether sure that he wanted the youth to start on this mission alone. He had been disturbed by his ignorance of what had happened in town and had regretted some of the things he had said to Ted. He was not sure of himself and this was enough to upset him. "Did Ted tell you where he was going?" he demanded.

"Said he was riding over Rainbow Butte way," drawled McCurdy. He knew Ed Wayne's moods, and suspected what was coming. But he knew, too, that his services were of great value to the stockman, in more ways than just running the ranch, had been, for that matter, for many years. Like Ted, he was not afraid of the ranch owner.

"I see." Wayne scowled. "How much did he tell you of what he was going over there for?"

"Said he was goin' over to see somebody," replied McCurdy. "But he didn't tell me who he was goin' to see. Took the big gray, so I don't expect he'll be long gone."

"Is that all he said?" Wayne asked sharply.

McCurdy looked at him coolly. "Now, listen, Ed, if you're tryin' to get something out of me that I don't know, you've got both feet stuck in the gumbo. I don't know anything, and that's all there is to it. You know me well enough. . . ."

"I know both of you well enough to know you don't keep anything from each other. But there were things I told Ted before I sent him out that I asked him to keep to himself. If he told you those things, then I've got something to tell you. If he didn't, then I haven't a thing to say."

"I don't know what the things were, so I can't answer your question straight," McCurdy retorted stoutly. "But I have strong reason to believe he didn't tell me any of those things. He wouldn't tell me what I wanted to know, if that'll help you any."

Wayne frowned doubtfully and tugged at his mustache. Then he tossed his head in a characteristic gesture that seemed to close the matter. "By the way, McCurdy," he said casually, "Ted told me he had been in a fight in town yesterday, which I knew he had, of course, the minute I set eyes on him."

"Yeah?" said McCurdy languidly. "Who was he fighting with?"

"Humph," said the stockman with a scowl. "I didn't let him tell me. I let on I wasn't interested in any more of his fights, and, if he wanted to go on tearing up, to go ahead."

"Well, then you haven't got any kick coming." The foreman nodded sagely.

"Of course, he told you about it," the rancher went on, "and I knew I could get the details from you later. I just asked him, if there was any shootin', and he said there wasn't. Did he tell you that?"

"Yep," replied McCurdy cheerfully. "I can vouch for that."

"All right, let's hear about the fight," said Wayne briefly.

McCurdy was carefully rolling a cigarette. He now lighted it just as deliberately. "So you want to hear about the fight, Ed? And you wouldn't let Ted tell you about it?"

"I thought it was best I didn't let him tell me," was the stockman's answer. "I usually know something about the way to handle my business." He was irritated by his foreman's tone.

"But he wanted to tell you, didn't he?" McCurdy asked blandly.

Ed Wayne was suddenly angry. "Look here, Mac," he snapped out, his face reddening. "I don't like the way you're acting this morning. I had my own reasons for not wanting him to tell me about it. And I won't let anyone else except you tell me about it. Of course I want to know, naturally have to know. You can see that. He told you . . . I'd lay a hundred head of shorthorns to that . . . so let's hear about it."

But McCurdy shook his head. "I won't do it, Ed," he said slowly. "Here Ted came back from town expecting that the news of the row had got here ahead of him, as it always had before. He was glad it hadn't. He told me . . . 'For once I'll have a chance to tell him myself' . . . meaning to tell you. He went in there to give you the details and you turned him down flat with a mean remark. Wait a minute! It won't do you any good to get mad. You wouldn't let him tell you himself when he wanted to, and now you want to double-cross him and get the story behind his back. Go right ahead and get sore, but you won't get the story from me, and I'll fire any man under me that lets out a word of anything he hears. That's flat."

Ed Wayne stared at his foreman in astonishment. Then he cooled again and tugged at his mustache, which was a sure indication of one of two things—either he was mad or thinking deeply.

"I suppose you know," he said coldly, "that I can ride into town, if I choose, and hear plenty."

"You can," McCurdy agreed, "and you can hear plenty that isn't so. You could have got the facts from Ted first-hand. He doesn't lie. Seems to me that instead of gettin' all het up about it, the squarest thing you can do is to wait and let Ted tell you when he comes back."

"Humph!" snorted the stockman. "Go out and look over things on the east range, for a change. The bunkhouse will still be here when you get back."

With this he stamped off toward the house, leaving McCurdy with a satisfied grin on his face.

Chapter Four

Ted Wayne sped eastward with the sun in his face and the endless green blanket of plains flowing before him. Riding his favorite horse, a magnificent gray, finest among the splendid thoroughbreds on the Whippoorwill, he sped over the grass at a swinging lope that would bring him into Rainbow with the twilight. He was in high spirits: a good horse, a trusty gun, an important mission before him, with danger lurking in the background—what more could a youth of strength and spirit desire? His mind was filled with the work entrusted to him by his father; he spurned the thought of using the letters his father had given him; he would find this Jim Hunter and bring him back to the WP if he had to rope him and drag him—so he thought.

The great domain of the Bar A, Pete Arnold's ranch, almost as large as the tremendous Whippoorwill, lay ahead, adjoining the WP on the east. Both ranches ranged south to the river and were divided by Alder Creek, which flowed almost in a straight line south from the scattered Crazy Mountains in the north. The creek boundary had been established years before, by Ed Wayne and Pete Arnold, and there had never been a dispute about water. Here was one instance where the affairs and association of two great stock ranches were tranquil.

Ted rode between grazing herds of sleek WP cattle. The sun was barely well started on its climb into the eastern sky when he reached Alder Creek. He paused for a drink of the clear, cold water, and also watered his horse. Then he was off again into the east. There was no boundary fence between the two big ranches. He swung a bit to the southward, where he picked up the trail the Bar A cowpunchers took when riding into town. He passed more herds. These bore the Bar A iron. Fine cattle, fine range. His thoughts flashed to Polly Arnold. If he wanted her, he could have her! She had told him so herself. She was Pete Arnold's only daughter, and he had no son. A wild, thrilling thought possessed him—to join the two ranches. But Ted put it aside instantly as unworthy of his love for Polly, just as he felt himself unworthy of her now. Well, he had more important matters to think about.

He came to a long stretch of open plain where there were no cattle. Winter range, this, closer to the home ranch, which was off to the southwest. He looked in that direction and saw a bobbing speck against the horizon's rim, which seemed close over a long, gentle rise in the plain. A lone rider, like himself, was abroad.

The speck rapidly assumed the outline of horse and rider, coming in Ted's direction. Some ranch hand on his way to the Bar A's west range or to town, he surmised. But as they neared each other, he found, with a leap of his heart, that the approaching rider was a girl. It wasn't long before he recognized Polly Arnold in the saddle of her spanking mare. Polly rode often, and alone, and far abroad, as he well knew. He greeted her with a flourish of his big hat and a bow as they reined in their horses on meeting.

"Polly, you look as sweet as honey, and ride the same," Ted greeted.

"That's a pretty compliment from a rider who must have started early in the morning." She laughed. "Going to the ranch?"

"Nope. Which reminds me that I haven't been over there for

some time," returned Ted, looking off to southward.

"You're always welcome, Ted," the girl said seriously.

"Well, maybe," said Ted, toying with his reins. "That is, in some directions, like yours, Polly. But I don't think your dad ever declared a holiday because I came over." He grinned amiably.

"That isn't fair, Ted," said Polly soberly. "Dad's never been anything but nice to you. He doesn't like some of the things you do, perhaps, any more than your own father does. But he doesn't dislike you."

"That's the girl," sang Ted gaily. "Can you get that horse over any closer?"

Polly flushed, then: "This is open country, but it may be full of prying eyes, just the same. Where are you going, Ted?"

"Out Rainbow Butte way. It won't take me long, I reckon. If I can, I'll stop on the way back."

But she was looking at him steadily. "Ted Wayne, are you going to Rainbow?" she asked.

"May have to go there before I get back," he returned. "What time did you get home last night?"

"It was late. But I thought you'd had enough of towns for a while, Ted. And now you're heading for Rainbow? Did you . . . have you had trouble with your father?" she asked anxiously.

"Not a bit, Polly. He hadn't heard about the trouble in town and wouldn't let me tell him about it. Said he wasn't interested . . . can you beat that? Said he wouldn't let anybody else tell him, either. That's straight, Polly."

The girl wrinkled her pretty brows in perplexity. But it was plain she didn't doubt Ted's statement in the least. "That's funny," she remarked. "Are you sure he hadn't heard of it, Ted? The news got out here."

"I'm sure, Polly," he assured her. "And it naturally would get out here, what with some of your men staying over and others taking this trail east. Don't worry, Dad scorched me with a few remarks on the side that sort of got under the skin. Want to ride along with me a ways?"

"About two miles, Ted, for I was about to turn back down to the house when I sighted you. I came on out of pure curiosity. But listen, Ted, it hurts me to see you riding off to Rainbow like this. We all know the kind of a town Rainbow is and the kind of a crowd that hangs out there. I . . . I can't help being worried." Her eyes were misty and Ted dreaded the sight of tears unless he could kiss them away.

"Can you keep a secret, Polly?" he asked quickly.

"Why . . . with you? Of course." Her eyes widened and the mist disappeared.

"All right, girlie," he said cheerily, "here it is. Dad is sending me into the Rainbow Butte country on business for him. It's important, more important than I can tell you, for I gave my word there were certain things I wouldn't tell to anyone. This job took the sting out of what he told me about the . . . the trouble. I'm not going into Rainbow to celebrate. But you mustn't mention any of this to anyone. Now what!"

Polly looked at him for a space, and her eyes softened, then shone. She edged her horse close to his and leaned from the saddle to meet his kiss. "C'mon, we'll race!" she taunted, and they were off, with Ted gallantly holding the gray in check just enough to keep the girl slightly in the lead.

When they had run the two miles and reined in, Polly shook her quirt at him and accused him out of laughing eyes: "You're a fraud, Ted Wayne. You held your horse back on purpose and I'm just as bad, for I let you do it. You know that gray can run rings around my mare, and everybody on our ranch, and yours, too, knows it. So there!"

"My horse is a gentleman," Ted retorted severely. "You wouldn't expect him to run ahead of a lady in a friendly race, would you? You going on to the house? Well, come here and get your prize for the race."

Five minutes later Ted was again speeding his lonely way east, with the purple pile of Rainbow Butte far ahead, and Polly was riding swiftly toward the Bar A ranch house with a song in her heart and another on her lips. But before she reached home she was seriously thinking about Ted's remark about her father, and Ted's visits. When she finally rode into the courtyard at the house, she felt vaguely disturbed. She turned her mount over to a hand and went to her room to change from her riding habit and to think.

Ted had to pass close to a large herd near the eastern boundary of the Bar A range, beyond which rolled the tumbled country leading to the badlands of the butte, and here he encountered Frank Payne, the Bar A range boss.

" 'Lo, Ted," Payne greeted, eyeing him sharply.

"Hello, Frank," Ted responded, reining in his horse. "How's tricks?"

"Good grass," replied Payne, which was a saying employed on the range signifying that everything was all right. "Reckon you feel a lot better today than Jake Barry. Anyway, you look a lot better."

Ted was instantly alert. "So you've heard about it," he said. "But how do you know I look better than Jake?"

"Seen him a while back," drawled Payne. "Rode past here about an hour ago with two others. Hittin' for Rainbow, I take it. Must have cleaned the Riverdale drugstore out of court plaster, by the looks of him. Could hardly see, by looks of his eyes. Got some water at the spring below here. One of the boys rode in last night with the news."

"Went on straight east?" Ted inquired.

"You have it. What're you doin' . . . followin' him up?"

Ted shook his head. "Don't want to meet up with him or any

of his crowd. I'm not looking for more trouble and I wasn't looking for trouble yesterday. He started it and I finished, and I guess I was lucky at that."

"What they tell me doesn't sound like luck," said Payne. "And it was smart of you to stop gun play. You know Jake and the crowd he travels with are bad medicine, I take it?" He spoke in a questioning tone of voice.

"Don't know much about 'em"—Ted frowned—"but I've heard that. Travels with the Darling outfit, doesn't he?"

"So they say, and that doesn't sound none too good. I'd keep one eye ahead and one behind, Wayne. Those people don't care how they get a man, as long as they get him."

Ted leaned forward in the saddle, his hands on the horn, and looked at Payne intently. "Do you know anything I ought to know, Frank?" he asked seriously. "I'm going over there on business and I'm not looking for trouble."

Payne thought for several moments. "Can't tell you a thing," he said finally, "except that Jake will be gunnin' for you as soon as he can see good enough to shoot straight. He can do that, you know, and . . . he's fast. He's runnin' with Darling's outfit all right, and I've heard roundabout that Darling has a bunch of men cached over east of the butte . . . more'n usual. You heard anythin'?"

"Not a word," replied Ted, catching a note of concern in Payne's voice. "You don't reckon he figures on working west of the butte, do you?"

"I'm the same as you," was the answer. "Don't know a thing. But seems to me I smell something in the air. For one thing, I don't figure Jake's idea in pickin' on you. Ever had any trouble before?"

"Hardly knew him," said Ted with a scowl. "Fact, I only knew him by sight. And he wasn't drunk like he tried to make out, either."

"What did your dad think about it, if I ain't gettin' too personal?" Payne asked.

"Doesn't know a thing about the business. Nobody beat me to the ranch with the story, and Dad wouldn't let me tell him. Acted queer about it, although he scorched me on the side. If it's going to be guns. . . ."

"Draw on sight!" Payne broke in sharply.

"And I don't like the idea," said Ted grimly. "Oh, I'm not afraid of him, but I don't like to be forced into a shooting like this. He thought he could break me into pieces when he called me out in Riverdale, and he got fooled. But when it was over, he didn't give me the word you're talking about. Well, I'll be moving on, Frank. I want to make Rainbow before dark."

"I'd take the trail on the west bank when I got to Rainbow Creek, if I was you," Payne suggested. "It's rough, but it's not much traveled and you'd be less likely to meet up with anybody. There's no sign of it when you first hit the creek, but turn down on the west side and you'll run across it in about a quarter of a mile. So long, Wayne, and I'm wishin' you luck."

"Thanks, Frank." Ted smiled. "Maybe I'll need it, at that."

Ted stopped at a spring a little after noon, watered his horse, loosened the cinch strap of the saddle, and ate the modest lunch he had brought along in his slicker pack. He rested for an hour while his horse grazed on the luscious grass, and then continued on his way.

He was now in the rough section southwest of the butte, which loomed close at hand, it seemed, swimming in a sea of color. There were clumps of alder and occasional cottonwoods, and in midafternoon he reached the wooded banks of Rainbow Creek. Here he took Frank Payne's advice and turned south on the west side of the creek without crossing the stream. He had to pick his way over hard going for some time until he came to the trail that had been described by the Bar A range boss.

It was slow going on this trail, and he was tempted more than once to push his way across the creek to the main trail on the east side. Late in the afternoon he brought his horse up suddenly, scanning the trail ahead. He dismounted so as better to read the sign he had seen. In the trail were fresh tracks left by horses a short time before. As he was puzzling over this, he heard a crackling in the brush along the creek. He flung himself into the saddle and dashed perilously along the trail, obsessed with the conviction that he was being followed. At the first opening in the brush, willows and tree growth along the stream, he turned in. For some time he waited, listening for the sound of hoof beats. None came. The sun was sinking fast in its drop behind the western peaks when he forded the creek and emerged on the other side. He had no sooner made the open plain, with the well-worn main trail in sight, than a gun barked in the timber and a bullet whined past his head.

He drove in his spurs and leaned low over his horse's neck, in the start of what he knew was to be a race to Rainbow.

Chapter Five

There had been no more shots as Ted swept along the trail across the plain, straight for the town of Rainbow. He looked behind, but saw no one in pursuit. Indeed, he had no fear of being overtaken from that quarter, for the gray could easily outdistance any horse on the range, and surely none of the Darling outfit could have one better. So he reasoned. But ahead lay the thin line of breaks where the creek joined the river, and where the town was located. It was a perfect spot for an ambush.

The sun had splashed into its pot of gold behind the western mountains, and Ted had lost time by taking the hard trail on the west side of the stream. He let the gray out and the horse ran for the pure joy of it, its mane and tail flying in the wind—a streak of gray in the golden glow of the sunset.

Ted pondered over the mystery of the shot from the trees. He linked it with the noise he had heard when he was examining the tracks in the west trail. But if anyone had wished to pot him, why hadn't he done so at that time when Ted was afoot and an easy mark? And how had this assailant known he was coming? Did Darling have a look-out stationed at the creek where the main trail crossed it? And the tracks in the west trail? Ted assumed that Jake Barry and his two companions had cut down from the Bar A range and made the trail at a point considerably below where he had come upon it. But these things were behind him. He gazed steadily ahead as he raced for the band of dark green that traced the course of the river to southward.

The twilight had come over that vast, brooding land when Ted reached the shadow of the trees along the river. Ahead he could see a single point of yellow light that shone in the town. The trail was wider here, and Ted spoke to the gray sharply and signaled with his spurs. The horse straightened out in a burst of terrific speed, and they plunged into the shadow. Ted was nearly thrown as his mount swerved suddenly to the left at a sharp bend in the trail. Then they were pounding across a wooden bridge and up a steep slope. Ted's gun was in his hand, but there were no shots, no signs of ambush. In another few moments they dashed out of the timber, with the lights of the town straight ahead. It was just come dark as Ted rode into the dusty main street of Rainbow.

After he had put up his horse, he made his way to the one hotel the town boasted and arranged for a room. There was no need to register; he paid in advance and was given a key. Rainbow apparently had no need for names of new arrivals. He crossed the street to a café and ate his supper. He doubted if many in the town would recognize him, and what if they did? And it seemed incredible that news of his coming could have reached town unless—and there was scarce possibility of this—he had been observed by hostile eyes leaving the Whippoorwill or crossing the Bar A range that morning. If Jake Barry were in town, he would be sure to keep out of sight with his face in such a condition as Frank Payne had described. His companions could hardly be expected to take up Jake's quarrel, for Ted knew full well that Jake would never sanction such a move. Therefore, Ted's first duty was to make the rounds of the various resorts in an effort to locate Jim Hunter, providing the latter was in town.

A visit to half a dozen small places failed to yield a glimpse of anyone even remotely resembling the disfigured features of the man Ted was seeking. He had purposely left the largest place of its kind until the last, as he wished to visit it late. This was The Three Colors, a resort of pretentious dimensions with three stripes of yellow, black and red painted across its high false front. Yellow lamplight streamed from its windows and wide-open doorway. Within all was in uproar, and Ted entered to find himself instantly swallowed by a milling throng about the gaming tables and the two long bars, one on either side of the big room.

The Three Colors was far-famed, and Ted drew in a swift breath as he stared about at the strange scene. It was totally unlike any resort he ever had been in—a combination of hurdy-gurdy, gambling hell, drinking place, and madhouse. Yet he carried in his pocket a letter to Miles Henseler, proprietor of the place. He realized why his father had given him a letter to this man, for if anyone in Rainbow would be sure to know if Hunter was in town, or have information as to his whereabouts, it certainly would be the proprietor of such a rendezvous.

Edging his way through the crowds about the tables and bar, Ted soon was convinced of the futility of locating his man in reasonable time, even if he were in the place. The groups of spectators about the tables were constantly changing. It was impossible to crowd in and get a look at the players at most of the tables. The bars were lined three deep. Under the yellow glow of the hanging lamps was bedlam. Ted decided to take up a station at the upper end of one of the bars and scan the faces of those who passed in or out or milled about him.

The bar he chose was the shorter of the two, due to the fact that a small room was partitioned off between its upper end and the front of the building. Bit by bit—almost inch by inch, it might be said—he edged his way through the crowd to the bar. The space he occupied was cramped, for he was backed against the outthrust portion of the little room. One of the bartenders served him shortly with a drink of white liquor without troubling himself to ask him what he wanted. Ted put a silver dollar on the bar and looked down the long line of faces as the bartender flipped the dollar into a box. There was no change. Here was a gold mine as rich as any to be found in the desert hills far to southward, thought Ted, as he managed to spill the drink upon the floor.

Then the door of the little room opened and a man came out—a big man, florid, broad of shoulder, with a big cigar between his thick lips and a massive gold watch chain across his wide expanse of chest.

Ted Wayne knew instinctively that this man was Miles Henseler. He had the unmistakable air that is always exhibited by the proprietor of such a resort. And Ted was favorably impressed. Not by the man's attire or features in general so much as by his eyes. He had shot a keen glance at Ted and it had roved all the way down the bar and about the room, but in the brief instant that their eyes had met, Ted had caught a gleam of honesty in the other's gray eyes that pleased him.

Henseler walked slowly along behind the bar, nodding to this one and that, and speaking a word to his bartenders. Then he came back in Ted's direction where there was an exit from behind the bar, a leaf that could be raised and lowered.

Meanwhile, Ted had been thinking. It might take him several days to find Jim Hunter, if he happened to be in town, at the rate he was going. And every hour he remained in Rainbow was fraught with the possibility of trouble. Rather than being so independent, wouldn't he be serving his ends better to present the letter to Henseler and find out what he could at once? Certainly it would hasten the completion of his mission.

As the big man reached the end of the bar and nodded to Ted to take his glass from the leaf of the bar so he could lift it to go out, Ted spoke in a low voice. "Are you Mister Henseler?"

The cool, gray eyes regarded him steadily. "Yes," was the reply, the word bit off short.

"I'd like to see you," said Ted in a voice that just reached the other's ears. "I have a letter from my father, Ed Wayne, of the Whippoorwill."

Henseler raised his brows with interest, looking closer at Ted. "Yes, I see the resemblance now," he said. "Come in." He lifted the leaf at the end of the bar, and Ted passed through and followed him into the little room, which proved to be a private office.

"So, you're Ed Wayne's son," said Henseler, taking a chair by the desk and motioning Ted to another. "Well, you've got old Ed's brand on your face and you're big enough. What's your name?"

"Theodore"—Ted smiled—"but they usually shorten it." He seemed to like this man from the start.

"Ted, eh? Well, young man, if you come over here to try to tear this town up like you've torn Riverdale up on occasion, you'll find yourself up against a different brand of talent. I see by your looks that you've been at it again. Rainbow's so tough, I have to be square to stay here."

Ted saw no joke was intended. Henseler was not looking at him, but he knew he was in deadly earnest. More and more he was liking this man who spoke with such smooth geniality, yet who ran one of the most notorious resorts on the north range and enjoyed the confidence of scores of desperadoes, gunmen, bandits—even Darling himself. Ted thrilled at the thought. He wondered if he couldn't arrange to get a look at the famous outlaw—the bandit, rustler, robber, killer, who laughed in the very faces of the sheriffs, and ruled the hardest band of cutthroats ever to ride the range north of the Missouri. He had listened to many descriptions of this outlaw, but all were vague, all were lacking in detail; they merely served to thicken the fog of mystery surrounding him.

"I didn't come to tear anything up," said Ted straightforwardly, "I came on business for Dad. Here's a letter for you." He handed the envelope to Henseler.

"How is the Old Man?" asked Henseler, splitting the envelope with a finger. "I haven't seen him in years."

"He isn't bad," drawled Ted. "Not bad at all."

Henseler looked at him quickly with a twinkle in his eyes, then drew out the letter. At this moment there came three short raps on the door. "Yes?" said Henseler in a louder voice.

The door opened and a bartender stuck in his head. "Mort Green wants to see you," he said.

Henseler's brow puckered for a moment or two. "Well, tell him . . . no, send him in," he decided.

He opened the letter, glanced at Ed Wayne's signature, and folded it again as the door opened the second time and a man came in. Ted recognized the type instantly. Green was a gambler, a cool, collected, inexorable gambler of what might be termed the middle school. He hadn't the glamour or picturesqueness of the old school, nor the flashiness of the new school. He wore an agate ring, which constituted his jewelry. He was dressed in a double-breasted suit, with a gray shirt of light wool, a dark blue tie, black shoes, and a soft gray hat. His gray eyes were cold, his nose and lips thin, the latter straight, his jaw square. Tall and slim, he radiated a certain elegance. Ted thought he had never seen a more beautiful pair of hands.

"Hello, Mort," Henseler greeted his visitor. Then, noting Green's questioning glance at Ted, he said: "This is the son of a friend of mine, meet Ted Wayne of the Whippoorwill."

Green nodded coolly at Ted and turned to Henseler. "Not so good," he said crisply. There was a slight edge to his voice. "May have to draw on K.C. again."

Henseler chuckled. "You will do it, Mort. Faro again? No, you don't have to tell me. How much?"

"Ten thousand," was the cool reply, as Green took out his cigarette case—the only cigarette case on that range.

Ted couldn't resist a look of admiration. Here was a man who had lost $10,000 and was as unconcerned as if he had lost $10. No wonder he never saw such men in Riverdale. But, no—it wasn't the amount lost. For Henseler had turned to the safe beside the desk, unlocked a drawer with a key taken from a vest pocket, and now drew forth a package of bills—yellow-backs, every one. He snapped off the rubber band, peeled of a number of the bills—a considerable number, it looked to Ted—and handed them to Green.

"Ten thousand," he said. "Count 'em."

Green put them in an inside pocket of his coat. "Later," he said as he turned to go. At the door he paused and looked at Ted. "Glad to meet you, Wayne," he said shortly, and went out.

Ted had gasped as he realized that the gambler had come in and borrowed $10,000 from Henseler as nonchalantly as Ted would borrow a dollar in case of necessity from a cowpuncher. And he had spoken to him as he left.

"Coolest, sweetest gambler I ever met," Henseler was saying. "Thought maybe you'd heard of Mort Green and would like to see him." With this he turned his attention to the letter Ted had brought and read it carefully, not once, but twice. Then he folded it and looked at Ted keenly. "Did your dad tell you what was in this letter?" he asked slowly.

Ted shook his head. "Just said to give it to you, for you might help me to find my man," he explained.

"I see." Henseler nodded. "You want to find. . . ."

"Jim Hunter," Ted supplied as Henseler paused purposely.

"Ever seen Hunter?" Henseler asked.

"No, but Dad gave me such a good description of him that I

believe I could recognize him on sight . . . if he hasn't changed too much."

"He hasn't changed," said Henseler dryly, flicking the ash from his cigar. "It's funny, Ed wouldn't. . . ." He paused and favored Ted with a quizzical look. "I was thinking he might have sent an older man, but from what I've heard of you, you're well able to take care of yourself. We get all the news out here, and you've figured in the reports from Riverdale more'n once. You're fast with your gun, eh, Ted?"

Ted shrugged his shoulders. "The boys on the ranch think so," he replied non-committally.

"Yes, and there's more than the boys on the ranch, as you say, think so." Henseler nodded soberly. "It's a bad thing for a man to have a reputation as a gunman, or as being extra fast with his shooting iron out this way, Wayne. It's downright dangerous. This is probably the easiest town in Montana to get into trouble in. There's red-hot trouble in every glass on my bars this minute, and nobody knows it better than I do. You've got to step slow and easy here. Did your dad tell you anything much about this Jim Hunter?"

"Not much," Ted confessed.

"Well, he's bad medicine himself," said Henseler, lowering his voice. "He has to be handled with kid gloves, as they say. The best you can do is to deliver your message and leave the rest to him." He sat thinking for a space.

"Then . . . he's in town?" ventured Ted.

Henseler frowned. "I don't know," he said. "And you don't want to try to find out too fast. I expect you started out to find him on your own hook, didn't you?"

"Yes, I did," Ted acknowledged. "But I thought it would take too long. Then I got a look at you and . . . well, I liked the way you sized up, if you'll excuse the expression. So here I am."

"And a good thing," said Henseler emphatically. "If you went around here trying to find Hunter by yourself, you'd probably run into a bullet. I don't know whether I can get hold of him or not, but I can usually find who I want to find in this neck of the woods, and I'll make a try. Did your dad tell you anything more to tell me?"

Ted shook his head. He was beginning to feel foolish because he knew so little, and he resented the attitude on his father's part in sending him on a mission that necessitated his answering most questions in the negative. "Dad told me practically nothing," he blurted, "and I blame him for it. It makes me feel like a fool."

"You don't want to think that way," soothed Henseler. "He expected you to come direct to me with this letter and not to go scouting around on the lonesome. I reckon he told you that this wouldn't be child's play."

"He did that"—Ted scowled—"but he should have told me why it wouldn't be child's play. I don't like this idea of going it blind. I could have talked more with him and probably learned more, and maybe he intended to tell me more this morning, but I left before the house was up. I had my reasons for wanting to get started before he could have a chance to change his mind."

"Well, your old man was always pretty smart and I don't suppose he's changed much," said Henseler. "He usually knows what he's doing. He was smart enough to send you to me, don't overlook that."

Ted found no answer to this and something in the older man's manner of speaking, and his look, restrained him. He felt himself equal to the occasion and wanted to say as much, but it would sound like boasting, and he hated the very word. He remained silent.

"Now that he has sent you to me," Henseler continued coolly, "the best thing for you to do is to let me help you along with this thing. I wouldn't wander around, if I was you. You've had a long ride and it's getting late. I suppose you've got a room? Good. Now the thing for you to do. . . ."

Henseler clipped off his words and sat up alert with a look on his face that showed plainly how alert he had been, regardless of his conversation with Ted. Now Ted heard what had startled the man—a queer, short series of raps, on the side of the partition, not the door.

Henseler stepped quickly across the little room and seemed to telegraph with his knuckles against the partition. Then he resumed his chair and leaned toward his visitor with his hands on his knees.

"The thing for you to do," he resumed slowly, "is to go to your room and go to bed and wait till you hear from me in the morning. Suppose you do that." The last four words were spoken more as a command than as a suggestion.

Ted resented being taken charge of—as he thought of it—but could think of nothing else to do other than to do as he was told. After all, his mission was to get the word to Hunter as speedily as possible. And the rapping on the partition—an important signal undoubtedly. He could sense that by Henseler's change of manner. And it certainly was to his interests to stand in with Henseler.

"All right," he decided, rising. "I'll do that."

Henseler stopped him at the door. "I know how you feel," he said. "You're sore because you think things are being taken out of your hands and you're craving action. But you're now in strange territory, Wayne, stranger than you may think. Take a tip from me and let me steer you and keep a tight tongue . . . but I don't have to tell you that. Good night."

As Ted passed out from behind the bar, he shot a quick glance about, but no one was near the partition. He wended his way out of the crowded place and made for the hotel with a heavy frown on his face. As he entered the small lobby, he stopped short and went cold, then hot with inward excitement.

Standing at the counter was a man with a disfigured nose, tall, and wearing a corduroy coat. Ted could not see the eyes, but, otherwise, here was the man his father had described as Jim Hunter.

Chapter Six

Wayne was so startled that he stood stockstill, staring at the man's profile. There was a small cigar case at one end of the short counter, and he quickly stepped toward this to cover his actions. He wanted to make sure of his identification by getting a look at the man's eyes. If it was indeed Hunter, he intended to accost him at once and make known his errand. But just as he reached the dingy counter, the man turned away and went out the door.

Wayne wanted to follow him, but the clerk was standing behind the counter, waiting for his order. He selected a cigar and lighted it while the clerk made change for a $5 bill.

"Who was that man who just left?" Wayne asked, flipping his match aside. It was a natural question, he thought, considering the man's facial blemish. Almost anyone might ask it.

"Dunno," replied the clerk, giving him a fishy glance. "Lots of people drift in and out of here."

"No doubt," said Ted with a wry smile. "Still, he's a man a fellow would remember."

The fishy look in the clerk's eyes had changed to a sharp scrutiny. "And there's men it's a good thing to forget," he remarked. His words and look conveyed a meaning that Ted Wayne could not fail to comprehend.

Instead of replying to this, Wayne turned and sauntered out the door. He was certain now that the man he had seen was the man he was seeking. He was not unmindful of Miles Henseler's admonition to go to his room and stay there until the resort proprietor saw him in the morning, but here was Hunter within his grasp, so to speak. Why should he wait when he had a legitimate message and the proper identification? Deep within him, Wayne resented being taken charge of, as he looked at it. He would much prefer to settle his business unaided. He was a man; his fists were sure; his gun hand was true.

He looked up and down the dim street. It was empty. He had an inspiration. Hunter might be leaving town. His presence at the hotel would seem to indicate that he had either just arrived in town or was about to leave. There was little sense in this deduction, but Wayne headed for the livery. If Hunter were not there, he might be able to worm some information out of the barn man with the aid of a gold piece. Such a man was most apt to know about the comings and goings of the visitors and denizens of the town.

The floating stars bathed the town in a soft light. The trees were tall and graceful shadows. All was a well of silence until suddenly a mockingbird began its errant nocturnal serenade. Wayne saw the dim light from the lantern swung in the entrance to the livery. Then a form passed quickly across its sickly beam, and Wayne recognized the tall figure of the man he sought. He hurried toward the barn to meet him, but the man swung down behind the buildings that faced the street. Wayne broke into a run. The man walked fast, and before Wayne could catch up with him he turned into a narrow alley. It was dark in the alley and Wayne could not see the man somewhere ahead of him. He stumbled over something and had to slow his pace. There was a dim square of light ahead that marked the street. Wayne saw the tall figure framed in this, and then his man crossed the street. Again Wayne ran and hurried across the street, following the other, who had entered another alley. At the far end of this was a faint glow of lamplight. This must be the man's objective,

Wayne reasoned. The mockingbird's song had died as suddenly as it had first sounded.

In the darkest point in the alley, with no light save the dull beam ahead, Wayne was suddenly hurled forward upon his face by the force of an impact from behind, a body that was flung upon him, striking him high in the back. Instantly there were others upon him, his arms and legs were grasped, a hand closed over his mouth.

The suddenness of the unexpected attack left him an easy prey for several moments. Then, as his assailants were in the act of gagging him with a handkerchief and drawing his wrists back to be bound, he rallied his full strength and a terrific struggle began. He wrenched his hands free, struck out, and grasped an ear, which he twisted with all his might. A howl of pain shattered the stillness of the night.

"Let him have it!" came the command in a hoarse voice.

Wayne didn't know if this meant to shoot him or to hit him on the head. But to do either was an uncertainty in the dark and the tangle of arms and legs and twisting, struggling bodies. He knew they had to knock him out one way or another quickly or take to their heels, for the yelling of the man whose ear he had twisted would speedily bring others to the spot. That this was the work of Jake Barry's crowd he didn't doubt for a moment, and even in those minutes of conflict he sensed the reason why Barry would want him captured and brought to him unscathed.

He had determined there were three against him, but could not be sure there in the inky black of the narrow alley. To hit him accurately was a problem for his attackers, for heads bumped together, arms and legs were entwined—guns, naturally, were useless. If the man Wayne believed to be Hunter heard the disturbance, as he must have, he evidently decided it was a common brawl, for he didn't come back to the scene.

"Get him!" the hoarse voice repeated.

Then Wayne went limp from a blow on the head as a beam of yellow lamplight suddenly shot upon the scene. Instantly the weight upon Wayne's body was lifted, and he heard the dull echoes of scurrying feet. He got up, dazed, and an arm was thrown about his shoulders. A hand upon his arm guided him into an open doorway. A door slammed behind him and he was shoved into a room that was dark.

"Don't talk," said a cool, low voice.

A match flared, and, when the lamp was lighted, Wayne saw it was on a green-topped table. There were several chairs about. It was unmistakably a card room at the rear of some resort. The beam of light had come from the rear door of the place that his rescuer had thrown open. And now Wayne looked closely at the man who stood back from the lamp, regarding him steadily. It was Green, the gambler who had borrowed the $10,000 from Henseler but a short time before.

Green motioned him into a chair and, as Ted felt of the lump swelling on the side of his head, said in a low tone: "Hurt much?"

Wayne shook his head. "Slipped off," he said wryly.

The gambler drew up a chair. "I saw you running after Hunter, and I saw those others following you across the street. I hurried around and through this place expecting to find . . . what I found." With this simple explanation he took out his cigarette case and drew out a smoke.

"I'm sure much obliged," said Wayne with a scowl as he remembered the odds against him. "Must have been at least three of them."

Green lighted his cigarette carefully. "There were that many," he said, continuing to speak in a low, easy tone. "Why were you running after Hunter?"

Wayne was thrilled to learn that he had been right in surmising the man he had followed to be Hunter, but he resented the question.

"I have some private business with him," he replied coldly.

"Well, you're going about the transacting of it in a very poor way," said the gambler dryly. "I suppose you know you were in for it if that bunch had got the best of you tonight."

"I suppose so." Wayne nodded. Why was this gambler so interested in his affairs? This question was answered when Green spoke again.

"Maybe you think I'm butting in, and I am. That was Jake Barry's crowd, or part of them, after you tonight. I haven't got anything special against Jake, for he knows enough to let me alone, but I'm not exactly stuck on his style, either. I heard about the ruckus over in Riverdale. Don't know how it started, and don't care, but I'm obliged to admire your handiwork, and that's why I'm taking an interest in you. I hope you got all this clear."

"I got it clear," Wayne returned bitterly. "Jake's out to get me any way he can. I licked him once and I can lick him again, and he knows it."

"Not in this town, you can't," said Green softly. "Wayne, you haven't got a chance here."

"Maybe not. Anyway, I'm not looking for trouble. I'm here on business, and, when I've finished my business, I'm gone. If Barry can get to me before then, all right. He can have any brand of trouble he wants."

The gambler's eyes were glistening. "He won't be out until that face of his looks like it used to," he observed. "I suppose Henseler tipped you off. You must know him or you wouldn't have been in his private office."

"Tipped me off to what?" said Wayne in surprise. Was Green merely fishing for information? Had he had some ulterior motive in interfering this night? Suspicion glimmered in Wayne's eyes and Green saw it—and smiled.

"Didn't he tip you off to keep under cover?"

"Say, I don't get you at all," flared Wayne. "And what's more, I don't like so confounded much mystery. You're on the inside here, and I'm on the level and out in the open. I want to see Hunter and I don't care a hang who knows it. If that satisfies you, all right. It's all I've got to say. You did me a favor tonight, although I don't know why, or I wouldn't tell you this much."

"I wouldn't tell anybody else, if I were you," was the cold rejoinder. "So far as I know, you're the only man in this town that is out in the open. You can make what you can out of that. Also, so far as I know, Miles Henseler and I are the only two here who know why you're here. This isn't Riverdale, by a long shot. I don't take an interest in every Tom, Dick, or Harry that happens to drift in here. Remember that. And it was a mere accident that I happened to get in on the play tonight. I didn't have to take a hand. You don't have to tell me a thing."

Green rose abruptly and Wayne looked up into the cool gray eyes of the gambler. The lips were expressionless, the lean face calm. There was nothing to indicate that the man was offended, yet Wayne had a feeling that Green was washing his hands of him. Behind that cold exterior there must be some feeling. Certainly there was a vast amount of knowledge. It struck Wayne on the instant that here was a man he might well try to make his friend.

He rose and held out his hand. "I didn't mean to be . . . I'm upset," he said simply. "I'm not used to having men play in the dark. I've told you all I can. I'm here to see Jim Hunter and I thought I recognized him by the description I had of him when he was in the hotel lobby tonight. Henseler told me to go to my room and wait for him until morning, but I thought I saw a chance to get to Hunter without delay. That's the lay."

Green took the hand extended to him for a brief instant. "I

thought so," he said. "And that's the thing for you to do. I'll walk to the hotel with you. You're safe with me. Jake has a bad bunch running with him. Every move you make is watched. You can bet your stack on that. And there isn't a chance in the world for you to see Hunter tonight. Fair enough?"

Wayne was convinced the gambler was speaking the truth. "Fair enough," he decided readily.

"Then come along," said Green. He led the way out of the room and out of the rear door into the black shadow of the alley. They passed quickly to the street, and, as they emerged upon the short main thoroughfare, a pistol barked in the darkness behind them. Green whirled and his gun blazed three times, the shots coming in such lightning order that they seemed almost a single burst of fire. He drew Wayne quickly in front of a building and headed for the hotel.

"Schoolboy work," he said scornfully. "Warning me off, I expect. That shot wasn't ordered by Jake, you can bet on that."

Wayne took off his hat and pointed to the bullet hole in it.

"Trying to scare you," scoffed the gambler, "and me, too. This town is tough, but it isn't tough enough to shoot a man down from behind. Not yet, it isn't." He kept his gun hand inside his coat, and Wayne knew his weapon was carried in a shoulder holster.

"I'm going to have to shoot it out with Barry yet," said Wayne in a matter-of-fact voice.

"I expect you will," Green agreed, "but Jake will want to tell you a few things first. That's why you're safe unless they grab you."

Wayne was thinking hard. If the gambler was ready to shoot in his defense, there must be something besides a mere interest in all this. In the instant Green had replied to the warning shot, Wayne had become imbued with a profound respect for the gambler's prowess with his weapon. Here was a man of guns as well as a man of the green-topped tables and purring wheels.

There were people in the street now, but they hurried on to the hotel, leaving a small throng to congregate behind them. Green sauntered in with Wayne and bought a cigar from the fishy-eyed man. They strolled into the little parlor, where a lamp was burning low on the table. Green jerked down the window shades. Wayne could not help but admire the cool, calm poise of the man as he took a cigarette from his case and lighted it with a hand steady as steel.

"That shot was an accident," he said slowly, sending a smoke ring spiraling toward the ceiling. "But Barry is out to get you, and I can tell you that flat. Watch your step. I think Hunter is going out in the morning, but Miles will likely be here beforehand. You better go to bed. Good night."

Wayne went upstairs, angry, perplexed, but most of all impressed by the queer personality of the man he had just left. His room was at the rear of the hall, with a window looking out on the courtyard between the hotel and the livery. He saw the pale yellow glow of the lantern in the entrance to the barn. There was no life. He did not light the lamp, but, after securing the door, pulled off his boots and lay down on the bed, fully dressed.

Chapter Seven

Pink streamers of the dawn were floating above the eastern horizon when Wayne woke from a restless sleep to the sound of guns. He sat bolt upright in bed, his hand seeking his weapon, before he realized sheepishly that the sounds he heard came from a thumping at his door. He rose hastily and opened the door cautiously. Miles Henseler pushed his way into the room.

"*Humph!* Thought you 'punchers were early birds," he grunted. "The sun will be up in a minute."

"I didn't have anything to get up for until you got here, as I took it last night," said Wayne. "I reckon you've been up all night."

"You said it," growled Henseler, "and looking after your business, or trying to look after it. I didn't connect with Hunter. Haven't any idea where he was after he got in last night. And now I hear he rode out of town less than an hour ago." He sat down on the edge of the bed and scowled. "How important is this business you got to see him about?"

"Dog-goned important," said Wayne irritably. "I'm sorry I stuck in here this morning. I saw Hunter last night and like a fool I tried to make too sure it was him. Where has he gone?"

"I don't know," replied Henseler. "He rode north. But now that I've started this thing, I'm going to see it through. I owe that much to your dad. I'll send a man with you and maybe you can catch him."

"Never mind the man," Wayne retorted, buckling on his gun

belt. "Just give me the direction. I don't want to act brassy, but I ride alone."

Wayne was not in the best of humor this morning. He had a notion that for some reason Hunter was being kept from him. He was disgusted with the veil of mystery that had been thrown over the man and his movements, and now he intended to find him and convey his message regardless of anything else.

"Don't be too independent," said Henseler sharply. "Your dad sent you to me for assistance, which I'm giving you. It wouldn't be any too safe for you to go cavorting around these parts, looking for Hunter on your own."

"I'm sick and tired of all this undercover business," said Wayne bluntly, pouring some water from a pitcher into the basin on the washstand. "I want to see Hunter, and today. All I'm asking is a tip as to where I can stand a chance of finding him." He began his ablutions with this terse remark.

Henseler's eyes had narrowed a bit and his face reddened. "You talk right smart for a man who's come to me for help," he said testily.

"Didn't mean it that way," Wayne retorted, using the towel. "But. . . ." He flung the towel aside. "Did you hear about my fuss with Jake Barry over in Riverdale?"

"Yes, and that wasn't so smart, either," said Henseler.

"He started it and I finished it . . . over there," said Wayne grimly. "If he wants to start it all over again here, I'll finish it for good. Some of his crowd took a shot at me from the dark last night. Maybe you heard about that? No? Well, I've a hunch you will. It looks like there was some kind of a conspiracy to keep me from meeting Hunter, although I don't know why. I'm not going to fan my ears in the sun, waiting."

He saw Henseler's face darken. His speech was having the effect he intended. If the resort proprietor got mad enough, he might tell him where he could find Hunter, and let it go at that, for better or worse. And this was exactly what happened.

Henseler rose from the bed. "All right, my young buckaroo," he said sternly. "You're the doctor. I've done my part, and your dad can't blame me for anything that happens. Jim Hunter rode out a little while ago before I could catch him. He went north toward the Rainbow Butte badlands. Maybe that'll mean something to you, but if it doesn't . . . go it alone, and good luck!" With this he went out, slamming the door.

Ted Wayne put on his hat with a grim smile of satisfaction.

At the expense of angering Henseler, he had learned the destination of Hunter and verified a suspicion that had been growing in his mind. So far as he knew, the only individuals who frequented the wild section east of the butte were members of the Darling gang. Since Hunter was evidently bound for the badlands, it might easily be assumed that he was going to see Darling. It might even be that Hunter was a member of the band, perhaps one of Darling's lieutenants. This would explain the cloak of secrecy thrown about him. Wayne remembered the mysterious rapping on the partition of Henseler's private office the night before. This had been no ordinary signal. Whoever had rapped was no ordinary person. It might have been Hunter. It might have been Darling himself.

Wayne hurried downstairs to the dining room. He felt better now that he was once more on his own, as he thought. There was no one in the dining room, so he went into the kitchen, where he had no trouble getting a breakfast of bacon and eggs, bread, and coffee. He gulped his food and would not have waited to eat had he not anticipated hard riding ahead this day. There was no telling where the trail would lead him. He took a substantial lunch to put in his slicker pack.

The liveryman was up and about and greeted Wayne with a cheery good morning. Wayne didn't know him, but, when he went to get his horse, the man followed him. Wayne looked at him closely as he took down his saddle. He was a tall, stoop-shouldered man with drooping gray mustaches and a face seamed and lined by exposure to range weather.

"I see your horse wears the WP iron," the man ventured.

Wayne nodded. "In plain sight all the time," was his comment.

"You're from the Whippoorwill, then," the liveryman said.

"Yep. My name's Wayne. Know anybody out there?"

"Guess you're Ed Wayne's son, then," said the other. "I used to know your dad, if you're young Wayne."

"I'm that same person," said Ted. "Reckon you're range stock. You look it, anyway."

"I've had rain in my face," said the liveryman dryly. "Your dad was a good sort. Good outfit to work for, I heard. Never threw a rope for Ed, though. Goin' back today?"

Wayne shook his head. He was speculating as to just how far he could go with this man. He decided to take a chance, since the liveryman knew of his outfit, and was to all appearances a former cowman.

"How long since Jim Hunter left?" he asked bluntly.

The liveryman didn't start or show any signs of uneasiness. He looked at Wayne coolly, quizzically. "Little over an hour ago," he answered with no attempt at evasion.

Wayne tightened his cinch strap. "I'm looking for Hunter on business, and these folks around here have steered me around the bush until it seems like school play," he said. "I was told straight he was headed for the breaks around the butte, or somewhere out there. If you'll keep it to yourself, I'll tell you that I'm going to follow him."

"Riders come in and out through this stable and it's none of my business where they're from or where they're goin' . . . so long as they pay their score," drawled the liveryman. But he continued to eye Wayne keenly.

"Would Hunter take the main trail on the east bank of the creek?" asked Wayne casually.

"Those who come and go don't admire to have their movements talked about much," said the liveryman. "They never tell me anything, unless it's some 'puncher who's just been in for a turn at the card tables. When did you get in?"

"Last night. I missed Hunter by a hair. It wasn't my fault that I missed him this morning. If you knew of my dad, you know he's a square shooter. He brought me up the same way. I'm trailing Hunter on business that has nothing to do with this town, or this part of the country, or anybody in it. It's important, or I wouldn't be starting out blind, alone."

"I see." The other nodded. "Well, there's two trails north. One is on the east bank of the creek, and the other turns off a mile beyond the bridge and runs northeast. I expect you can read sign in the dust." With this, the liveryman turned away, walking slowly to the front of the barn.

Wayne was jubilant. In his subtle way, without committing himself or giving any tangible information about Hunter, the liveryman had, nevertheless, given him an excellent tip. He had not mentioned the second trail idly, and Wayne felt sure that was the trail Hunter had taken. By pushing his horse he should overtake his man before noon, perhaps by midmorning.

He led his horse to the front of the barn and paid his bill. "Who'll I tell dad I saw over here knowing him?" he asked.

"It's right in plain sight on the sign outside," was the answer. "Fred Hastings. He cussed me out once as the worst rep ever on his range, so I guess he'll remember me."

"Dad doesn't always mean what he says, but he never forgets a man," said Wayne, extending his hand. "I'll tell him I saw you over here."

"So long," said Hastings. "If you take that trail to the right, you'll find it damp going before you hit the real breaks. I'd try to catch up with my man before I hit the broken country, if I was trailin' anybody up there."

"Thanks," said Wayne gratefully, swinging into the saddle. "So long."

He cut around the outskirts of the little town and made the main trail north almost at the bridge. He had seen very few people about and didn't believe his exit had been witnessed by anyone except the liveryman. He felt sure Hastings would keep his own counsel. North of the bridge he checked his horse and leaned from the saddle to scrutinize the trail. Sure enough, the sign was there—fresh imprints of a horse's hoofs, and its rider was heading north.

Wayne tickled his big gray with the spurs and raced along the trail. It had been so dark when he had arrived the night before that he had seen no trail intersection, but this morning he was watching carefully for the trail Hastings had said led off to the right, toward the northeast. The sun had climbed above the rim in the east and the plain spread out like a sheet of gold, with the green band of timber along the creek to the left, and the pink and purple outline of Rainbow Butte far ahead. A deeper shadow lay about the butte than clothed its lower slopes, and Wayne knew this marked the badlands country that he might have to penetrate—the stronghold of the outlaw, Darling, and his nefarious band. There was no sign of a horseman ahead, no telltale spiral of dust. But Hunter had an hour's start, and Wayne did not expect to catch sight of him for two hours at least, despite his own fast pace.

He came upon the intersection of the northeast trail so suddenly that he wondered that he could have made the distance so quickly. He dismounted and found the tracks he was following did, indeed, turn off on this branch trail. But there was another set of tracks that appeared just as fresh. He mounted and rode back a short distance, and found there had been two sets of tracks for some time during his ride. He had no mind to trace the second set back to where they joined the main trail, for the element of time was too important. He galloped back and swung into the northeast trail, conscious that there were two men ahead of him.

He shook out his reins and rode like the wind, with the sun mounting steadily. However, though the big butte and the tumbled land about it marched steadily toward him as he sped along the thin ribbon of trail, he caught no glimpse of dust or riders ahead. If Hunter was maintaining a similar pace, he must be racing to the breaks on an important matter. As to the other rider, Ted could only conjecture. He was unable to tell by the sign in the trail if one rider had preceded the other, or if they were together. It might be that one of Jake Barry's companions was on his way to Darling's headquarters. Probably Hunter was hurrying there, too. But Wayne had no desire to run into any of the Darling band.

Wayne had rode so hard from the start that he had to ease his pace. The trail had veered to the east, and now he came to the rolling plain, with gullies and coulées, leading up to the fantastic ridges of the badlands country. He swung over the first of these and seemed to drop from a clear sky into the shadows of the breaks. There was a cool lane, with poplars on either side that led to a fragrant meadow in which Wayne found the first of the famous Rainbow Butte springs. It was the wild surroundings, the marshy ground, the deadly quicksand soap holes, which made it impossible for stockmen to take advantage of these springs. And, indeed, it was not necessary, for they fed two small streams that didn't dry up save in an exceptional year of drought.

Wayne stopped at the spring to refresh himself and water his horse. He found fresh tracks, but only one of the riders had stopped here. He pushed on, renewing his fast pace when the trail permitted. It wound about ridges and over them, through shadowy ravines, about the ghostly soap holes, across patches of dry gravel that no horse could negotiate noiselessly.

Noon found Wayne in what he thought must be the wildest part of that wild section—the heart of the breaks. The ridges were higher and rock-ribbed with gnarled pines struggling to maintain their hold with talon roots. The trail was very narrow, but as hard from use as an old buffalo trail. The telltale sign still was in it, but Wayne had seen no one ahead and realized that he had had too late a start. Caution now was necessary to the utmost degree. If he were approaching the rendezvous of the Darling gang, there most certainly would be look-outs stationed at points of vantage to forestall an unexpected arrival of strangers. Wayne kept on, although he was beset with misgivings. It would be foolish to turn back, perhaps foolhardy to push on. He wondered if he actually had anything to fear from Darling. An explanation of his presence in that section would be the awkward part of it if he were taken into camp. Shortly afterward his dilemma seemingly solved itself.

He came into a ravine so short and wide that it was practically a basin. The skirts of the ridges sloped gently down and were green with a growth of fir. From the slopes on either side he could have a good view of the trail and anyone riding in either direction. There was a spring and a trickle of water on the lower slope to the left. Wayne decided to wait here until dusk.

He watered his horse and led the animal through the trees up the left slope until he reached a shoulder of the ridge. Here was a grassy knoll above the trees that would serve as an excellent look-out station. It likely had been used as such more than once, for he found the cold ashes of dead fires.

He unsaddled and hobbled his horse, although he felt sure the gray would not stray from him. While the animal grazed, he ate his lunch. Then he lay down on the knoll in the shade of a single fir that grew upon it, and smoked a cigarette. The sun began its slant to westward, and Wayne dozed. He roused himself time after time, then dozed again.

The wind whined in the firs, and the soft grass deadened the sound of footfalls as Wayne finally slept.

Chapter Eight

Wayne opened his eyes, but instead of the sun, and the blue sky, and the green of the fir branches, he saw only the black bore of a rifle covering him. The soft drowsiness of the warm afternoon had betrayed him and lured him to dreamland. Here he was, sprawled out under a tree, covered by a rifle, of all weapons. There were two shadows, one on either side of him, and so he knew his captors numbered three. The man who covered him with the rifle was bulky, with a thick stubble of beard that prevented Wayne from identifying him as one he might have seen before.

"Well," said Wayne pleasantly, "what're you going to do? Stand there and pose, or shoot, or what?"

"Get up!" came the sharp order from behind the rifle.

"Just what I was going to do," said Wayne, "if you'll move that thing so I won't bump my head on it. Seems like close quarters for a Thirty-Thirty, but we learn something every day."

"You'll learn something before you get any smarter," said the man with the gun as Wayne got to his feet. "Tie him up."

Wayne now took notice of the other two men. They were younger than their companion. He could not remember ever having seen either of them before. The question uppermost in his mind was whether he was in the hands of the Darling band proper, or a captive of Jake Barry's crowd. This he hoped to learn by adroit queries, if he could taunt the men into talking.

After securing his hands behind him with thongs tightly

bound about his wrists, Wayne's captors caught up his horse, took off the hobbles, and saddled him.

"Much of a ride ahead?" asked Wayne casually. "You've got my gun, and there are three of you, and my hands are tied. Maybe you better tie me in the saddle, too. That horse is trained for emergencies like this."

"Don't worry," the bearded man snapped out. "You're not goin' to ride. You're goin' to walk for a change." He gave an order to the other two in a low voice, aside.

"As easy as all that?" said Wayne. "Then we're not going far. Cow boots aren't made for walking, and we're all wearing 'em."

"Keep that smart tongue in your mouth," said the leader angrily, "or I'll knock it down your throat."

"Oh, no, you won't," Wayne taunted. "You're not a big stick. You've got your orders. Why don't you gag me if you can't stand conversation? A man who has to shoot from the shoulder instead of the hip isn't so much."

"I'll put you where you can talk to yourself," was the big man's comment. "You're just fresh and covering up your scare with bluff." Then, to the others: "All right, we'll go."

"Why not," sang Wayne. "We want to get there before sunset."

No attention was paid to this remark. One of the men tied the reins of his bridle to the saddle and caught up the reins of Wayne's horse to lead it. Another took the reins of his own horse. The horses of the trio had been left at the edge of the tree growth. The man with the rifle evidently had carried it to cover Wayne from a distance or shoot down his horse.

The big man turned to the captive. "We're goin' up a slick trail," he said. "You can jump off any time, or try to make it into the woods, just as you please. Or you can walk along peaceful-like, and not get hurt. Fall in and follow that lead horse."

"That won't be hard," drawled Wayne. "It's bony enough."

This touched a raw spot, for the leader swore and took a step toward Wayne. But he thought better of whatever intention he had. "That's a horse for this kind of business," he blurted wrathfully. "If yours slips over the edge, it'll be because it don't know its business. Move along. I'll be right behind you to take up the slack if you start anything."

"You're a brave man, I can see that," was Wayne's sarcastic comment as they started.

One of the younger men of the trio led the first horse. The big man followed directly behind Wayne, leading his own horse. The third man brought up the rear, leading Wayne's horse with his own following.

The queer procession proceeded up the knoll to the rocky spine of the ridge above. In a few minutes Wayne learned why they were afoot. He had expected a bad trail, but the trail they came to was the most perilous he ever had negotiated.

The ridge twisted off to the left and appeared to divide. At this fork there was a precipice, a sheer drop of three or four hundred feet. They turned to the left, upon a narrow shelf of rock with a rock wall rising from the shelf. A misstep here, and man or horse would plunge down upon the massed boulders hundreds of feet below. It was the famous Devil's Hole of which Wayne had heard rumors. Few had seen it. None who he had ever met had been there. One thing he had ascertained before they came to this dangerous trail was that the trail they followed was little used. It was not probable that this trail led to the rendezvous of Darling. He was being taken to a place to be held a captive until. . . . Jake Barry! He felt sure that the man he had whipped in Riverdale was behind this business. He had tried to take him in town and had lost out through Green, the gambler. Wayne recalled the tracks of the two riders. One was Hunter. The other might easily have been a messenger for Barry. They knew he was following Hunter, and Barry had sent a man ahead in event that he followed his man into the badlands country. A man might have been watching from the very knoll where Wayne had decided to await the coming of dusk.

Now the dangerous going demanded his closest attention. He was not so much concerned about himself, for the trail was comparatively safe for a man afoot, but not so for a horse. And Wayne's horse was larger than the mounts of the trio, range bred and ridden, and unaccustomed to trails such as the one he was on. Wayne felt if he lost his horse he could kill whoever was responsible with a clean conscience. But such a trail could not continue any great distance. Wayne sighed with relief when he saw the end across a perilous slope of fine shale. He recognized this as the most dangerous point and held his breath as they crossed it on a hard-packed ribbon of path made by elk and deer, providing those wild animals were in this tumbled wilderness. They came out upon a wide cut between mounds of boulders.

"All right, we'll ride on in," said the leader. "Put him on his horse."

Wayne's hands were untied and he was told to mount. "You won't be goin' out of here fast enough but what we can stop you with a club," said the big man with a sneering grin. "How's the scenery?"

"Wouldn't be bad if it wasn't spoiled by that dirty mug of yours," returned Wayne, patting the neck of his horse.

"You'll sing a different tune before long," the other said savagely.

"Watch out you don't join in the chorus," Wayne flashed grimly.

"Cut it out, Boyd," said one of the others. "If you're goin' to smash him one, smash him, but this talk won't get us anywhere."

Boyd turned on the speaker. "I'm runnin' this business," he snarled. "No young whippersnapper is goin' to tell me what to do. He'll get smashed enough when the time comes, so don't worry. Now we'll get goin'."

"What do you think of that, whippersnapper?" Wayne put in.

The young fellow was uncertain whether to be angry at Wayne, as well as with Boyd, until he caught Wayne's guarded smile. "It ain't up to you to go around callin' people names," he shot at Boyd as he mounted. "If you don't like what I say, you can lump it!"

The big man's face darkened, but he held back the sharp retort that was on his tongue. Wayne saw he didn't want dissension among his companions.

"Ride ahead," he ordered the youth. "You follow him," he told Wayne, "and don't forget I'm still behind you."

"That's where you belong," said Wayne, falling in.

They rode through the cut and into a forest trail. On the left, Wayne could see the wall of rock still towering above them. Once the trail climbed high enough for him to see over the tops of the firs on his right, and beyond them was nothing save the distant rim of Devil's Hole. He assumed that the dangerous trail by which they had come was the only exit from whatever place they might be going.

This proved to be the case, for they came out of the tree growth into a circular meadow, hemmed in by the rock wall, except on the side where they had entered it and on the side toward the Hole. There were two cabins here and a small corral. Water trickled from a spring at the base of the wall on the left. The meadow was carpeted with luscious grass. Wayne felt a concern he didn't show. The whole Whippoorwill outfit could comb the badlands about the butte and fail to find this place.

"This is it," Boyd called to Wayne as they drew rein at the corral. "Hop down and turn your horse in. There's the way out, any time you want to try to make it." He pointed to the opening in the trees across the meadow where the trail entered the timber, drew his rifle from the scabbard on his saddle, and signaled to a companion to look after his horse.

"Oh, I'll stay for supper, anyway," drawled Wayne.

He noted, as he attended to his mount, that the place was to all appearances deserted, save for himself and his captors. Heavy padlocks secured the doors of the cabins. *Why the locks?* Wayne wondered. He was convinced that, if Darling had ordered him taken, or if he had merely been captured by look-outs for the band, he would have been taken to a place near the outlaw's headquarters, perhaps to the headquarters itself. He couldn't be sure, but more than ever the conviction seized him that Jake Barry was responsible.

With the horses in the corral, Wayne was led to the smaller of the two cabins. Boyd unlocked the door and motioned him inside. As he entered, Wayne caught the young fellow who had talked back to Boyd staring at him curiously. Wayne deliberately winked. The door was pulled shut behind him and the padlock clicked.

A glance about the room showed two bunks on opposite sides with a table between. On the table were some candles and a pile of tattered magazines. There were two small benches. The single window, facing the trail, was barred with two thick saplings. On a shelf over the window was a greasy pack of cards.

Wayne sat down on one of the bunks, on which was a straw tick and a blanket, and rolled a cigarette. The sunlight was fading rapidly. Wayne surmised he was high on the eastern shoulder of Rainbow Butte. One thing was certain: any visitors would have to arrive before dark, because the narrow trail above the Hole could hardly be negotiated except in good light. A bright moon might be all right; starlight would be too dim. Barry could hardly be expected until next day—if it was Barry who was to come.

The gathering twilight brought the faint odor of frying bacon and strong coffee. Wayne wondered who would bring his supper. If Boyd came. . . . But Wayne put aside the thought of a sudden onslaught and possible escape. He would wait for a break.

When the supper came, it was the young fellow who had defied Boyd who brought it.

Chapter Nine

Wayne surveyed the young fellow with frank interest. He merely glanced at the bacon, biscuits, boiled potatoes, and coffee that were put on the table with salt and pepper and sugar. It was a good enough supper for a hungry man. He caught the other looking at him repeatedly with that gleam of curiosity in his eyes.

"Boyd outside?" he asked, careful to speak in an undertone.

"Nope, and I'm not supposed to talk," was the guarded answer.

"Maybe you'll answer one question," Wayne suggested. "I'm entitled to know, and nobody'll ever get wise that you told me. When is Jake coming?"

Even if the young fellow had decided not to reply, Wayne would have known by the momentary startled expression in his eyes that he had hit a verbal bull's-eye. His visitor looked about hastily, and then murmured: "Tomorrow."

Wayne nodded and his smile flashed. "Thanks . . . for the supper." He added the last three words quickly as a shadow slanted across the floor from the open doorway. It was Boyd.

"Has he got his grub?" demanded the big man with a heavy frown. "Yes? Well, what you goin' to do? Stay here and watch him eat it? He's old enough to eat alone."

"And then some." Wayne nodded, forestalling any reply from the young fellow. "If you were so interested in my supper, why didn't you bring it yourself? Your man, here, just got the things on the table."

"Yeah? Well, then, he can beat it." Boyd signaled with a thumb for the young fellow to leave. When they were alone, he turned on Wayne, his face dark, his eyes narrowed.

"You're getting' away with a lot," he shot through his teeth, "because, like you said without knowin' you hit the nail on the head, I've got my orders. If I didn't know you was goin' to get yours, and plenty of it, I'd hand you a package myself. You've played a high hand over on the west range, but you're east of the butte now, you sap, and you're just plain dirt, see?"

"Throw your gun on the table and I'll slap that big mouth of yours," said Wayne.

Boyd fumed. The words he wanted to get out choked in his throat. Then, realizing the futility and foolish stupidity of his situation, he turned to the door.

"Maybe you'd rather shoot it out," Wayne taunted, "especially since I haven't got a gun."

Boyd stepped out and pulled the door shut, snapping the padlock. Wayne had a feeling that he would see no more of him until Jake Barry arrived. He turned to his supper and ate a hearty meal. When he had finished, the shades of twilight had deepened so that a light was necessary. He lighted two of the candles and lay back upon the bunk to smoke.

After a time he again heard the rattle of the padlock, and, when the door swung open, he saw the third member of the trio. He was not as young as the man who had brought his supper and he had a harder look. "Had enough?" he asked gruffly as he stepped to the table.

Wayne had noticed that the man's holster was empty, and remembered that the young fellow's holster also had been empty. He had laid this to the probability that he had been working in the kitchen or wherever the meals had been prepared. But now he realized that Boyd was taking no chance of having a man attacked and his weapon taken from him. As a matter of fact, Wayne hadn't thought of this, for he knew the trail would be guarded, and, in any event, he would not leave the place without his horse.

"Where's your gun?" he asked, ignoring the other's question.

"It's handy enough, if I need it. Don't worry."

"Nice sociable bunch Jake trails with," Wayne said pleasantly.

If he expected the man to betray any interest in this remark, he was mistaken. Gathering up the dishes, the man left without a word, and Wayne heard the padlock snap for the last time that night.

The wind moaned dolefully in the firs and stunted pines as he lay down to sleep. But the sleep that had come so easily that afternoon with the warmth of the sun about him failed to come this night. His thoughts continually reverted to Henseler and the gambler, Green, in Rainbow. He could not bring himself to believe that Henseler had not seen Hunter. He remembered the mysterious rapping on the partition of the former's office. It could not have been Hunter who had given that signal, for he had left the resort immediately and had found Hunter in the hotel lobby. If Hunter had seen Henseler, it was possible that he had refused to meet Wayne. Green's warning had not been idle talk. Just what Barry intended to do, now that he had him in his grasp, Wayne could only conjecture. He remembered, too, that Jack McCurdy, the foreman of the Whippoorwill, had said he would start a search for him if he wasn't back in three days. Wayne smiled at this recollection. McCurdy would have scant chance of finding him, even if he tried. Then Wayne thought of his father's queer instructions. And why did he want to see Hunter, who, by all indications, was mixed up with the Darling gang? He thought of Polly Arnold.

It was midnight before he slept.

Wayne woke at dawn in an altogether different frame of mind

than had possessed him the night before. He got up and looked out the window until the dazzling sunlight filled the meadow. He was in a dangerous mood. Not for a moment did he feel the slightest fear about the coming of Barry. He was eager for the man's arrival.

He whirled as the padlock rattled. The same man who had taken the dishes the night preceding brought his breakfast.

"Have a good sleep?" he asked with a grimace meant for a grin.

"Put those things on the table and cut the talk," was Wayne's sharp reply. "And tell Boyd I want some water to wash with."

"Sure," sneered the other, putting the food and coffee on the table. "Soap and a towel, too?"

"Get out before I break your neck!" Wayne stepped quickly toward the man, who retreated to the door. As he pulled it shut, Wayne laughed. "Yellow!" he exclaimed aloud. He felt that the young fellow was not altogether against him, and now, with the second man showing plainly that he was afraid of him, he decided he would have only Boyd to reckon with in event that he made a break to get away.

As he was eating breakfast, he formulated a plan to get on the outside of the cabin. It was to be the simple expedient of knocking the man out when he came for the dishes, and dashing out the door. Almost under the window outside was a stout stick. It was all he needed for an attempt to take Boyd unawares.

But the opportunity to put this plan into effect did not materialize. No one came for the empty dishes. The morning wore away to noonday with Wayne fretting and pacing the floor. Boyd had ignored his request for water, or the message had not been delivered. The afternoon slipped slowly along until the sun was low in the west. Wayne was at the window when three riders cantered into the meadow. His lips tightened as he recognized the huge form of Jake Barry in the lead.

When they rode up to the cabins, Wayne saw that Barry's eyes were much improved. Both were discolored, but the swelling was down, so that he could see clearly. The two men with him had been in Riverdale, as Wayne quickly made out. They passed from view as they drew up at the larger cabin, and shortly afterward the horses were led past to the corral.

Within half an hour the padlock sounded its message, and the door swung open to reveal Barry's bulk against the light. He was wearing his gun, as Wayne instantly noted. His face was bruised and swollen, but the eyes shot an unflickering flame of hatred. He stepped inside the cabin.

Wayne didn't give him a chance to speak first. "Let's have it," he said curtly. "What do you want with me? You must know you're taking a big chance, so you must be willing to take it. How'll you have it?"

"You're the one that's taking chances," said Jake in a thick voice, husky with anger. "You took your biggest one when you edged over into my territory. I suppose you thought your friend, Green, could keep you out of trouble till you had your own lay set. I'm goin' to give you trouble, and give it to you so you can't dance away from it."

"All right," said Wayne sharply, "let's have it."

"I just want to tell you. . . ."

"Cut the mouth warbling," Wayne broke in. "You haven't got anything to tell me that I want to hear. I'm not listening to any of your bellyaching. Bring on your trouble and let's have it over with, but I'll tell you one thing. You can't get away with this. Let's have the bad news."

Jake was boiling mad. If he had intended to postpone what he had in mind another day or two, that intention fled before the look in Wayne's eyes and the contempt in his voice.

"All right," he managed to get out with an oath and a vile

name directed at Wayne. He stepped out the door. "Come and get it!"

Wayne was through the door in two bounds, but he didn't reach Barry. As he made the open, Boyd flung himself upon him, and the two men who had accompanied Jake helped hold him.

"This way," Barry told the men.

Holding Wayne by either arm, they followed Barry to a thin trail that entered the timber on the side of the meadow toward Devil's Hole. Wayne walked behind Barry with a gun pressed against his back. A few beads of cold sweat broke out on his forehead. They were going toward the edge of the precipice, the sheer wall of rock that fell away into the Hole. Did Barry intend to throw him over? It could be done, and his body probably never would be found. He had never heard of anyone having been down in the Hole. A man could be thrown in there and he would pass out of the picture, leaving no trace as to the manner of his disappearance.

They had not gone far when they came out into an opening. The clear space was in the shape of a semicircle, with the trees about, except in the front. Before them was the awesome edge of the precipice and the void above Devil's Hole. It was small, this open space, so small that a man could cross it in any direction in a score of steps.

The gun was withdrawn from Wayne's back, and the men stood back, spreading out fan-wise. Jake Barry was taking off his gun belt. A mean grin was on his swollen lips and his eyes were flaming with malice. Tossing the belt to one of the men, he strode toward Wayne.

But Wayne stepped quickly aside. His own eyes were darting a greenish flame. Barry intended to throw him over the cliff into the Hole. He could see it in the larger man's eyes, in the very manner in which he walked. His intention fairly shrieked its menacing message.

Barry laughed. "Not much room to dance here, eh, boys?" he called. Then he made a lunge at Wayne.

Wayne knew the only chance he had was to get in some telling blows to Barry's eyes for the second time. But the man was right in that there wasn't sufficient room for anything approaching expert boxing. Barry could rush him, taking the blows as they came and, in that narrow space, succeed, more than likely, in getting a hold on him. Once in the grasp of those arms of steel, Wayne wouldn't have the ghost of a chance.

The ruby glow of the sunset was staining the rock walls, and a pink mist seemed to float above the yawning depth of the Hole. Wayne realized he was about to fight for his life. He avoided Barry's rush and, in doing so, stepped close to the edge of the timber. His best chance seemed on the instant to plunge into the shelter of the trees. But a hand caught him and threw him back. He staggered, and recovered just in time to side-step another vicious rush and to take a glancing blow on the left side of his head.

"You rat!" he cried. "Six to one! Barry, you're yellow!"

He leaped in as Barry poised for another rush. Wayne had his back to the precipice now. He wasn't six feet from the edge. He could go over in dodging Barry's blow or in avoiding his rush. He could wait. Barry lunged forward just as Wayne made his leap. But instead of landing a blow, or clutching Wayne, he went down on his hands and knees. For Wayne had dropped to the ground and Barry had stumbled over his body.

Wayne knew any attempt to wrestle with the big man would be folly, for Barry was more than a match for him in strength. In the instant of a mind picture he saw Jake lifting him aloft and hurling him over the cliff. He was on his feet before Barry could get up, and, as the latter rose, Wayne drove a blow behind the ear with every ounce of strength he possessed. But Barry merely shook it off and rose to his full height. But not before Wayne had succeeded in getting in a second blow. This caught Barry fully in the face, and the blood spurted. But Wayne now was away from the edge of the precipice.

Barry walked slowly around the outer ring of the clear space with Wayne in the center. The big man was recovering from the pain of Wayne's last blow. Wayne expected to hear any minute the order for the men to close in on him. He didn't think for a minute that Barry would continue the struggle any length of time unless he felt sure of getting his hands on him.

As he walked about, Barry slowly closed in, then, when he was opposite the rim of the Hole, he made another rush. Wayne leaped aside as Barry made a grasp near the ground, expecting his adversary would try another trick. This time, Wayne's side-step carried him to the trees, and he whirled on the man who reached for him, landing a straight right to the jaw. The ferocity of the blow, as powerful, almost, as Wayne could deliver, seemed to lift the man off his feet. Then he went down in a heap.

But this had taken time, and before Wayne could square away for his dash into the trees, one of the others hurled himself upon Wayne's shoulders, sending him to his knees, almost over the man he had knocked out. As the crushing weight came down upon him again, Wayne glimpsed the butt of the gun in the holster of the man on the ground beside him. With a violent heave and twist he wrenched himself free and came to his feet with the gun in his hand.

Boyd came on the run as Wayne backed to the edge of the trees. Barry was shouting, but no one seemed to hear. Then Boyd's right hand darted low and his gun cracked from his hip. The weapon's report seemed long-drawn, for Wayne's gun spoke almost at the same instant as he went down on his left knee and hand. Boyd went backward as if he had been struck with a club. He fell on his back on the grass.

Another bullet whistled past Wayne's head as he leaped forward to meet Barry. He had the big bruiser covered, and called sharply: "Put 'em up, Barry, or down you go for keeps!"

Barry raised his hands. He had gone into the fight unarmed and, in the excitement of what had happened so swiftly, he had not secured his gun.

Wayne stepped behind him. At his rear was the edge of the yawning chasm. Just in front of him was Barry, holding his hands aloft, and beyond him the four others were grouped, all holding their guns in their hands, staring stupidly at Wayne and their helpless leader. Boyd lay still upon the grass with a bullet in his heart.

"Tell your men to drop their guns, Barry," Wayne commanded sternly. "You were six to one against me. Now you're five to one. I'm taking no chances. You'll do as I tell you to do, or I'll bore you in the drop of a hat and make it four to one and shoot it out!"

"Drop 'em," snarled Barry.

The guns fell from the hands of the quartet in front.

"All right, you." Wayne motioned to the young fellow who had brought his supper the night before. "Pick up those guns, one at a time, and carry 'em that way to the edge of the Hole and throw 'em over. I've got Jake, here, covered, and I can get the two of you if you try any kind of a trick. Stick up your paws, the rest of you!"

Wayne stepped a little to one side of Barry, where he could keep an eye on him, on the young fellow, and on the other three. He had picked the youngest member of the gang because he didn't believe he would attempt to evade the order. In the present situation, however, none in the clearing had a chance against Wayne's gun if he should have to open fire. The young fellow did as he had been told, carrying the guns, one by one, to the edge of the precipice and tossing them over.

"Don't forget Boyd's," said Wayne grimly. "He won't need it any more. He has Jake's gun, too, if I am not mistaken. Throw 'em over."

Wayne was not forgetting the rifle Boyd had carried at the time of the capture, or the probability that there were more guns in the large cabin. But he didn't intend to let any of the gang reach the large cabin. As the young fellow threw the last gun away and returned to his place in line with the others in front of Barry, with his hands elevated, Wayne spoke again. His words were crisp, the tone icy: "Barry, you're still five to one, due to what common sense you've got. I'm going to herd you into the cabin where you had me penned up. Those four men out there are going to walk single file ahead. You're going to walk just in front of me. If any of 'em makes a break, I'll drill you and take my chances. I've got too much at stake and the odds are too big against me. I'm going out of here, one way or the other. By the trail or on the road to kingdom come. If I have to take the road, I'll take you with me! Now, you tell 'em."

Barry gulped. "Accidents'll happen," he said hoarsely. "Go ahead as he says, you fellows."

As Wayne stepped behind Barry, there came a startling interruption. A tall man, with the lower part of his face covered by a black silk handkerchief, stepped out from the entrance to the trail. His gun was in his holster, but Wayne had leaped from behind Barry to cover him at first sight.

The mysterious newcomer held up a hand and stepped to one side of the trail. "March!" he said curtly to the gaping five. Then he leisurely drew his gun, without looking at Wayne, and backed along the trail ahead of the men, covering them from the front.

Chapter Ten

Barry and his four companions marched slowly through the aisle in the forest with the mysterious stranger ahead and Wayne bringing up the rear. The latter could not imagine who had come to his rescue. The masked man was about Jack McCurdy's build, but Wayne knew it was not Jack. There were certain characteristics he would have recognized in the Whippoorwill foreman, and the latter's eyes were dark, not a cold gray such as those that looked out over the black handkerchief. The man wore a black sateen shirt. These were seldom, if ever, worn by the WP outfit. Wayne was more than partly inclined to believe that this was a ruse. But if the man was one of Barry's crowd, he could have shot from the trail, and have wounded Wayne, if he didn't want to kill him.

When they came into the meadow, the stranger stepped aside, sheathing his gun, and looked askance at Wayne.

"Into the small cabin," Wayne ordered.

The stranger fell in with him as he followed the men to the cabin. When the four ahead of Barry were inside, the masked man drew Barry aside with a jerk, and pulled the door shut.

"Keep him covered," he said sharply to Wayne as he snapped the padlock. But as he turned, Barry, who had watched him closely from the start, pulled down the handkerchief with a lightning move. Barry laughed derisively and Wayne was too startled to move or say a word. The man before him was Jim

Hunter, smilingly untying the handkerchief at the back of his neck.

"You didn't have to do that, Jake," said Hunter. "I'd have had it off in a minute, anyway. I thought it was just as well that those other four didn't know who I am, and I still think that way." He turned to Wayne. "Put up your gun. He'll stay with us. And we'll get your horse and his. Come on to the corral, Jake. You're goin' out with us. I didn't want to leave you fellows locked up here, for somebody might forget where the place is, and that cabin is a stronger jail than it looks. Get moving."

Barry swore. "I suppose you're a friend of this rat," he sneered.

"Looks like I was a friend of yours," said Hunter dryly, "considering the way he had you sewed up when I arrived. I reckon, if I hadn't showed, you'd be in that cabin for the night, or next week, or more maybe, if you didn't stop a slug of lead."

"You're long on talk today," said Barry viciously.

Hunter stopped at the bars of the corral and faced Barry, his eyes hard, his face stern. "I'm not goin' to talk any more to you," he said, cutting his words off short. "Boyd's back there in the grass, dead. You've done enough with your personal grievance. This is pretty raw. If you can't fight it out like a man, forget it."

Barry's bruised and bloated face went black, and his thick lips trembled with the reply that he managed to keep back only by a tremendous effort. It was plain to Wayne that Barry was afraid to talk back to Hunter. For Hunter's tone had been that of command, and Barry had glanced away from the look in the tall man's eyes. "You two saddle up," said Hunter. "My horse is across the meadow."

When the mounts were ready, Wayne signaled Hunter aside. "I want to see you alone on a matter," he said.

"I know." Hunter nodded. "Green told me. We'll have time later."

They crossed the meadow, Wayne and Barry riding, and Hunter walking ahead. Hunter had been careful not to look in the direction of the small cabin when his face might be seen. There had been shouts from the imprisoned quartet, mostly jeers at the enraged Barry.

"What're you doin', Jake, giving us the double-cross?" came a voice Wayne thought he recognized as coming from the youngest of the men.

"Who's your friend?" called another.

Barry bit his lip and didn't reply. His face was white under its tan. Not once did he look at Wayne, but the latter sensed that, if thinking could kill, he would be a dead man instantly.

When they reached Hunter's horse, tethered among the trees at the opening of the trail, Hunter took his corduroy coat from the saddle and put it on. The coat would have been a giveaway, but Wayne surmised that Barry had suspected Hunter's identity from the start.

"You go ahead, Jake," Hunter ordered when he had mounted.

"You've got a lot of crust!" Barry exploded. "Anybody would think. . . ."

"Cut it!" Hunter broke in crisply. "Whatever I've got, you lack. Ride along ahead there, and we'll walk around the rim. You can talk to yourself, and cuss at the birds comin' back from the valley. Slope!"

They cantered along the trail between the trees to the wide space at the start of the dangerous trail across the shale, and here they dismounted. It was sunset, and the purple shadows already were playing on the narrow shelf of rock that they had to traverse. Below them yawned Devil's Hole. Wayne looked down only once and shuddered.

"You say I'm coming back from the valley?" Barry asked

Hunter with a scowl.

"If you want to," was the casual answer.

"It'll be gettin' pretty dim for this trail in here," said Barry. "What do you want me to go to the valley for?"

"Not a thing," said Hunter. "Not a thing, on second thought. I'll just see you on your way up from the other side. Since you've got to lead your horse, you won't be turning back too quick, unless you jump over him."

"I haven't got any reason to follow you," Barry flared. "I don't see why I should have to go any farther than this."

"No?" Hunter's tone was cold. "Well, I do. And that'll do for you. Go ahead, Jake. You know the way. It's right in front of you."

Barry started, leading his horse, then stopped and called back to Hunter, who was following with Wayne in the rear. "What's the sense in my taking my horse along if I'm coming right back?" he demanded.

"I just told you," Hunter retorted. "Move along before I prod that nag of yours and put you on the run."

They went out upon the shale, slowly, careful of their steps. Once across the shale, they came upon the narrow shelf of rock, and moved slowly around the upper side of the dreadful chasm. Once again Wayne breathed a sigh of relief when they reached the end of the perilous trail.

The sun had set, and already the twilight shades were gathering. By the time Jake had returned to the cabins, it would be too dark to go out again by that treacherous shelf of rock. Thus it was that Hunter was making sure they would not be followed.

"All right, Jake, you can beat it back," said Hunter. "If I was you, I wouldn't say anything about it being me who was behind that mask."

"Yeah?" sneered Barry. "And who'll I say it was?"

"Tell 'em it was Jack McCurdy from the Whippoorwill,"

Wayne put in. "He's due here about now, looking for me."

"Not a bad idea." Hunter nodded.

But Barry paid no attention to Wayne. He spoke again to Hunter. "There's Boyd, you know." For the first time Wayne detected genuine concern in Jake's voice.

"I don't know a thing," said Hunter with a wave of his hand as he caught up his reins to mount. "He wasn't with me, and I haven't even seen you, as far as that goes. You can make up your own story or just let him drop out of sight. I'm not goin' to do any talking. If those rowdies with you keep their mouths shut, you're sitting pretty. My part in this business is finished, so far as you're concerned."

"I suppose I ought to thank you for that," Barry commented in a voice brimming with sarcasm.

"You've got more than that to thank me for, but you're just naturally too dumb to see it," was Hunter's rejoinder. "I'll watch you start back, Jake."

As Barry turned again to the trail, his eyes met Wayne's for a long moment. But in the brief space he put into his glance a venomous gleam that could mean but one thing—plain murder. Then he started on his way, leading his horse out upon the shelf of rock where it was impossible to turn back unless he killed his mount to clear the path. This he could not do, for he had no weapon.

Wayne and Hunter sat their horses, watching him go. "Where'd they get you?" Hunter asked quietly.

"Up on the ridge," replied Wayne. "Yesterday afternoon. I was waiting till dark before I went any farther looking for you, and the heat put me to sleep." He wanted to ask Hunter how he had found out where he was, but decided to let the older man lead the conversation.

"All right, let's ride along," said Hunter, and turned his horse into a narrow opening in the trees.

Wayne soon found they were following a different trail than the one by which he had come. Instead of going back up the ridge, they were veering to the north and going down steadily. A thrill came to him as he speculated whether or not they might be going to the Darling headquarters. Regardless of what might happen, he wanted a look at the notorious outlaw. Hunter knew he had a message for him, because he had said as much. He would ask for it in due time. Wayne was content to wait.

It was dark when they finally came out of the timber at the head of a long ravine. They crossed a ridge and dropped down into another ravine, which widened rapidly until it became a valley. They rode down this, and finally Wayne made out a cabin ahead with a lean-to shelter for horses. When they came to it, Hunter drew rein. "We'll lay up here," he said, swinging from the saddle.

They put their horses in a small corral behind the cabin. This cabin, too, was padlocked, and Hunter brought forth a key. Inside he lighted a lamp on the table, and Wayne saw a neatly furnished room, with two bunks, a stove, dishes and provisions, two chairs, and clothes hanging from hooks on the wall near the door. Evidently this was Hunter's own cabin, and occupied regularly.

Hunter cooked the supper while Wayne told what had taken place in Riverdale at the time of his fight with Jake, and gave the details of the affair in town and what had happened after his capture.

"Suppose," said Hunter, looking at him quizzically, "that Jake had made a break when you had him dead to rights. What would you have done?"

"Shot him down," replied Wayne promptly with a frown. "Might not have killed him, but I'd have put him on the grass."

"It's a wonder Boyd didn't get you," muttered Hunter.

"I felt the breath of his bullet and knew I couldn't take a

chance," said Wayne briefly. "I . . . I never shot a man before. It doesn't leave you feeling any too good."

Hunter looked at him quickly. "You were bound to come to it sooner or later," he said. "And it always makes a gun expert more careful when he can boast a notch. I don't mean boast in your case. That was just my way of putting it. But . . . well, I've been through it."

Wayne looked at the disfigured features of this man who was feared and respected. His lips were drawn tightly, his face grim, as he put the supper on the table. Was he an outlaw? Wayne didn't know and he could think of nothing to say.

"Now, why were you looking for me?" asked Hunter as they sat at table.

"Dad sent me to find you an tell you that he wanted to see you at the ranch. He said to bring you back with me. I saw Miles Henseler and that gambler, Green, in town and they wouldn't tell me. . . ."

"Yes, I know," Hunter broke in. "Don't worry. They knew what they were doing. I was back in town last night and trailed Jake today, which is how I happened on the scene. I wouldn't have stepped out there if I hadn't been afraid that Jake would make some kind of a slip. You handled that business like an old-timer."

Wayne disregarded the compliment. "Will you go back with me?" he asked.

"I don't suppose old Ed said anything about why he wanted to see me?" Hunter frowned.

"No, but he made it plain that he does want to see you."

"Humph," grunted Hunter. "Well, I suppose I'll have to go over there. I suppose you know you took a chance in coming into this section in here." He looked at Wayne sharply.

"I've heard that Darling and his bunch hang out in here," said Wayne boldly. "They're dynamite, aren't they?"

Hunter put down his coffee cup suddenly. "Get this straight, here and now," he said evenly. "You haven't been here at all, understand? You met up with me on the trail outside. Just forget about that fool play of Jake's. And wrap your questions up in your tongue before you let 'em out."

Hunter didn't look at Wayne as he said this, but his manner of speaking lent emphasis to his words. The quiet statement did not seem to require any answer or comment and Wayne remained silent.

"We'll get started at daybreak," Hunter announced when they had finished supper.

Wayne washed the dishes, and within half an hour they turned in. Wayne did not lay awake, thinking, this night. He had escaped death at the hands of Barry and he had performed his mission. He only regretted that he would have to leave that section without a glimpse of Darling. Hunter fairly radiated wild adventure, despite his calmness and cool demeanor; the breaks seemed to teem with it—Wayne yearned for it. His first visit—and he had killed a man!

It still was so dark that the lamp was necessary when they got up in the morning. Hunter fried bacon and beans, made biscuits and coffee, and they had breakfast with the first glimmer of the dawn gray in the window. Shortly afterward they rode down the valley and crossed a ridge to the east. In an hour they were on the trail by which Wayne had entered the badlands district. They saw no one. "If we meet up with anybody, let me do the talking . . . if there is any," had been Hunter's instructions.

At noon they had lunch at the spring on the eastern edge of the Bar A range. The herd that Wayne had seen three days before had been moved. As they rode westward across the Bar A, a small group of riders came in sight, with a whirling dust cloud spiraling behind them. They were traveling fast. Wayne wondered if it could be Jack McCurdy and some Whippoorwill men. He saw Hunter was interested. Then, as the horsemen came on at a ringing gallop, he recognized the big form of Pete Arnold, owner of the Bar A, in the lead.

Chapter Eleven

As Arnold and the five men with him drew close, Hunter checked his pace and nodded to Wayne, who rode in close to him. "Remember what I said about the talking," Hunter told him. "Leave the best part of it to me . . . if there is any."

It was soon apparent that there was going to be some, for Arnold turned in his saddle and called back to his men and they reined their mounts in to a walk. Hunter and Wayne kept on at an easy trot. The Bar A men halted as the pair came up.

"Hello, Ted," Arnold greeted with a brief nod. He hardly heard Wayne's amiable rejoinder. His eyes were for Jim Hunter.

"Haven't seen you in a long time, Jim," he said.

"That's because you don't come over Rainbow way much, I take it," said Hunter coolly. "Not that I'm always there, but it's about as far west as I get."

Wayne saw instantly that each had spoken with restraint. It wasn't dislike, exactly, but there was a certain coolness between them. They seemed to look at each other searchingly. Arnold—a portly man who lacked the rugged appearance of Wayne's father—was dressed in a gray worsted business suit. The collar of his soft white shirt was open. His trousers were pulled over his cow boots, and his stockman's Stetson was low over his eyes. Wayne had seen him dressed in this fashion on most of his visits to town and thought he might be going to Rainbow this afternoon.

"Well, we haven't much to offer you in the way of excitement over here," said Arnold. "You wouldn't get much kick out of a herd or two just feeding."

The way this was said convinced Wayne that it was no idle comment. He saw Hunter stiffen in the saddle, and the men with the Bar A owner looked at him sharply.

"I got more than one kick out of it when I was workin' cows," Hunter returned. "And those kicks crippled me for range work. You doin' well, Pete?"

"Tolerably well, when I've got the grass," said Arnold. "The grass over close to the butte isn't so good this year."

"No?" Hunter appeared but mildly interested. "Well, you've got all the way from here to Canada to range. You shouldn't complain."

"I suppose not," said Arnold shortly and turned his attention to Wayne. "Been over to Rainbow, Ted?"

"Just getting back."

"Tell your dad I'll be riding over that way to see him in a day or two. I've got to go to Rainbow myself." His gaze shifted to Hunter. "Going to drop in and see old Ed?"

"I was thinking that might not be a bad idea," said Hunter, "so long as I'm over this way for the first time in years. I met up with his son, here, back a ways and maybe I'll ride home with him."

"So long," said Arnold. He touched his horse's flanks with his spurs as he nodded to Hunter. "So long, Ted." Then he rode on his way eastward, followed by his men, while Hunter and Wayne resumed their lope into the west.

Wayne couldn't help but believe that the information that Arnold would drive over to see his father in a day or two was given for Hunter's benefit. Arnold had been looking at Hunter when he spoke. And it wasn't necessary to send word that he was going to the Whippoorwill. Ed Wayne was at the home ranch practically all the time and easily accessible. It was the first time

Wayne ever had carried such a message.

Whatever Hunter thought about the chance meeting, he kept to himself. Wayne knew the two men had talked between words, so to speak, and it was Arnold's remark that the grass over close to the butte wasn't so good this year that impressed him most. Was anything wrong on the Bar A range? The men he had seen on his way to Rainbow were certainly moving Bar A cattle away from that part of range that Arnold always used in summer.

Oh, I'm thinking things, he told himself with a shrug. As they passed north of the Bar A home ranch, he looked eagerly down the road that led from the benchland to the house. He saw no one. Polly would hardly be riding in the heat of that July day. But she would be riding that evening, and Wayne realized that he wanted to see her very much. So much had been crowded into the last three days that it seemed a year since he had seen her. And he wanted her to know that he was back with no story of wild exploits to follow him. Jake Barry would be the last man to talk about what had happened. Hunter was a man of his word, Wayne felt. He decided to see her when she took her evening ride.

In a short time they turned off the road leading from the Bar A home ranch to Riverdale, and swung northwest toward the WP range. During the ride to the ranch from where they had met Arnold, Hunter didn't speak a word. But as they approached the Whippoorwill ranch house in the late afternoon, he drew close to Wayne and broke his silence.

"If it's all right with you, you needn't say anything about what Arnold and I said, Wayne. Pete and me don't hitch."

"It's all right with me." Wayne nodded. "I'm not even going to mention that Arnold said he was coming over to see Dad. If it comes up, I'll say I forgot or something." He frowned. He was rather incensed at the Bar A rancher because of his attitude toward him when he went over to see Polly. "Playing his cards behind my back," was the way he had put it to McCurdy once.

Ed Wayne was in the courtyard to receive them, having seen them coming up the lane. He waved to Ted, but his spoken greeting was to Hunter. "Come in the house, Jim," he invited cordially. "We'll go out on the porch till supper is ready. Ted, take Hunter's horse, will you?"

Ted took the horses to the barn and put them up. When a hand showed a little later, he sent the man to get him another horse to use that night. Then he went into the house to wash and change his clothes.

Supper, with Ed Wayne, Ted, and Hunter at the table, witnessed an animated conversation between the rancher and his guest. From the talk Ted learned they had known each other well during the early days on that range. Hunter was older than he had thought. They dealt mostly in reminiscences, and the younger man gathered that the pair had been involved in more than one wild escapade. For some reason that he could not fathom, he sensed that this talk was, in a way, for his benefit. But why?

Supper over, the stockman and Hunter went into the big living room. So far, Ted's father had not sought a word with Ted alone. He went out to the barn and saddled the horse that the man had brought in. He rode down the lane and straight across the open plain toward the Bar A ranch house. Polly Arnold was just riding up to the benchland when he sighted her.

Polly turned off into the northeast, riding fast in the cool evening breeze that came with the first drifting veil of the twilight. Wayne gave chase, but the horse he was riding was not his regular mount, and Polly stood fair to outdistance him. He waved his hat, and after a spell the girl slowed her pace.

"You know, I've only got one horse that can run with yours," he told her, when he caught up with her. "Did you want to leave me behind, Polly?"

She was looking at him gravely, he thought. She did not seem her natural self, the whimsical, laughing, taunting Polly that he loved. *Now what was wrong?* he wondered.

"Let's ride up to Nine-Mile spring," she suggested.

"But that's quite a distance," he demurred. "And I want to talk with you, Polly. It seems ages since I saw you last. So much has happened." He shouldn't have said that, he realized as the words came out. "Won't you get down and sit with me a few minutes on this knoll? Look! There's a first star way up in the west."

He was off his horse in a moment, and Polly yielded. She even allowed him to help her down from the saddle, which was most unusual. And when she was on the ground beside him, he took her in his arms and kissed her and held her for what seemed to be a long time to both of them. Then they sat down on the warm grass, with the freshening breeze in their faces, and the horses grazing with reins dangling.

"You were gone quite a while, Ted," said the girl.

"Only two days after I saw you," he said. "But it does seem long. Polly, right out here on this clean prairie, with the wind in the grass, and the twilight sort of wrapping us up, I want to tell you that I love you more than ever. You're my girl!"

She looked at him quickly and the old light was in her eyes. Polly always seemed more beautiful to Ted in the twilight, or moonlight, or in the soft gleam of the hanging stars. She threw an arm about his shoulders and kissed him. The world was sweet, so Ted Wayne thought. And Polly Arnold must have thought so, too.

"Now," she said as his arm slipped about her, "tell me all that happened to keep you so long on a business trip to Rainbow."

The first brave star seemed to pour an icy waterfall upon Wayne's spirits. That slip of speech he had made had tripped him. Now he was caught in a predicament. There were but two things he could do: tell Polly everything, which he had promised not to tell anyone, or lie to her, which he did not wish to do.

"You ever been in Rainbow?" he asked.

"No, Ted. But I'd like to go over to see it, since Father says it's such a bad place. Surely a girl would be safe over there, don't you think so, Ted?"

"I don't see why not," he replied. "It's a tough town and all that, but I don't think the real and would-be bad men there are looking for chances to be rude to women. I didn't see many women, as a matter of fact. Come to think of it, I didn't see any except those who were working in the hotel."

"Did you gamble, Ted?" the girl asked quietly.

"I didn't turn a card," said Ted with the truth ringing in his voice.

"Oh, I don't care if you gamble some, Ted," said Polly, stroking his free hand. "My father gambled when he was young, and so did yours. It's the other that bothers me, makes me afraid that you will have some great trouble. You're so . . . so aggressive. Did you have any fights?" Her eyes searched his.

"No!" Surely that scuffle in the alley when Barry's men had attacked him could not come under the category of a regular fight, and the struggle with Barry on the rim of Devil's Hole, well, he would have to lie. He would have to lie to protect the true course of their love, that was all. He had a growing presentiment that his trouble with Jake Barry was not over, not finished. If it came to a finish, he could tell Polly all. In time he could tell her all, anyway. He would leave it to her sense of fairness to forgive him for lying to her under the involved circumstances.

"I'm so glad, Ted," Polly was saying. "Oh, how I dread the ruckuses you get into. I don't say that you look for trouble, Ted dear, but trouble seems to be riding herd on you most of the time. You never can tell. You'd be sure death with your gun, Ted, if anyone tried to draw on you in one of those affairs. And . . . oh, Ted, boy, I don't know what I would do or think if you were to kill a man. I could never think of you the same again. I guess it would kill me, too."

Wayne became cold all over for a few moments. He saw Boyd lying in the grass, his frozen features turned up to the sky. He hadn't thought of the reaction the knowledge that he had actually killed a man might have on Polly Arnold and their close relations.

"Never mind, girlie, I'm not looking to killing anybody," he said, managing with an effort to keep his voice steady. "Now, let's talk about something pleasant. Polly, we can find other topics, for I'm going to marry you one of these days . . . maybe when you least expect it, now that you've promised me." He drew her closer to him and kissed her hair.

She was silent for a space, then: "Father seemed upset when he came home for supper, Ted. He said he met you and a man riding from Rainbow."

"Yes?" Ted was nonplussed. So Arnold hadn't gone to town at all. He had lied to him when he had said he was going in, or he had changed his mind after leaving them. If the latter was the case, then the presence of Hunter must have been responsible.

"He doesn't like the man you were with, Ted," the girl went on slowly. "He said he had thought he wasn't the right kind of a man to be in your company, but after . . . after some of the things that had happened lately, he wasn't sure. Don't blame Daddy, for he seems to be hard-worked these days. He's out on the range more than he has been in years."

"I don't see why he should object to my just riding along with a man going in the same direction." Wayne frowned.

"He said the man was a Jim Hunter. Is that so, Ted?"

"Yes, that's who it was."

"Daddy says Hunter used to be a square cowman, but he found easy money more to his taste," said the girl. "He said he has become a professional gambler, and is running with that terrible outlaw, Darling, in the bargain. Said he wouldn't leave his own range while Hunter was near it."

Wayne started. So Hunter was responsible for Arnold's sudden change of mind. He had told Polly these things to cause her to doubt Wayne. The young scion of the Whippoorwill bristled. "It seems to me that your dad goes out of his way to paint me any color except white," he said. "Just because I happen to be riding along with this Hunter isn't anything against me, is it?"

"I didn't say it was," Polly returned with spirit, catching the resentment in Wayne's tone. "And Father didn't say that. He was speaking of that man. He said he wouldn't put rustling past him, either." She added the last in a vexed voice.

"I don't know anything about him," said Ted stoutly. "And I'm not saying anything against your dad, exactly. But if he had anything to say, he should have said it to my face right there in front of Hunter, or have waited and told me when he saw me afterward."

Polly withdrew from his arm and rose suddenly. "Ted, you're disagreeable tonight. I'm going home."

Wayne was on his feet in an instant, trying to grasp her hands. "Polly! Are we going to let such a silly business disturb us?" he pleaded. "Now, don't you think it's silly?"

"I don't think it's silly, Ted Wayne, when you talk in cryptic fashion," she answered, walking to her horse and catching up the reins. "You're keeping something from me, and goodness knows what it is. You worry me to death, and there's no reason why I should keep on worrying indefinitely."

"But, Polly! What is it you want to know?"

"Nothing," she replied shortly, swinging into her saddle. "Oh, Ted, maybe I'm not myself. It's not far and I wish you'd not ride with me to the bench above home tonight." Her lips were quivering. "So long," she murmured, and rode away at the fastest gallop of which her splendid mount was capable.

Wayne knew there was no chance to catch her with the horse he was riding. He started back to the Whippoorwill, tight-lipped, grim-faced. He was going to ask a few questions of his father and Jim Hunter. He was going to break out of the dark.

At that very moment, Ed Wayne and Jim Hunter were seated close together in the WP ranch house living room under the yellow glow of a lamp, talking earnestly.

Chapter Twelve

Ed Wayne was smoking a thick, black cigar. Jim Hunter was sticking to his brown-paper cigarettes, which he rolled, lit, and re-lit at constant intervals. The men spoke in tones that hardly carried beyond the table at which they sat.

"You know, I'm not expecting you to tell me anything, Jim," old Ed was saying, "unless you want to. It's been a long time since I've seen you, and, when I saw you last, you were jake, so far as I knew."

"I played the game," said Hunter. "I never could get the start you did because I was too wild. I needed something to take it out of me, but that something never came along. I was fast with my gun and tough with my fists, and I needed excitement as much as I needed food. I kept on that trail, and it's a trail that's bound to lead to one of two things . . . soft money, as they call it, or a six-foot trench, providing they're decent enough to bury you. I've had one foot in the trench for a number of years now, Ed."

The stockman nodded. "They tell me you're running with Darling," he said casually. "Just how bad is Darling, Jim?"

Hunter's gaze never flinched. "He's as bad as they make 'em," he said simply. "That's talk you'll understand from me, Ed."

Ed Wayne nodded again. "So I've heard. That's about all I'm going to ask you about him. You could tell me a lot more, but I don't see why you should."

"Don't worry, I won't." Hunter smiled grimly.

"You know, Jim, I didn't send for you to ask about Darling, or his gang, or what they're up to. I sent to ask you to do me a favor . . . a personal favor. You'll remember . . . now, I hate to bring this up, Jim . . . but you'll remember back some years I had a chance to lend you a hand, and. . . ."

"Put it straight," Hunter broke in. "You saved my life at the risk of your own, and against big odds, to boot, Ed. We shook on my promise to come if you ever needed me. I'm here, and glad of the chance to make my promise good if I can."

"That wasn't the only reason why I sent for you," old Ed said slowly. "You're about the only man I know who I believe can do what I want done, and do it right. Besides that, I've got to have a man I can trust. I feel that I can trust you, Jim. And I've got to have a man who is tough, tough as cactus, Jim, and with plenty of spine. I reckon that's you, too. This is going to be delicate business, Jim, if you take the job on."

"Sounds interesting," was Hunter's comment. "You've got to be guessing both way from the jack. It . . . maybe you want to hire my gun, Ed?" Hunter's gaze was keen.

But the rancher shook his head. "Not exactly," he said. "You might have to use it, but I hope not. I'm hoping there won't have to be any shooting, but I've got my doubts. And maybe I'm making a mistake, dang it! But you know you said you were following a wild trail when we were younger, and nothing happened to steer you off it?"

"That was the way it was," Hunter affirmed.

"Well, Jim," said old Ed earnestly, leaning toward the other man with his hands on his knees, "that's just the situation my boy Ted is in. He's wilder than an electric storm, and I need a lightning rod. Now . . . do you begin to see what I'm getting at?"

Hunter was silent for a spell. "You want me to be the

lightning rod," he decided aloud.

"You've hit it." The stockman nodded. "I suppose it's a whole lot my own fault that Ted's so wild. I haven't kept any check rein on him. He can't go to town without getting into some kind of a mess. He was in one a few days ago after the Fourth. I don't know what it was and I don't want you to tell me, if you know. I told him I wouldn't let anyone else tell me after I refused to let him tell me himself. Yes, I can see by your look that you know about it. I reckon it was bad. I can tell a lot by the way men act and what I see in their eyes. Ted showed it was bad, and my foreman, McCurdy, showed it was bad. I'll let him tell me about it in case there's something I should do. But these scrapes he gets into have got me worried. Sooner or later there's going to be a shooting, and you know what that means. I've got a big ranch here, Jim, and it's stocked to the limit, almost, with good cattle. I haven't got a scrub in my herds. I want Ted to have all this someday, but I don't want him to pass out before he can get it, and I don't want him to throw it away after he gets it. That's why I sent for you."

"I can understand everything except what it is that you can possibly want me to do," said Hunter, genuinely surprised. "If it's a lecture, you should know better. I know that young fellow's stock and he isn't bad."

"Not yet," said old Ed gravely. "No, I don't want you to try any silly lecture. I want you to take him out and give him what he wants till he gets his fill of it, and shows it by his own actions. Now, if you think that isn't a big order, I'll tell you that the wages will be ten thousand dollars and expenses, with no limit on the last."

Hunter raised his brows. "It's a big order," he confessed. "Just how far would you want me to go?"

"Go the limit," replied Ed Wayne tersely. "Give him all this wild stuff he wants . . . the wilder the better! I'll even pay the gambling bills. If this experiment turns out all right, and brings Ted to his senses, fifty thousand will be cheap."

"When you say the limit, you're saying a mouthful, Ed," said Hunter. "And it'll get around that he's traveling in fast company. Folks'll talk. It'll hurt, Ed."

"That may all be, but if the boy has the stuff in him, he'll work out the solution. I'm banking on Wayne stock, and Ted has it, Jim. If he doesn't come through. . . ." Old Ed looked steadily into Hunter's eyes. "I'd just as soon lose him," he finished soberly.

Hunter pursed his lips. In his quiet tone, Ed Wayne had succeeded in putting tremendous feeling, possibly without realizing it. Hunter was struck by the gravity of the mission that the rancher wished to entrust to him. He hadn't told him about Ted's adventure in the badlands near the butte, or his night adventure in town. He felt that the stockman should know about these affairs, for, if Hunter took Ted in charge, he would be sure to meet up with trouble in the same direction again. That would mean but one thing: gun play. He cleared his throat. "How do you know Ted will fall in with this idea?" he asked.

"I'm not goin' to let him suspect anything," said Ed Wayne. "I'm going to make him think he's doing it of his own accord. I'm going to make him mad, Jim . . . deliberately make him mad. He's sort of quick-tempered, anyway . . . gets it from me, I suppose. It's up to you to steer him. Lead him along by easy stages. Put him right in with the Darling gang."

Hunter half started from his chair, his eyes wide. "You don't want me to go that far, do you?" he gasped. "That outfit isn't just bad, it's wicked."

"I know," said old Ed grimly. "They're a bunch of cut-throats, without principle, without scruples, and, so far as I know, without fear. A month with a bunch like that would cure him."

Hunter smiled wryly. "You seem to have a good line on 'em,

Ed," he said quietly.

"I think I have, Jim. And that's why nobody could make me believe that you're in with Darling clear up to the hilt. For one thing, I don't believe you'd rustle cattle. You know I've naturally got more respect for a man who'd touch a bank or an express shipment than I'd have for one who'd trail a loose rope."

Hunter frowned. "Suppose we leave me out of it so far as anything except your proposition is concerned," he suggested coldly. "I'm telling you straight that I haven't sprouted any wings since you knew me last. Maybe you're picking the wrong man for this job."

"I'm willing to take the chance," said the rancher firmly. "If you don't want to tackle the job, say so. I don't want any half measures, which is why I sent for you. But it's a big order, like I said, and you won't make me sore if you turn it down. In fact, I half expect it."

"I can't turn it down!" exclaimed Hunter, his frown deepening. "That's the devil of it. I don't feel that I could trust the job to anybody else, even if you could find somebody. You've got me interested in this thing in a personal way. You know, I suppose"—his tone became whimsical and he looked at Ed Wayne quizzically—"that I've got a reputation over east as a gunman and suspected outlaw?"

"Seems I heard something to that effect." Old Ed nodded. "I'm more than just a member of the Cattlemen's Association, you know."

"Your investigation department isn't any too well informed," said Hunter dryly. "I suppose Pete Arnold's head is stuffed with information. He's the woman gossip breed."

"I don't know anything about that, Jim," said old Ed. "I've never gossiped with him. And I don't think he's got much use for Ted, since Ted and Polly Arnold are pretty thick."

Hunter looked up quickly. "So? Well, Arnold and me never

could run in the same traces." He paused, and old Ed remained silent. "I guess I'll have to take this job on, Ed," he said finally. "Now then, how're we goin' to go about it?"

For another half hour they talked in low tones. Ed Wayne brought forth a bottle of old bourbon and they took a drink. Then Hunter went to the bunkhouse where he was to sleep.

Ted Wayne had thought better of the impulse to burst in upon his father and Jim Hunter. After all, just what did he want to know from Hunter that he had the right to ask? He couldn't very well delve into the man's personal affairs openly. Even if he was certain and had proof of all he suspected, he could not bring the older man to task about it. He had been sent to find Hunter and deliver his father's request that Hunter come to see him. This he had done, Hunter had agreed, and there Ted's interest in the man's business should end, except as to natural curiosity. Hunter would be leaving shortly and Ted regretted that his acquaintance with such an interesting character should come to an end.

He inquired for Jack McCurdy, but the foreman was out on the range. He walked about the courtyard between the ranch buildings and was in front of the big barn when Hunter came out of the ranch house and crossed to the bunkhouse. Wayne wondered just how much Hunter had told his father, but refrained from asking. He went into the living room. It was vacant, but the light was shining from the little office opening off from it. When Ted was seated across the desk from his parent, he found it was not to be so easy to say what he thought he had to say as he had expected.

"Well, I found him," he ventured by way of an opening.

"Yes, Hunter says you caught up with him in the badlands over there," his father remarked, examining a paper on his desk.

Then Hunter hadn't said anything about the trouble near the butte, Ted thought. "It wasn't as easy as you may think," he said with a frown. "Did Hunter tell you anything about the trouble I had in finding him?"

"He said you missed him in town and had to chase out after him," his father replied.

"Oh, yes?" Ted was irritated to hear this. "Well, it wasn't my fault, in a way, that I missed him in town. You put so much mystery into this thing, along with your friend Miles Henseler over there, that I wanted to be dead sure I had the right man before I tackled him. That's one reason why I missed him in town, and the other is because Henseler stalled me off."

"He must have known what he was doing," said Ed Wayne calmly.

"What's the idea in all this mystery about Hunter, anyway?" Ted demanded. "It seems to me, if he's such a dangerous person, and so touchy and all that, that you could have given me more of a line on him and how to go about your job."

"You seem to have done very well," his father observed.

"Is this Hunter in with that Darling outfit?" asked Ted.

His father raised his eyes for the first time since Ted had started speaking. "Just why do you ask that?" he countered.

"Because it looks to me as if he is," Ted retorted stoutly. "What's he hanging around Rainbow and those badlands for? There's only one outfit that stays in the badlands over there any length of time, and that's Darling's gang. I can't see why the owner of the WP should be wanting to see a member of that crowd."

His father's eyes grew cold. "We've known each other a long time," he said slowly, looking Ted in the eyes. "We knew each other before you were born. I'm not sure what he's doing now, but I was sure of what he did in the days when we were more or less together. That's one reason why I wanted to see him, and the other doesn't concern you. You can tell me something, though."

"What's that?" Ted asked angrily.

"Who'd you have this last fight in Riverdale with?"

"Haven't you heard yet?" Ted's brows went up. "Didn't Hunter tell you?"

"I didn't ask him to tell me, and I haven't heard," replied his father sternly. "I don't mind saying that I might have let you tell me the other morning if you hadn't lit out so early, and I did ask McCurdy, who wisely kept his mouth shut. So now you can tell me yourself." His eyes shot the question.

"Jake Barry!" Ted exploded. "That's who I had the fight with. Maybe you know how tough he is. I saw to it that we discarded our guns and the only way I could get the best of him was to close both his eyes so he couldn't see. I suppose you know that he is one of Darling's men."

His father's eyes were snapping. It was no mean trick to beat Barry in an encounter, and he felt rather inclined to be proud. But he couldn't permit this feeling to interfere with his plan. The fact that it was Barry, however, who Ted had made an enemy worried him a little.

"I suppose it started in the usual way," he said sarcastically.

"I don't know just what that crack means, but Barry started it with his mouth," said Ted, his face darkening. "I don't think you'd have wanted me to take the slurs he shot at me. Tried to make out he was drunk, but I know the whole thing was intentional, although I don't know why." Ted was mad.

"It seems as though somebody is always picking on you," his father observed. "This last stunt wasn't very wise. Barry isn't a good choice for an enemy."

Ted stared at his parent with a look of incredulity, as if he were trying to believe his own ears. "You mean to say I . . . I should have stood there . . . and taken it?" he stammered, his face turning red.

Old Ed looked at the narrow slip of paper he was fondling. "You should use judgment in these affairs, if you have to have them, which I take it you do," he said tersely. "I won't stand for this continual round of brawls any longer. Every stockman on the range is wondering why I've stood for it so long. You've got so wild you're practically no use on the ranch."

"Then I better get off of it!" Ted exclaimed hotly.

"Maybe you'd better," said his father. His tone was quiet but decisive. "You seem to want to run wild, so go and run wild." He pushed the slip of paper across the desk. "There's my check for five thousand dollars. You won't have any trouble cashing it. If you don't take it, I'll know you're a fool and not independent. Go ahead and run wild somewhere else besides around here. Take up with Hunter, if you think he's so bad. He might be able to teach you a few tricks, at that." The stockman smiled wryly, then he looked at Ted coldly "There's just one thing to remember . . . don't come back here unless you're ready."

Ted's first impulse as he fingered the check was to tear it up and throw the pieces into his father's face. Instead, on second thought, he folded it carefully and stowed it in a pocket. "I guess it'll be worth a loan of five thousand to get rid of me, the way you feel," he said grimly. "I'll be going in the morning."

His face was white as he left the little office and went out upon the porch into the cool night air. But his mind, angry as he was, was made up instantly. He would take his father's dare. He would trail with Hunter, if Hunter would let him. If he wouldn't, he would follow him, anyway. For the first time in his life he was completely on his own. Adventure spread its far-flung carpet of mystery before him, and he stepped out upon it.

Chapter Thirteen

Ted Wayne walked under the stars among the lilac bushes and shrubs, and the few flower beds that his mother had planted and his father had kept up through the years. The night wind whispered in the leaves of the cottonwoods that formed the wind break. The grass in the yard was soft and thick, well watered. He saw the lights in the living room and office go out, and then a yellow beam shone from the window of his father's bedroom. He shrugged. His father was throwing him out, with a string attached to the process. *Don't come back here unless you're ready!* Then he had been wrong these many months? His wrath flamed again. He thought his father would rather he had taken the vile things Jake Barry had said, rather than make an enemy of the man because he was in with a crowd of cut-throats and bandits, outlaws every one, Yes, Hunter, too—probably. And what had his father wanted of Jim Hunter?

Somehow or other, Ted didn't like the idea of his father's sending for this man. He had seen them through the doorway of the living room, talking in low tones, and whatever had been said didn't appear to have left Ed Wayne in any too good a humor. Still, he couldn't bring himself to believe that Hunter was as bad as Arnold had painted him. The Bar A owner, in blackening the man's character, had sought to injure Ted in the eyes of Polly. That was what Ted Wayne thought. His anger swelled again and the reaction drew him to Hunter rather than made him more suspicious.

He looked up at the dark windows of his own room. He had no desire to sleep there this night. He doubted if he would sleep at all. In the morning he would make a pack of the few things he intended to take along. His plans were vague. But the exhilaration of being free continued to grow. Why not go out and run wild, as his father had suggested? But he resolved to stay away from Riverdale. His activities must fit in with the proper environment. He walked around to the bunkhouse.

Jim Hunter was in bed in one of the bunks. His clothes and gun hung on the back of a chair near at hand. The lamp on the table was burning and Hunter was awake, looking at a paper he had found. He nodded to Wayne as the latter entered.

Wayne pulled off his boots, threw his hat on the table, hung his gun belt with its empty holster on a peg above a bunk at the side where he could see Hunter. He would fill that empty holster with another tried-and-true gun of his own in the morning. Jake Barry owed him a gun, perhaps his own gun. Wayne sat on the edge of the bunk, stealing glances at Hunter, who now seemed oblivious of his presence. For the first time doubt was kindled in his mind. Why should he want to trail along with this man, even if he would let him—which he probably would not? Why go out upon this wild adventure, as he thought of it, at all? And, if he changed his mind, go back to his father and say he didn't want to go? Never! His teeth came together with a click. His frown bunched into a scowl.

"You act like you're in the dumps."

It was Hunter's voice, and Wayne started. The man wasn't looking at him, but he seemed to be aware of Ted's mood. Now he shot a glance over the paper. It was keen and calculating, and seemed to read Wayne's mind. Wayne felt that he resented it.

"I'm not in the best of humor," he said.

"No? Well, you ought to be." Hunter's tone was short.

"Yeah?" Wayne bristled. "What makes you think so?"

Hunter simulated surprise. "Why, here you are back home, safe and sound, nice house to live in, good horses to ride, money to spend, I suppose, and a big ranch that'll someday be yours to play with. What more do you want?"

"And a lot you know about it," Wayne returned with a light sneer. "I suppose you think I'm sitting in clover."

"I should say you're floundering in a bed of roses," was Hunter's rejoinder, and Wayne thought he detected resentment in the older man's voice. "When I was your age, all I had was a horse, and saddle, and gun . . . and I had to make 'em good. Oh, yes, on second thought, I had a girl or two. I reckon it must be a girl that's bothering you. Maybe it's that Arnold girl. She's neat enough."

Wayne kept back the hot reply that was on his lips. "I saw her tonight," he said, instead.

"I had an idea you were on some such errand when you rode away," said Hunter dryly. He was playing his cards with a skill that was more than adroit; it was superb.

"Pete Arnold didn't go to Rainbow. He must have changed his mind soon after he left us. He rode back to the Bar A ranch house and told Polly a thing or two."

"So?" Hunter showed interest. "Tried to blast your rep because you was ridin' with me, maybe."

"Just about." Wayne nodded. "You just about hit it the way I figured. What he hinted about you was plenty. An in doing that he might as well have included me, I guess. Pete doesn't hang out any flags when I go over there to visit."

"What did he say about me?" Hunter asked sharply.

Wayne hesitated, but the look in Hunter's eyes led him on. "Oh, he merely said you were not the right kind of a man for me to be riding with, he thought, but after what had happened lately . . . meaning my fight with Jake, I suppose, among other things . . . he wasn't sure. A nice crack at me, you see, and I care a lot. And he intimated pretty strongly that you're sort of married to the green-topped tables and fond of easy money, and hooked up with Darling." The fact that Hunter's eyes had narrowed and his lips tightened was not lost on Wayne. "He closed by saying he wouldn't care to leave the range while you were around close."

Then, to Wayne's surprise, Hunter laughed with genuine mirth. "Pete's getting too fat," was his comment as he turned back to his paper. "What's the idea of you sleeping out here when you've got a room in the house . . . to keep an eye on me?"

"I won't have a room in the house after tonight," said Wayne sourly.

Hunter put down his paper. Old Ed had carried out his intention so soon? "Why not?" he demanded. He looked about again, to make sure they were alone in the bunkhouse.

"Dad had to get a stepladder to get on his high horse tonight," said Wayne grimly, "and I guess I jerked the ladder out from under him. He landed with a thump that bounced me out."

"Disinherited?" asked Hunter, picking up his paper again.

"Dad's sore because of a few scrapes I've been in," said Wayne. "From the talk between you and him at the table tonight, he was no angel when he was young. But he can't think back that far when he's talking to me. Told me to go and run wild. Said maybe you could teach me a few tricks." He was crafty enough not to look at Hunter as he said this last.

"Well, maybe I could," said Hunter, rousing in his bunk. "Looks like he was sore at me, too."

Wayne was inwardly excited. If he could get Hunter angry, the man might take him along with him. He might in the end find out why his father had sent for Hunter. Anyway, pure curiosity stimulated his desire to go with this man.

"I'm getting out tomorrow morning," Wayne said.

"Where you going?" Hunter asked, frowning.

"To Rainbow . . . first," Wayne announced.

"I'm going back that way myself," Hunter confessed. "If you're up early enough, you can go along . . . providing you're not afraid that your rep will be blasted forever if you ride with me again."

"I . . . might as well trail along," said Wayne, suppressing his exultation with difficulty.

The entrance of the barn hand brought the conversation to an end. Hunter threw away the paper and turned with his face to the wall, satisfied, but doubtful of the outcome of old Ed's experiment. Ted Wayne crawled into his bunk, jubilant. The barn hand looked curiously at the pair, blew out the light, and went to bed.

They had breakfast in the ranch house very early, before, as Wayne thought, the stockman got up. He did not see his father when he went upstairs for his things. Ted finished first and went out to see about the horses, excusing himself on that pretence. He did want to attend to the horses so they could get an early start, but he also wanted to leave word with the barn hand for Jack McCurdy. "Just tell him I had a little ruckus and I'm going away for a spell," was the message.

Old Ed was up, although he didn't particularly want to see Ted. But in the interval, while Ted was gone, he spoke with Jim Hunter. He wanted to know how Ted had taken it.

Hunter instantly detected worry and doubt in the rancher's eyes, uncertainty in his voice. "Oh, you're wondering if you hadn't better back down on the proposition, eh?" said Hunter. "Well, I don't know as your son would let you. He's pretty well heated up. Oh, I fixed it all right. We're riding out *pronto.*"

"I think it's for the best," said Ed Wayne. "You know I'm

trusting you, Jim."

"Now look here," said Hunter, frowning with irritation. "You've hung this job on me and you've got to agree to let me go about things in my own way, understand? And if anything misses fire, you're not to blame me, is that agreed? If it isn't, I'm layin' down on you here and now."

"It's agreed," said old Ed. He shook hands with Hunter. Then he watched the pair from an upstairs window until they were mere dots on the plain to eastward that melted into nothing.

It was a glorious morning. The vast plain was a bowl of gold, with emerald rim, and a floating, purple plume that was Rainbow Butte. The horses wanted to run, for it was a morning to quicken the spirits of beasts as well as men. As they were speeding across the Bar A range, they soon became aware that they were not the only riders abroad. From southward came a horse at full gallop, and, even at that distance, Wayne stirred uneasily in his saddle as he thought he recognized the outline of the rider in the saddle. He looked quickly at Hunter, and the older man merely nodded that he had seen. He did not increase their pace. He was splendidly mounted, and Wayne was riding his own horse. They might have avoided meeting this rider had Hunter seen fit to do so. It was not long before Wayne's suspicion was confirmed. Polly Arnold, lured by the beauty of the dawn, was out for a ride. Perhaps she suspected who Wayne and Hunter were. A frown gathered on Wayne's brow. It was a meeting he would have wished to avoid. But now it was too late.

"Why, Ted!" the girl sang as she pulled up her horse, compelling them to stop. "Are you riding east again?" She put something else—another question—into her eyes as she looked from him to Hunter.

At the moment Wayne could think of no plausible excuse for

his riding out this morning. "Yes," was his answer. Then he felt a rebellious surge within him. One would think he had to report his goings and comings to this girl before he could do anything. It wasn't fair to Polly, who had his interests very much at heart, and to whom he was, so far as he knew, engaged, but he didn't think of it as Hunter gazed quizzically at both of them. He didn't want to appear foolish before Hunter.

"Going to Rainbow again?" Polly persisted sweetly.

"I . . . I'm going to finish my business," he said, and then wondered how it sounded.

"Oh, I see." Her eyes lost their luster behind a cool, steady gaze directed at Hunter. "You're not very free with your introductions this morning."

Wayne saw no way out of it. Her father would describe his companion and she would recognize the description. "This is Jim Hunter," he said coldly. "Polly Arnold, Mister Hunter."

"Good morning, ma'am," said Hunter.

"Why are you taking Ted away?" Polly asked.

"He's free, white, and twenty-one, and handy in the bargain," said Hunter with a slight drawl. "I don't think anybody would be taking him away far . . . unless he wanted to go."

"That's not answering my question," the girl said, her fine eyes snapping.

"I don't see why you should have to ask Mister Hunter any questions, Polly," Wayne put in.

"Ted, have you had trouble at the ranch?" she asked in a different tone.

Anger tugged at the threads of his self-control. Hunter's face bore an amused expression. "Really, Polly, I don't think that question fits, either," he replied.

"You don't want to answer it!" she accused. "I'll ask your father!"

"You've got too much sense to do a silly thing like that," he told her sharply.

Then the girl of the range showed her temper—a temper that was a natural heritage of a girl who could shoot and ride with many men and still retain her adorable feminine traits.

"You're throwing what sense you've got, Ted Wayne, to the winds," she said. "And this man is helping you do it."

"Polly! You're talking before a stranger." He shook out his reins and his face paled.

Without another word, the girl whirled her horse and rode swiftly away in the direction she had come.

"There's one that's worth holding on to," was Hunter's brief comment as they resumed their ride.

Wayne didn't answer. He was angry—angry at Polly, angry at her father, angry at his own father—and disgusted with himself. Well, now, nothing much mattered. He saw that Hunter was keeping an eye on him, and he resented it. The glory of the morning seemed to fade. He saw only the yellow plain, the colorful outlines of the butte far ahead, the green band of timber along the river in the south. It was going to be a hot day.

CHAPTER FOURTEEN

Hunter did not follow the same trail Wayne had taken to Rainbow. He turned off above the spring on the Bar A southeast range and cut straight south toward the river. Whether this was a shorter way, a better trail, or an indication that Hunter did not want to meet anyone, Wayne could not conjecture. But he assumed that this must have been the way Jake Barry and his companions had gone the day they had preceded him on their return from Riverdale. In any event, it looked as if he already was learning some of the secrets of that wild district.

The new route did not prove to be shorter, but it was screened by timber on both sides a short distance below the spring where there was much marshy land. It was a dim trail and wound along the north bank of the river. Several times they passed intersecting cattle trails and Wayne wondered that Arnold would range his stock so near the river with its frequent breaks. It recalled to his mind the remark the Bar A owner had made to Hunter about the range near the butte not being so good this year. Somehow, that remark stuck in Wayne's mind. The statement was simple enough, but it was the way in which Arnold had put it, and the look that had accompanied it, that had made such an impression upon him. And now, for the first time, a doubt assailed him regarding Hunter. It was reported that Darling was no cheap rustler, that he stole cattle wholesale when he operated along that line. If Hunter were a member of the Darling gang, hadn't he, too, been mixed up in rustling?

Wayne felt he could overlook almost anything except the stealing of cattle. Yet he couldn't bring himself to believe that Hunter would rustle. He was, to all appearances, a cowman of the old school. Still, the great herds of more than one big outfit had been started with a running iron.

They emerged from the foliage along the riverbank in the late afternoon and rode across the bridge. Here Hunter again made a detour, going around the town on the west and entering on the south side, away from the river. Thus they avoided the main street and came into an alley, a narrow way between the buildings that Wayne recognized as the same alley into which he had followed Hunter and where Mort Green, the gambler, had aided him in the fight with Barry's men.

They stopped at a small green house that fronted on the alley. Its two front windows were heavily curtained against the dying sun. There was a narrow porch and three steps.

"Wait for me," Hunter instructed. He went up the steps and knocked at the door. In a few moments it was opened and he disappeared inside.

Like everything else connected with Hunter, this house and Hunter's queer rapping on the door, and his vanishing were mysterious. Wayne was convinced this was the place Hunter had been heading for when he had followed him, four nights before. And now that Wayne was back in Rainbow, he wondered just what he would do. The inspiration of the preceding night deliberately to follow Hunter, if the man tried to shake him, did not seem reasonable in the light of broad day. In its stead he was seized by another idea. Suppose he were to get into trouble—trouble of his own making, if necessary—and look to Hunter for help? He discarded the idea immediately. Such a man as Hunter would not want to mix with a fellow who could not take care of himself. And Wayne needn't have worried his brain in this respect, for even then events were shaping themselves, events over which neither he nor Hunter would have any control. Wayne's first great adventure was being made to order with none of the principals to be involved aware of it.

Hunter came out shortly. "We'll ride over and put up our horses," he told Wayne. "Then we'll come back here. It's a place where we can get a good home-made meal . . . without grease."

This sounded good to Wayne, not merely because of the promise of a good meal, but it indicated that Hunter was not shaking him for the time being, at least. Above all things, he wanted to get acquainted with this man.

It was hot, and the street was dusty. There were not many people about. They rode to the livery where Wayne started as he saw Fred Hastings, the owner. He had forgotten to tell his father he had met Hastings. But then, the man might not ask him about it. As it turned out, Hastings merely nodded, possibly because of the presence of Hunter. They walked back to the little green house at the end of the alley.

Hunter rapped on the door and it was speedily opened by a woman who admitted them at once. Wayne was struck by the cozy appearance of the room he entered. It was the full width of the house and must have been nearly half its length. The heating stove glistened in ebony and nickel. When not needed to furnish heat, it served as an ornament. There was a big couch with its head smothered in fancy pillows, easy chairs, a mahogany table with a tasteful runner and a vase of flowers upon it, deep rugs, a well-filled bookcase, an ornate phonograph, a small stand on which was a square of onyx holding a gold nugget in a depression in its top. The pictures were copies of great masters. It was a home-like room, a friendly room—and not the kind one would expect to find in a wild town such as Rainbow.

"Missus Trippett, this is Ted Wayne," Hunter introduced.

The woman fitted into her surroundings perfectly, thought

Wayne as he bowed slightly and took her hand. She was a buxom woman, pink-cheeked, round-faced, with blue eyes and beautiful hair that was snow-white. She radiated cheerfulness and hospitality.

"So this is the man who handed Jake what was comin' to him," she boomed in a voice that filled the room and contrasted strangely with its quiet tone.

Hunter looked at Wayne who was plainly showing his surprise. "You'll find you've got a reputation here," he said dryly. "The news of what happened over at Riverdale couldn't keep."

"That's right," beamed Mrs. Trippett. "If somebody doesn't ride into this town with news, the birds bring it, or a jack rabbit gallops in with a note tied to his ears. When my husband, Tom, was alive, he used to say all he had to do was to go outdoors and the wind would whisper the news in his ears. He found a river full of gold like that chunk you see on the stand over there and they had to kill him to get it away from him." She twisted a corner of the white apron she wore over a blue house dress. "But you folks must be hungry. Jim'll show you where to wash up, Mister Wayne. It won't be long till you can eat."

She led the way through a small dining room to an immaculate kitchen and Hunter beckoned to Wayne to follow him to a little covered porch outside.

"You'll want hot water, Jim," said Mrs. Trippett. "Take the tea kettle from the stove. And try to rub out them dust rings on your neck before you use the towel."

Hunter grinned at Wayne. "We're at home here," he said simply.

Wayne took this to be a friendly advance and welcomed it with a flashing smile. "Right good of you to bring me here," he told Hunter. The fact that Hunter had seen fit to bring him to the house showed that the man had more than passing interest in him.

"The madame'll tell you about her late husband now and then, but a lot of it's good stuff," said Hunter when he brought the hot water. "She's a good sort."

"I can see that." Wayne nodded.

By time they had washed and returned to the living room, and smoked a cigarette, Mrs. Trippett called them to supper.

A gorgeous lamp was lighted in the center of the table, for the sun was behind the western peaks and the trees shaded the window. It was an excellent meal of meat and vegetables, with home-made pickles and jellies, apple pie, and strong coffee.

"Tom always said more homes was broke up with weak coffee than with strong tempers," said Mrs. Trippett as she filled their cups. "You won't need any stick in that to make you sit up."

She took a chair near the window while they ate. She seemed much interested in Wayne. "You don't look heavy enough to lick Jake Barry," she observed. "He's a bull if there ever was one."

"I reckon I was lucky," said Wayne with a smile.

"There ain't so much luck in fist fightin'," said Mrs. Trippett, shaking her head. "Tom used to say that fists was made to fight with and guns was made to kill with. You better be careful, Mister Wayne. That Jake ain't above takin' a pot shot at you or gettin' you mixed up in a gun play."

"I've got to take my chances," said Wayne. "I'm not looking for trouble."

"Them's the ones that run smack into it lots of times," said the woman. "You're too young and well set up to be stoppin' hot lead. My Tom used to say it paid to turn corners slow."

"I'll take the middle of the street." Wayne smiled. It was a common saying, but Hunter glanced at him quickly.

"There's a punch in most things the madame says," he remarked. Then, to the woman: "You haven't heard anything about Jake, have you?"

"Well, I don't think he's in town," she replied. "Somebody was sayin' he'd gone away to heal up."

Wayne was led to wonder just who came to the little green house. He was convinced that just anybody wouldn't be welcome there. Was it patronized exclusively by members of the Darling band? And it wasn't a boarding house, for there couldn't be more than two bedrooms in the place. He wondered if he would be welcome there at some future time if he were not in Hunter's company.

Twilight had fallen when Wayne and Hunter finished their supper and went back to the living room. Mrs. Trippett occupied herself with clearing the table and washing the dishes. Wayne heard her humming as she went about her work.

"You'll let me pay for this," he suggested to Hunter, thrusting a hand in his pocket.

"No, I have a ticket here," said Hunter. "It isn't a regular eating house. Where are you going to put up?"

"I guess the hotel is the only place," replied Wayne. "I left my pack at the barn, as you know."

"You better get your room," Hunter suggested. "Suppose I'll put up there tonight myself." He blew a smoke ring absently. He didn't want Wayne to know he was practically taking him under his wing. He wished to go slow, and was not altogether sure of his procedure. "Of course, it's none of my business, but I was wondering what you figured on doing tonight." There was nothing in the look he gave Wayne to signify more than an idle interest.

"I'm going to gamble," Wayne told him readily.

"Well, that's easy enough to do here," Hunter said. "And Henseler's place is as square as any. I'm going to stay here a while myself."

Wayne could not mistake this for other than a friendly dismissal. "I'll be sliding along," he said, rising.

"You goin'?" said Mrs. Trippett in the dining room doorway. "You can come back when you feel like you've got to have something substantial with no frills, but don't bring any cowpunchers, or card sharks, or gun twisters with you." Her tone, despite the admonition, was one of invitation.

"I want to see you again, Missus Trippett," said Wayne. "And I want to thank you."

"Well, that's something, too," said the woman, her eyes brightening. "Tom used to say that thank you was the two easiest words in the language to say and the two hardest to say like you meant 'em. Good bye."

When Wayne had left to get his pack at the livery and engage a room at the hotel, Mrs. Trippett's manner changed. "What about him?" she asked Hunter.

"He's the son of Ed Wayne, owner of the Whippoorwill," was Hunter's noncommittal reply.

"Yes, I know. But what's he doin' over here with you?"

"He isn't with me," said Hunter with a wave of the hand. "Just rode in with me from over west of here. Is Green up yet?"

"He isn't here. I haven't seen him since supper yesterday. I hope you two are not goin' to get this Wayne into a sky-high game. He seems like a straight-out fellow."

"You know me better than that, madame," said Hunter severely. "But if Green drops in, tell him I want to see him. I'll be hanging out at The Three Colors tonight, I expect."

Ten minutes later Hunter left the house. He walked to the end of the alley and around the rear of several buildings until he reached the rear of The Three Colors resort. He entered and passed through a hall with doors to private card rooms on either side and found Miles Henseler at the end of the bar near his office. After a few words with Hunter, the resort proprietor excused himself to the men who were with him and took Hunter into the office. They were closeted together nearly half an hour before Hunter came out alone, and after a quick survey of the big room left the place.

Wayne had seen fit to remain in his room at the hotel until dark. Now he pulled down his window shade and lighted the lamp. His pack was open on the bed and he took out his cleaning kit and carefully cleaned and oiled his gun. The weapon was one he had not carried for some time, but it was a duplicate of the gun he had lost. He counted his money and found that his celebration in Riversdale had left him a little more than $300 in cash. In addition to this he had the check for $5,000 his father had given him. He took this from a pocket, looked at it, and replaced it. He had a vague feeling of being terribly alone. Homesickness?

"Bah!" he said aloud. "What I need is some excitement."

He had done a lot of thinking in the two hours while the twilight gathered and night closed in. His father and Polly Arnold were uppermost in his mind. He was angry with old Ed, but not bitter; he felt a growing resentment toward Polly. Now he shook off these thoughts, donned a soft gray shirt with a blue neckerchief, and buckled on his gun belt. The present was here; the future was just around the corner. He had not told Hunter not to say anything as to how he had come to leave the ranch as he believed Hunter would keep what he knew to himself.

He set off at once for The Three Colors. Men who recognized him on the dim street turned for a second look. When he entered the resort, he saw instantly that he attracted attention. Men looked at him curiously or with undisguised interest. Hunter was right. He did have a reputation in this outlaw town this night, where before he had been unknown. The outcome of his fight with Jake Barry had pushed him into the limelight. He found the sensation not unpleasant. In fact, it gave him a thrill.

Miles Henseler greeted him cordially at his customary station at the lower end of the bar on the right side of the room. He even shook hands with Wayne—and the whole crowd knew at once that Wayne was not without friends.

"I'd like to see you privately for a minute," said Wayne.

"Sure . . . anytime," said Henseler, leading the way to his office. When they were seated, he said: "I should have told you the other morning that Jim would probably be back that night, but you made me sore. It was the first time I'd been mad in a month. I'm not perfect any more than anybody that comes into my place is perfect."

"That's all right," said Wayne, although in his heart it wasn't all right. "Give me a thousand out of this and keep the rest in the safe." He drew the check for $5,000 from his pocket.

"Sure," said Henseler, glancing at the signature. "I'd like to have a fistful of these. No, you needn't endorse it now. You can endorse it when you draw the rest. And if you need more, you don't have to ride back to the ranch. Just let me know. Your ticket can ride here for what you say."

"Thanks," returned Wayne. "But I don't figure on running into debt."

"Here you are. Five centuries and ten fifties." Henseler handed him the roll of bills and Wayne added the $300 he had had in cash. Then he counted the whole. "Correct," he said. "Have a drink?"

After two light drinks with Henseler he sought a place in a stud game. This was easily found and his entrance into the game filled it with seven players. Wayne knew no one at the table, but he saw at once that he was welcome. What was more, a group of spectators quickly collected and the table became a popular one with onlookers. Wayne bought $100 worth of chips, for the game was not a steep one. He was alert; his glances darted about constantly from under the pulled-down brim of his big hat. He saw Miles Henseler pass the table, but he did not see the look the resort proprietor gave his dealer. If he had, he might have been suspicious—for no reason at all. He won steadily, but not in any large amounts.

The players at the table changed as the night wore on. But no sooner did a man quit the game than another was ready to slip into his chair. And all this time Wayne was really playing under a handicap because his mind was not fully on his game. Would Hunter seize the opportunity to shake him? And why should he expect Hunter to take up with him?

As the game progressed, the bets gradually increased in value. The fresh talent entering the play was more aggressive. The last player to buy in before Wayne left the game took $1,000 in chips just before midnight. Thus the whisper went around that a back-room game was in full blast out front and the ring of spectators became three deep. And the last man proved to be Mort Green.

This, in itself, was enough to cause a mild sensation. Mort Green playing out front. His play was ordinarily in a rear room where a limit was unknown and a man's cards were worth anything he could make them worth. And he nodded to Wayne when he had tossed a $1,000 bill to the dealer. "Make most of 'em canaries," he had said, jerking a thumb toward the stacks of yellow chips worth $20 each.

This roused Wayne. At last his mind was fully on his game. He could play stud, and, while this was as stiff a game as he had ever sat in, it was, so far as he could determine, absolutely square. True, there had been two boosters, or house men in, and one of these had given up his seat to Green, probably at a signal. But Wayne had reason to believe that the gambler was a privileged character here.

It was an hour after midnight when Wayne again took keen cognizance of the room beyond the circle of interested spectators. The noise of the crowd had died down. There was almost a complete silence in the place. Wayne looked up to find Green's eyes looking straight into his. There was a warning in that gaze as much as if the gambler had shouted it at the top of his voice. Wayne saw spectators looking startled, first at him and then over his shoulders and the heads of other onlookers. There was a stir behind him as men hastily shifted their positions. Then he heard the stamp of boots and the clink of spurs.

He kicked back his chair and got to his feet as an aisle opened through the crowd like magic, reaching from the card table to the bar. Jake Barry was striding toward him. Wayne stiffened and their gazes locked. He had expected this meeting, but not so soon. Perhaps it would make a good beginning for the adventure upon which he had entered. The thought rather pleased him. Green said afterward: "I'll swear he looked glad when he saw Jake coming."

Barry stopped within three paces of him and planted his big hands on his hips. On his thick lips played a grim, sneering smile.

"You're back again, eh," he shot through his teeth.

"You're able to see again, you ought to know," Wayne shot back.

The crowd gasped and a sigh seemed to stir in the room. Men closed in behind Barry, but Wayne didn't know whether they were companions of his or not. One thing, however, was sure. Barry could not try any underhand work in the presence of the throng.

"Listen, you!" Barry pointed a stubby forefinger at Wayne as he snarled the command. "You're off your pie-and-cake playground and on a he-man range, get me?"

"I suppose you're trying to make me think you're top he-man, is that it?" Wayne returned coldly.

Spectators now began to move back from the table and those directly behind Wayne and Barry, respectively, got into a jam in their sudden effort to get out of what might be the line of fire. Only Mort Green remained where he was sitting at the table, his hands outspread on the green cloth, his face inscrutable.

"Think what you please!" thundered Barry with an oath. "But remember this. I'm givin' you notice to get clear of town by time the sun sinks tomorrow!"

"And suppose it's cloudy," said Wayne with a cold, queer smile.

"Then you can figure time," flashed the infuriated Barry. He turned on his heel and now had clear passage back to the bar.

But Wayne leaped, caught him by the shoulder, and whirled him about. "Why wait for tomorrow?" he demanded.

"I don't want anybody, 'specially your pa, to think I didn't give you a chance," sneered Barry.

"Yeah?" said Wayne in a tone of derision. "You mean you want to try to get the drop on me. Listen, Jake, get an earful of this. I hadn't intended to leave town tomorrow and now I don't intend to change my plans. But I'll make you draw in the open, and, if you do, I'll lay your length in the dust. This is twice you've started trouble with me in a town and there won't be a third time. I'm giving you a chance, if you only knew it, and maybe I'm too charitable."

"You're givin' me a chance, if you stay," Barry managed to get out.

"You've got that twisted," said Wayne grimly, his eyes glowing coals of dangerous fire. "I'm giving you a chance to think it over and beat it."

He turned his back, picked up his chair, and sat down at the table across from Green as Miles Henseler battled his way through the crowd from the rear, swearing horribly.

Chapter Fifteen

"What's the trouble here?" Henseler demanded as he reached the table where the players were resuming their places before the stacks of chips.

"Jake Barry just made a speech." The answer to the proprietor's question came in Green's cool voice. "He gave Wayne, here, his notice and Wayne threw it back at him."

Henseler glared around. "Where is he?" he cried angrily. There was a shuffling of feet and a swelling murmur of voices, but no one ventured to answer the question. Henseler seized a chair that had been vacated at a nearby table and stepped upon it so he could survey the crowd. But Barry was not to be seen.

"He's gone out," came a voice from the front.

Henseler got down and looked first at Green, then at Wayne. "I won't have any trouble in my place," he said.

"You ought to know," Wayne returned coldly.

"Yes, and Jake ought to know," fumed Henseler. "And now I'm telling *you* so that you'll know." He glared about at the sea of faces. "I'm making a new rule here and now!" he shouted, banging the table with his fist. "Any man that starts a fight in here, doesn't come back! He's siwashed! I have had trouble enough to keep this place running as it is, without gettin' the white-ribboners at the county seat stirred up." He wet his lips and continued to look about him with a scowl.

Wayne noted that Green, whose deal it was, was calmly shuffling the cards. Once, when he caught the gambler's eye, he thought he detected a glimmer of amusement. Possibly Henseler had laid down this rule before. He could tell it wasn't said for his benefit.

The player on Green's right cut the cards and the gambler dealt swiftly and smoothly. Henseler turned away and went back to his office, grumbling. The place again became noisy. There now was a real topic to discuss. Jake Barry, a gunman of more than passing note, had given Wayne his orders and Wayne had stood up to them. This made a meeting inevitable at sundown the very next day. The Three Colors hummed like a gigantic beehive.

Wayne tipped the corner of his hole card and the ace of diamonds smiled at him. He shoved in the $1 check it cost to stay with fingers steady as steel. All the players stayed including Green. On the first upturn of the cards, Wayne received another ace, giving him aces back to back, the ace of diamonds down and the ace of clubs up. Two kings were turned up, one in the hand of a player on Wayne's left and the other in Green's hand. With the only ace in sight, Wayne bet $50. The player on Wayne's left stayed, two others ahead of Green dropped out, but Green raised the bet $100. The other men in the game up to Wayne turned their cards, but Wayne saw the raise and boosted it another $100. The other player with a king stayed and so did Green. Green's king was the king of diamonds. They were not playing with the joker, nor did straights count unless they were all of a suite. A straight flush beat a flush naturally. Thus, on the second run of the cards, only three were in the game and there was $750 in the pot.

On the next deal all three drew small cards, but Green drew a diamond, giving him two diamonds in sight. The two others had off-color cards. Wayne bet $100 and the two players with him each stayed, bringing the total value of the checks in the center of the table to more than $1,000. The crowd of spectators now were looking on breathlessly. Here, indeed, was a back-room game in front! When Henseler became aware of this, he, too, came back to the table to watch.

On the fourth run of cards, Wayne drew a jack, the man on the left drew a deuce, and Green drew the eight of diamonds. He now had three diamonds in sight with the possibility that he had a fourth in the hole. Wayne did some rapid thinking. He had the man on his left beaten even if he held two kings back to back, as he suspected. He had Green beaten if he held kings back to back. But he couldn't have two kings of diamonds and therefore, if he had two kings, he didn't have the making of a flush. But why should he have stood Wayne's $100 raise, or have raised himself, on the second card if he didn't have two kings. He might have raised on ace and king of diamonds, although it would not be good playing, but Wayne had the ace of diamonds as his hole card. Then Wayne came to the conclusion that Green was trying him out. But why do it in such a public manner at such expense?

As high man, Wayne bet $100. He had won considerably and was playing on velvet. The man at his left stayed, showing that he did have two kings. Green stayed without raising, which seemed a queer play to Wayne, if Green had four diamonds. Green also was winner in the game, while the checks belonging to the man at Wayne's left dwindled to one stack of $10 blues. This amounted to $200.

As Green prepared to deal the cards, the third man spoke suddenly. "I'll cut the pack," he said.

Green's eyes flashed once. Then he placed the pack in front of the player, who cut deep. Three cards, completing the hands, shot deftly from Green's fingers.

It was Wayne's turn to bet, regardless of the fact that he had high card, for he was first from the dealer's left on the last card out. He had drawn a trey and had no pair in sight. The man on his left had drawn a small card that didn't pair in sight. But Green had drawn his fourth diamond—a jack. He had a possible flush.

He took out his silver cigarette case and calmly lighted a smoke. Wayne studied that jack of diamonds without concern for the third man's hand, for that player could not beat him. The onlookers hung upon the play like vultures. Even the hardened Henseler was visibly affected. There were two reasons for this. First, it was an interesting situation; second, Wayne was a stranger, but evidently knew his cards and was facing the most accomplished gambler in town; third, he was playing coolly and excellently, despite the fact that Jake Barry had declared himself only a short time before, and this would seem to indicate that he had no qualms whatsoever over the prospect of meeting the gunfighter. The money on the table was the least of the factors that made the situation interesting.

Wayne pushed out a stack of blue checks, which would tap the man at his left. But the third player turned down his cards. There was a possible flush, or possibility—yes, certainly—two aces against him. Green waited a full minute before he pushed in the blues to meet Wayne's bet, and then followed with two stacks of canaries, worth $1,000. For the first time in the game he smiled faintly. It was just a suggestion of a smile, perhaps, but Wayne saw it. It decided him instantly. He pushed in two stacks of yellows and looked at Green with raised brows. He had called the bet.

In his same cool, easy manner, Green turned the four exposed diamonds over upon his hole card, backs up, picked up the five cards, tore them in two, and thrust the pieces in a side pocket.

"That's enough," he said quietly, as Wayne reached for the $3,757 in checks in the center.

An audible intake of breath came from the spectators. Green and Wayne both cashed in their checks and pushed back their chairs. Nothing seemed strange about their leaving the game.

"Have a drink?" Wayne asked.

"We'll make it two," replied Green as they started for the bar.

"I see you found Hunter," the gambler remarked casually.

"Yes," said Wayne with a sly smile. "I'm much obliged to you for telling him I was looking for him." He wondered if Green had seen Hunter the night of the attack or had told him when he came back to town from the badlands, before he followed Jake out. But he had no inclination to ask. "I guess Henseler also told him," he added. If Green wanted to think that Wayne suspected they had both kept him from meeting Hunter that night, all well and good.

Green ignored the remark. "Here's a go," he toasted, lifting his glass. Wayne drank with him, noting that he took but a taste of the liquor as he did himself.

Green signaled the man behind the bar as Henseler moved toward them. Wayne had seen in the mirror above the backbar that scores of pairs of eyes were upon him. It gave him the first thrill of his big adventure. He had come to town to find he had a rep, as Hunter called it, and his stock had gone up like a kite since Jake Barry had challenged him. The card game, too, had made him better known. But he would have liked to put his hand in the side pocket of Green's coat to secure the torn cards that were there.

If Green had been beaten with two kings, having had them from the start, why had he played to make Wayne think he had the making of a flush, and had finally made it? It wasn't like an experienced gambler such as Green was to bluff in this way. Had he been trying to draw out on the others and gain two pair? That didn't sound like his style of poker. And if he really had had the flush and had let Wayne take the pot, then—why?

Henseler joined them. "I wouldn't take too much stock in that flare-up of Jake's," he told Wayne. "It wouldn't surprise me any if he didn't show up."

"No?" said Wayne coldly. "Well, if he doesn't show up, he wants to beat it out of town and stay away while I'm here. You don't know all the inside of this and Barry has wished something on himself." He was surprised at the vindictiveness in his tone. Was he actually looking forward to this meeting that could mean but one thing, gun play? He knew that Barry was practically disgraced—was disgraced—because of his defeat in Riverdale: No man there or in Rainbow might care to tell him so to his face, but he had lost prestige and standing. This would be enough to drive a man of his breed to the border of madness. Wayne was satisfied that the one reason why Jake had not pushed the trouble to a finish tonight when he accosted him in the resort was that he sought an advantage in the draw—a favor from Lady Luck. This, Wayne was resolved, he should not have.

Henseler had said something to Green, and now he spoke again to Wayne. "If this business has to go through, don't stage it in my place," he said.

"Oh, hang your place!" Wayne said in disgust. "This isn't a church. Do your own worrying. You've got a tough place in a tough town. What do you expect?"

"I expect. . . ."

"Cut it," Green broke in. "Wayne isn't likely to pick out stuffed quarters for fast work, and Barry's no fool. These spells of yours don't make a hit with the crowd, Henseler."

The resort proprietor scowled, but held his tongue.

Green turned to Wayne. "Suppose we go and get a snack to eat," he suggested. "I know a pretty fair place."

"Sure," Wayne agreed. He didn't look at Henseler as they went out with the stares of the crowd focused on them.

To Wayne's astonishment, Green led the way straight to the little green house at the end of the alley where he had taken supper with Hunter at sunset. This house, then, was the retreat of a favored, important few, of which Green was one.

Although it was past midnight, there was a light showing at the bottoms of the windows and Green's knock was quickly answered.

Mrs. Trippett beamed when she saw Green and Wayne. She nodded pleasantly to Wayne. He surmised by her manner that she considered him in good company. There was a light in the dining room for which Green headed. " 'Lo, Hunter," Wayne heard him say. So Hunter was there, too.

"You can come right in and set down," Mrs. Trippett invited. "I've got a lunch on the table. 'Tain't much, but I reckon you can fill up on it. And there's some hot tea. How did you make out at your gambling?"

Wayne smiled. This woman seemed to know much. "I won," he told her. "I had beginner's luck in a new town."

"My Tom always said the luck was mostly what you made it," was the woman's comment, as she preceded him into the dining room, and Wayne thought to himself that this applied peculiarly to Jake Barry, after his declaration of that night.

Hunter, who was eating at the table, nodded to him as he and Green sat down. Wayne looked at the gambler who nodded toward Hunter. "Tell him," he said.

"Jake called the turn tonight and set the time for sundown tomorrow," Wayne told Hunter.

"I heard about it," said Hunter shortly. Although Wayne hadn't known it, he was in the resort when Barry had given his notice. Fifteen minutes afterward a rider, mounted on one of the fastest horses on that range, had crossed the bridge outside town at a ringing gallop, bound for the Whippoorwill with a message for Ed Wayne. The message was brief and to the point, and would be at the WP by sunup. The rider had definite instructions on that point.

"I think Jake's imagination is running away with him," Green observed, following a short silence.

"Are you goin' through with it?" Hunter asked Wayne in a listless voice.

Wayne's brows arched in surprise. "Of course I'm going through with it," he answered, somewhat curtly. "What else could I do?"

"It might be arranged so that Jake would forget about it," said Hunter mildly.

"I don't want any such arrangement, and I don't want anybody trying to make such an arrangement," said Wayne, coloring. "If Jake doesn't show up, he'd better get out of town. I'll make him remember it if I have to take his gun away from him."

Both Hunter and Green were looking at him keenly. "I suppose you know," said Hunter, "that he's a greased thunderbolt . . . greased lightning, I mean . . . with his gun, and has friends."

"Lot of good they'll do him," Wayne retorted scornfully. His lips drew tight and he shook his head slowly. "No, I've got to do it."

"Do what?" Green asked.

"If Barry shows up and doesn't get the drop on me in some underhanded way," said Wayne slowly, looking at his plate, "I'm going to have to kill him."

Green pursed his lips and Hunter stared. This wasn't bravado; it wasn't overconfidence; it had all the authenticity of a carefully considered statement of fact. Wayne's implicit faith in his ability to do just what he said he was going to have to do, with the one stated provision, was amazing. Anyone could read unmistakably in his eyes that he wasn't bluffing.

The gambler thrust a hand into his side coat pocket on the right, drew forth the halves of five torn cards, and tossed them face up on the table.

Wayne pushed back his chair, staring at the pieces of the cards. There were the two halves of the king of diamonds, the halves of four other cards, three of them diamonds and the other the seven of clubs.

Green hadn't had a flush; he hadn't even had two kings.

Wayne's eyes narrowed. "What was the idea?" he asked.

"The seven of clubs is my lucky card," the gambler replied coolly. "I never pass it up. But tonight it threw me down, in a way."

Wayne smiled grimly. A gambler of Green's caliber tossing away the amount he had on a fool superstition? Rot! "Now let's have the real reason," he said, rising.

"Sit down!" Hunter recommended.

Wayne remained standing, ignoring the order.

Green made a gesture of conciliation. "I was thinking of Jake," he said to Wayne whimsically. "I wanted to see if you had it . . . the guts, I mean, and the common sense. I guess you've got a chance."

Chapter Sixteen

After a long pause, during which neither of the older men looked at him, Wayne finally resumed his seat. He was scowling in doubt and perplexity, for he still failed to understand thoroughly the purport of Green's explanation of why he had deliberately lost the pot. If it was a test, it was a queer test. And it had served to win admiration for Wayne from the spectators.

"Sure all sounds mighty fishy to me," he said at last. "But I can't forget you did me a good turn the other night, Green."

"You might as well forget it," said the gambler dryly. "I have." He calmly lit a cigar.

"Looks to me, Wayne, that you've no call to get heated up over anything," drawled Hunter, looking the other squarely in the eyes. "If we didn't have an interest in you, we wouldn't be here. You can be sure of that. And . . . whether you know it or not or give a dog-gone . . . we're not bad friends to have. Maybe we ought to be given some consideration."

"Oh, I don't mean to get sore at anybody, you men especially, but. . . ." He wavered in indecision, looking at the two of them.

"You see, it's like this," said Hunter in his slow drawling voice, tapping on the table and looking down at his moving fingers. "I feel responsible for all this, in a way. You came over here at your dad's orders to see me and give me a message. And when you thought you'd been double-crossed in getting in touch with me the other night, you followed me to the butte next day and got into that other mess."

As Hunter paused, Wayne looked sharply at Green, but nothing about Green indicated that he knew what had happened above Devil's Hole, although Wayne suspected he knew all about it. "I'm not blaming you for a thing!" Wayne ejaculated. "I wouldn't have the right to, anyway." He still yearned for Hunter's friendship and confidence. And, naturally, Hunter had had nothing to do with the affairs of the night—so he thought.

"Nobody's saying anything about blame," Hunter went on with a wave of his hand. "I'm just explaining that I feel responsible for what's happened. If you hadn't come to see me, this business with Barry never would have come up. Isn't that so, Mort?" He looked quickly at Green.

"That's right," agreed the gambler. "And I feel a certain responsibility, too." He looked at Wayne directly. "I should have fixed that night meeting with Hunter. I would have fixed it if I had thought anything like this was to come about. Oh, don't look that way. Hunter was due back the day he left. Did come back that night, in fact. So I guess you'll agree that Hunter and me are responsible . . . to a degree."

"If that's the case, you might as well include Henseler," said Wayne with a wry smile. Then his expression and the tone of his voice changed instantly. "If you want to know who is responsible," he said curtly, "I'll tell you. It's Jake Barry. He was responsible from the start. Now, he's got to finish." His eyes were flashing.

"We'd rather not see you go through with this," said Hunter. "It isn't necessary in your case. You're not a gunman or anything like that."

"And you know you don't mean what you're saying!" Wayne exclaimed scornfully. "They know me as Wayne of the Whippoorwill. I've heard 'em call me that when they thought I wasn't listening. The Whippoorwill has a pretty good reputation, if I do say it, and my dad never backed down from a man in his life.

So, such talk is nonsense."

For a moment there was a sparkle of admiration in Hunter's eyes. Again he looked at Green and some message seemed to pass in that look. He turned to Wayne. "Then you'll have to have friends," he said quietly. "I suppose you know that."

Wayne appeared somewhat startled. Then he looked at the older man thoughtfully. "My father gave me letters to two men who he said would help me to find you. One was Henseler, and the other. . . ." He bethought himself suddenly of the remaining envelope. This he drew forth. It was addressed to Mortimer G. Webb. He studied the superscription. Mortimer G. He stared at the gambler. They called him Mort Green. Was not Mort short for Mortimer? And could not that middle initial easily stand for Green? And was it not possible, if it were he, that Webb would prefer to be known simply as Mort Green?

A smile played on Wayne's lips. "My father," he repeated, "gave me letters to two men. These must be friends of his or he would not have trusted them in this way. Therefore, shouldn't I expect them to be my friends in an emergency like this?"

"I should think so." Hunter nodded. Without another word Wayne tossed the second letter on the table before Green.

The gambler glanced at the superscription. "Took you a long time to get wise," he snapped, as he tore open the envelope, took out a sheet of paper, and scanned what had been written on it.

Wayne felt relieved. This explained Green's interest in him and possibly his queer play of that night. A friend of Ed Wayne's would naturally be a friend of his son. So with Hunter. As to Henseler, Wayne had his doubts. The way matters were going he had no desire to jump at any conclusions.

"I half suspected you had this for me," said Green. "If you had given it to Henseler, he would have told you who I was the first night I saw you. You had nothing to gain by keeping this in your pocket, and it might have caused me embarrassment if it had been found on you." He tore the letter to bits and threw the pieces out the open window.

Hunter leaned his elbows on the table and spoke in guarded tones. "This thing has to be arranged," he said, looking at Wayne closely. "It can't just happen, you might say . . . not in this town. Barry has friends here and they're none too good. That fellow, Boyd, you shot up above the Hole has friends, too. None of 'em wants you to win this little shootin' bee. Barry knew what he was doing when he called you. Right down in the bottom of his heart he thinks he can beat you to the draw and the spot. And maybe he can. But whether he can or not, he isn't going to take a chance. He wants your hide with a hole in it, and don't fool yourself into half believing he'll forget about the little appointment he made with you. You called the turn when you said he was afraid to take a chance with you in The Three Colors tonight. No, he wasn't afraid . . . don't get that in your head . . . but he wouldn't take the chance." Hunter took out tobacco and papers. His face looked almost hideous in the lamplight because of its horrible blemish. "Right now, that ornery bunch is scheming out just how it's to be done," he concluded with a nod at both of them.

"I wouldn't doubt it." Wayne frowned.

"I know it!" said Hunter sharply.

"And so do I," Green put in with his silky poker voice.

"That's why," Hunter went on, after putting a light to his cigarette, "this thing . . . this meeting . . . has to be arranged. You can't just walk down the middle of the street, expecting Jake to come walking from the other end. And you can't just stand somewhere and wait for him to come along. We've got to go at this a little different." He inhaled deeply and wafted a smoke ring upward.

"I suppose because this Barry is a member of that cut-throat

Darling's gang, that outlaw will be along with his gang." Wayne watched Hunter through narrowed lids as he put in this bold shot.

But Hunter never batted an eyelash. "Darling isn't that kind," he said. "And this isn't any of his affair and wouldn't be, even if Barry was running with him, as to which, I don't know."

"I take it you don't know much about Darling," said Green, showing a sudden interest.

"I only know what I've heard," Wayne returned, biting his lip with annoyance for having brought up the name of the outlaw. "It's well known he's a killer, and a rustler, and a general all-around bandit with a gang of desperadoes trailing with him. Isn't that so?"

"He's bad," Green agreed.

"He's worse than that, if you meddle with him," said Hunter sharply. "Let's get back where we belong . . . to what we was talking about."

"I don't like the idea of somebody making arrangements for me," said Wayne, sensing the foolishness of his statement even as the words came from his tongue.

"It's no longer a question of what you like," said Hunter curtly. "We're going to see fair play and it's up to you to do the fighting when the time comes. Until then, you'll take orders."

"Whose orders?" Wayne flared.

"The orders of your friends . . . whether you want to, or not," Hunter replied grimly. "You must think this is fun for us, Wayne. And for all you know, we may be taking a little chance ourselves. But you can do this. You can go with us or you can go alone. It's for you to say . . . now."

"Oh, I've got sense enough to trail along." Wayne smiled. "What's the plan?" Although he could not know it, in that smile and speech he won Hunter's friendship. And that was no mean acquisition.

Hunter rolled and lit a fresh cigarette while Green puffed moodily on his cigar. Once more Hunter leaned with his elbows on the table and spoke slowly in a moderate tone. "You stay here in this house tonight." He smiled in turn. "You're dangerous enough to have wandering about town, but that isn't the point. If something was to happen to you before the time for meeting Barry . . . see? Anyway, it'll be daylight in a few hours. Green lives here. I'm going out and scout around and find out anything I can. Henseler's ears are wide open at The Three Colors, too. Get a good sleep and I'll be back in the morning. I'll come clean and say I don't know what our play will be yet, but I do know one thing. We're going to bring Jake to a certain spot when the time comes and none of his hanger-ons, to say nothing of himself, is going to have a chance to take a pot shot at you or pull any other dirty work. Listen, Wayne, there's more behind this than you think. That sounds like mystery, and it is mystery. It's as much mystery to me as it is to you. But I can read sign when it's on the tip of my . . ." He scowled, and Wayne knew he had meant to say nose. Yet there was nothing amusing in the slip. Hunter was too deadly in earnest. "Anyway, you lay low," said Hunter, rising. "I'm goin' to browse around. You know. . . ." He ceased speaking and looked at the two of them quizzically. "There's a chance of me getting mixed up in this thing myself." He started out as Mrs. Trippett came in. "Feed this buckaroo an antidote for gunpowder in the morning," he said in parting, jerking a thumb toward Wayne.

Green laughed. "Jim's a queer bird," was his comment.

Mrs. Trippett stared at Wayne. "So you've tied yourself up in a shootin' match," she said severely. Then, with an air of resignation: "Well, my Tom used to say, if a man had to shoot it out, shoot it out on the outside." She nodded as Wayne grinned. It was her way of conveying advice.

"I'm going to bed," Green announced. "You better follow suit, Wayne."

"I'll show you your room," said Mrs. Trippett.

Wayne said good night to the gambler and followed the woman into a small, comfortable room. She lighted a lamp on the table, and he sat down to pull off his boots.

Mrs. Trippett fussed about the room and seemed in no hurry to leave. Wayne surmised that she had something to tell him and paved the way by remarking: "You hear news fast as it's set loose, don't you, Missus Trippett?"

"Oh, Jim told me when he came in. It was straight talk he was givin' you and Jim Hunter's a mighty good man to have for a friend."

"I know that," said Wayne soberly. "Do you think he is my friend, Missus Trippett?"

"He wouldn't bother with you if he wasn't," the woman snorted. She looked about and lowered her voice. "You can forget I said it, but there isn't any love lost between him and that Barry crowd."

Wayne nodded in understanding. "And Green?" he suggested.

"The same," Mrs. Trippett affirmed. "But they'd stick with you, anyway, I expect. Watch this Barry. He's slippery as a snake. He'll wear two guns and try to make you think he's goin' for both of 'em to rattle you, but he's only good with his right."

Wayne yielded to a sudden inspiration. "Do you know this man, Darling?" he asked casually.

Mrs. Trippett hesitated. "Don't talk about him," she advised finally. "It ain't policy."

"Do you think he'll be in town?" Wayne persisted. "I'm just curious, that's all."

"He's . . . liable to be," was the answer. "Now you go to bed and I'll call you for breakfast." She left before Wayne had an opportunity to question her further, but he felt that he had learned what he wanted to know.

The dangerous possibilities of the impending meeting with Jake Barry did not prevent Wayne from sleeping soundly until nearly noon. Meanwhile, the town of Rainbow thrilled to its biggest sensation in years. There had been clashes between gunmen and free-for-all fights that had ended in tragedy; men had been "given notice" before. But this was different. Wayne was not a reputed gunfighter, but the scion of a great stock family. Even the roughest element conceded that he could back out and retain his face to a great extent. That he did not choose to do this, raised him sky-high in the estimation of most of the denizens of that tough town. On the other hand, he was not supposed to have much chance. True, he had gotten the best of Barry with his fists, but with guns—that was another matter. Moreover, Barry had a big following. Men who belonged to his crowd flocked into town. And other men swarmed into Rainbow. The riders who came from the wild district about the butte were not few. Comments in general were guarded, but there was an underlying sentiment among the groups in the resorts and street that Wayne didn't have a chance. But in some mysterious manner the word got about that Jim Hunter was backing Wayne. Men began to think hard when they heard this rumor.

Neither Wayne nor Barry appeared on the street during the morning or early afternoon. Barry was circulating among his friends, cheerful and confident—almost bragging. But there was a queer gleam in his eyes, an alertness in his manner, that to some betrayed nervousness. He was wearing two guns.

Wayne remained in the little green house. There had been conferences with Hunter and Green. His hand and eye were steady as steel. Then, 5:00 P.M., Jack McCurdy, foreman of the Whippoorwill, rode into town at the head of fifteen WP cowpunchers, and Rainbow shivered with excitement.

But when McCurdy met Wayne in the little green house, the latter's face was pale with anger—and Jim Hunter nodded approvingly at Green.

Chapter Seventeen

Wayne made a gesture to Hunter and Green. "Maybe I better talk to Mac, here, alone." He saw McCurdy frown as the others went out, and then he stepped close to the WP foreman and put his question straight and to the point. "Mac, how'd you happen to come here just now? Have you heard what's up?"

"Of course, I have. We're here. . . ."

"How'd you hear it so soon?" Wayne broke in, pressing his lips together.

"One of the boys told me." McCurdy frowned. "You don't have to act so huffy about it."

Wayne smiled. "Was one of the boys in town last night?"

"Not that I know of, but he gave me a tip that you and Barry was to match guns tonight and that was enough for me. I didn't wait for any more details. I rounded up a bunch of the boys and lit out for here as fast as four good hoofs could bring me. Now. . . ."

"Just a minute," Wayne interrupted impatiently. "You know none of the boys were in that you know of, and there's no reason why any of them should be in. It took powerful fast riding on a mighty good horse to get word to the ranch in time for you to get here, and that's the only way the news could get there. Do you know who took the word to the ranch?"

"I do not!" exclaimed the WP foreman angrily. "And I don't give a whoop. What's the matter with you? Do you think I'm lying?"

"Not exactly," Wayne returned, cooling down. "You've never lied to me, Mac. But I'm thinking maybe you're keeping something from me. Somebody went out there with the message, and somebody sent that messenger. I'm entitled to know about it."

"Well, you can't find out anything more from me than that a man rode into the north camp at sunup and told me. That was all I needed to know. We were on our way *pronto.*"

"Does Dad know about it?" Wayne inquired casually.

"I don't know that, either. Maybe he sent the man up for all I know. I'm not interested. We're here to see that you get a square deal. We'd be fine friends if we didn't back you up at a time like this. I reckon you know you're in a town that's as hostile as a rattlesnake."

"Yes, I know that." Wayne nodded thoughtfully. Who could have sent the messenger? One of three men: Henseler, Green, or Hunter. He eliminated Henseler at once. He had his doubts as to Green. But Hunter—by the guns, it must have been Hunter!

"How'd you come to run into Barry again?" asked McCurdy.

"He ran into me," Wayne answered shortly.

McCurdy scowled. "This thing supposed to come off tonight?"

"No need to suppose anything. Unless Jake beats it, it will come off."

"Where?" McCurdy demanded.

Wayne laughed queerly. "I don't know. You see there are a lot of people interested in this business, it seems. That is, interested in arranging it for me. Now you come in with a crowd from the ranch and they'll say I sent for help. Makes it look sweet for me." His eyes narrowed. "Just remember, Mac, I don't want the boys getting into any fights on my account."

"Don't worry about the boys," McCurdy snapped. "They can

look after themselves and I'm here to give the orders. You needn't try to lord it over me, either. I've been in a few shooting scrapes and this is your first. You don't have to have a lot of people arranging things for you. When the time arrives, just come along with us and he'll have to come out in the open."

Wayne smiled. McCurdy didn't know about Boyd. He shook his head. "There's one thing I won't stand for and that's a bodyguard. Great snakes!"—he waved his arms in disgusted resignation—"you'd think this was a rodeo exhibition or something." Then he laughed.

"Darling's in town," McCurdy announced casually.

Wayne started. "Yeah? In for the show, expecting me to get mine, I suppose," he said sarcastically.

"I don't know what he's expectin', but he's here. And that means he's brought a bunch with him. And don't forget, my young buckaroo, that Barry travels with that outfit."

"Meaning that, if Barry doesn't get me, one of Darling's men will, I suppose," Wayne mocked.

"Stranger things than that have happened and don't you forget it." McCurdy nodded. "Come and take look out this window."

He led Wayne into the next room and drew aside the curtains of a front window. Wayne swore softly as he saw half a dozen WP men lounging outside.

"There's a couple more out back," said McCurdy. "And the rest are circulating around, keeping their ears open where the listening is good. Don't start to holler, for it won't do you any good, Ted. We're not here to fight your battle, but we propose to see that you get a square deal. If we have to pack you back across a horse, it won't be because you were potted from the sidelines. You know I . . . the outfit thinks a lot of you, Ted. You've run with us ever since you could straddle a horse. It seems to us that we've a right to be here."

McCurdy's tone, as well as his words, made an impression on Wayne. He held out his hand. "Don't get me wrong, Mac. You can't blame me for being a bit upset. Only, don't make the look-out too . . . too conspicuous. I've always wanted a chance to use that word. It's one of my few big ones."

His smile brought a grin from his friend. "Now you're beginning to act normal," said the latter. He looked Wayne over with a critical eye. "You're steady enough," he decided. "When the time comes, don't wait a fraction of a split second. And they say this Barry packs two guns." He frowned.

"And I've heard that one's a dummy." Wayne grinned.

There was a knock on the door and they went back into the dining room as Mrs. Trippett came to answer it. A moment after she had admitted someone, she came in to them.

"There's a man to see Mister McCurdy," she announced.

McCurdy went in, and, when Wayne looked through the doorway, he saw the WP foreman talking in an undertone with a man near the window. A short space later, McCurdy let the man out. When he turned, he was frowning deeply.

"Well, I reckon it's my turn to feel peeved," he said. "I suppose you will, too. Now who do you think's in town?"

"Dad, I suppose," replied Wayne dryly.

"Worse than that," growled McCurdy. "Polly Arnold just rode in and is over at the hotel. Saw one of our men at the livery and said she wanted to see you, and, if you didn't come to see her, she'd start out to look you up."

For several seconds the two men stared at each other.

"Well, of all the. . . ." Wayne dropped into a chair and laughed heartily, to the other's astonishment. When he could manage to talk, he said: "Mac, all we need is a band!" And his laugh rang out again.

"I don't see anything so funny about it," grumbled McCurdy.

"That, Mac, is because you haven't got a sense of humor."

Wayne chuckled. "I expect a messenger any minute now to say that the Old Man and Pete Arnold just arrived in a buckboard with the horses' tails braided and tied with red, white, and blue ribbons."

"This is no place and time for a girl," McCurdy snapped. "And that young firebrand . . . jumping coyotes! There's no telling what she might do. The thing is what'll we do?"

"No." Wayne smiled. "The thing is what'll I do. Well, you bet I'm not going to have her chasing around town looking for me . . . not in this town. I'm going over to see her. I've got time."

McCurdy scowled darkly, and then he slammed his big hat on the table and swore. It was cow-country profanity of the highest order, with no irreverence intended. But it was the only way in which the cow boss felt he could thoroughly express his feelings. "What in the devil is she doin' here?" he demanded finally.

"Why, didn't you hear?" Wayne sat up in his chair in mock astonishment. "She came to see me."

This was too much and the big foreman flew off into another profane burst of exasperation.

"She probably wants to see me at least once again before . . . you know," Wayne taunted with a grin. "It was just what I needed, Mac, old hoss thief. This thing is getting so serious it was threatening to get on my nerves." He rose and drew aside the curtain. "Sun is still up," he said cheerfully. "I'm going over."

"I'll go along," said McCurdy.

"I wish you wouldn't, Mac," said Wayne earnestly. "I wish you boys would keep in the background. I know why you boys are here, and, after what you told me, it's all right with me. But, for my sake, don't make it look like I sent for you."

"Well," said McCurdy, scratching his head, "all right. Go ahead."

As he started out, Hunter came in the door. Wayne stopped short, his cheerful mood vanishing. "Hunter, I want to ask you a straight question. Did you send word to the ranch?"

"If you want to know who went to the ranch, it was Fred Hastings, the liveryman," said Hunter crisply. "He used to know your outfit." With that he pushed past Wayne, nodded at McCurdy, and went into the kitchen.

Wayne looked at McCurdy and smiled. "Another friend," he said, "another town friend, I mean. Used to know Dad so he took it on himself to slope for the ranch with the news. And Dad sent a man up to tell you. That's how you got your information."

"That may all be," said McCurdy, "but he didn't send any instructions. Or, if he did, I didn't wait to hear 'em. I did this on my own, and if the Old Man fires me, that's all right, too. If you're goin' to keep both your appointments, you better get moving."

"There's just one thing," said Wayne thoughtfully. "I wonder how Polly found out about it. Hastings wouldn't be stopping at the Bar A before daylight to tell them."

"She probably saw us riding in and took a chance that something big was up," growled McCurdy. "She's everywhere on the range, and can hear things a mile away. We'll take her back with us tomorrow. But, go ahead. Get this fool girl business over with as quick as you can . . . and don't let it affect your gun hand."

Wayne's laugh broke again. His cheerfulness returned. McCurdy had heard him laugh when going into a battle with his fists, but this was a different brand of hilarity. He looked at Wayne sharply as they went out the front door. Then he made a signal behind his back.

Wayne paid not the slightest attention to the cowpunchers loitering about. He walked swiftly up the alley to the street, keeping an alert look-out. He saw a WP cowpuncher at the street intersection. Then he crossed the street and hurried to the hotel. There were two WP men in the lobby. He stepped to the desk and asked a question.

"In the ladies' parlor, upstairs, in the front," was the respectful answer.

Polly Arnold was sitting by the window in the little room with its few stuffed chairs and center table. It had been a wild impulse that had caused her to ride to Rainbow. All her life she had been a slave to wild impulses, it seemed. It had not altogether been a wild impulse that had prompted her to tell Ted Wayne she would marry him. This thought, in company with many others, bothered her. Just how much did she think of Ted Wayne? Enough to ride to Rainbow in foolhardy fashion! Now that she was in the town, she doubted the wisdom of her move. There was no sense in it. She was a fool! The realization angered her. What would her father think? How could she explain? Just because she had seen Wayne riding east with that outlaw, Hunter, and then had spied the WP men riding in, she had suspected—what? Ted could take care of himself without her. She had no reason to expect. . . . Suddenly she became angry and struck her riding boot with her crop. There were steps on the stairs in the hall. She turned quickly as Wayne breezed into the room and closed the door.

"Come here, Polly!"

He held out his arms. Polly was a beautiful thing to look at. Now that he was exiled from home, nothing in the world seemed so desirable as this girl. But he had to play fair. . . .

"Not until you tell me what you're doing here," said Polly, rising.

Wayne tossed his hat on the table and stepped close to her.

"Let's make a trade," he bantered. "You tell me what you're doing here first."

Polly bit her lip and flushed. In that moment Wayne took her quickly in his arms and kissed her. She broke away with flashing eyes and half raised her riding crop. "You're taking a liberty," she said with trembling lips.

"I thought . . . well . . . I didn't mean to do that," he stammered.

For a space there was silence between them. Polly was angry and Wayne was nonplussed. In the moment of that embrace and kiss something seemed to come between them. It puzzled him, and the girl was uncertain of herself. But she was the first to recover.

"Ted, I risked a lot to come over here," she said in a slow, earnest voice. "I saw you riding over this way with that terrible man, Hunter. I saw some of your 'punchers riding over here. I just couldn't seem to stand it, and like a fool I came here to find out what you were doing. I thought, if you wouldn't listen to anybody else, you might listen to me."

"I've always been ready to listen to you, Polly," he said soberly.

"Then why are you here, and why don't you go home? Something is wrong, Ted, or the WP men wouldn't be here. What is it?"

So she doesn't know, thought Wayne. She had come on a chance. And she had risked a lot. But what was he to do about it? Only one thing—McCurdy would have to look after her, invent a plausible lie to tell her father, and take her back home with the outfit.

"You shouldn't have come here, Polly. Were you over to the ranch?"

"No. But I should have gone."

"Father and I had a break," he confessed. "I suppose you suspected it was coming. It was over that last trouble in town.

So, you see, I can't very well go back."

She stared at him with frightened eyes. "But . . . there must be some way." She paused as he shook his head.

"Not at present, Polly . . . perhaps never. That's why I've got to hold myself in check and play fair with you. I don't want you to risk any more for me, Polly. McCurdy will look after you and take you home when the outfit goes in the morning. Leave it to him to make up a story that'll hold water. You. . . ."

"But I've got to go back tonight," the girl interrupted. "They'll be looking for me. They may even ride over here from the ranch. I thought, if I found you, that you would take me back."

"That would make it all the worse," he pointed out. "Don't you see?"

She flushed, and then her face paled. "Oh, I'm a fool!" she exclaimed, stamping her foot angrily. "You won't tell me anything, so I know you're wrong. You don't care enough about me to. . . ." She tossed her head. "Ted Wayne, you've gone bad! Father always said you would, and he was right. I'll tell him so!"

"Your father is a smart man in a good many ways," said Wayne grimly.

"He's smart enough in that way," she retorted scornfully. "I'm taking back what I said that day in town. Pity for you went to my head."

He winced at this. "That's your privilege, Polly."

There was a soft rapping upon the door. Wayne started and glanced quickly out the window. The sun had set. He stepped quickly to the door and opened it. Hunter was there, beckoning to him.

Polly glimpsed him and sprang forward with her riding crop upraised, fury in her eyes. "It's your fault, you beast!" The crop was snatched from her hand and she was pushed back as Hunter pulled Wayne through the door, closed it, and, to Wayne's surprise, turned a key on the outside.

"You don't want to be late?" Hunter asked in a low, even voice.

Wayne didn't answer. He led the way along the hall and down the stairs, his face deathly white.

Chapter Eighteen

The western sky was afire and all over the land spread that brilliant glow that signals the setting of the sun. A freshening breeze stirred the dust in the street and set the leaves of the cottonwoods aflutter, their undersides dancing like silver spangles. Pink and blue and purple veils drifted about Rainbow Butte, and its crest wore a golden crown. The air was soft with the faint aroma of warm earth.

Rainbow swarmed upon the street. It was well known that Jake Barry had not left town. He had taken pains to be plainly in evidence during the late afternoon. The arrival of the WP cowpunchers had created a sensation and he had sneered and jeered, and openly accused Wayne of sending for help. This rumor, however, had been spiked by Hunter and Green and their friends. It was generally conceded that Wayne was entirely on his own.

That the prospective meeting of Wayne and Barry should attract more interest than any similar affair in the history of the town was but natural. There had been many clashes between professional gunmen, most of them impromptu, but this meeting was different in that it involved the scion of the largest rancher in the north range. Moreover, Barry was out for revenge. He had lost an immense amount of prestige because of his defeat in the fight with Wayne. Always a bully, he had few friends in town outside of his own coterie of followers, who were also disliked. There was an underlying sentiment against him. Another factor was his connection with the Darling gang, which was well known, but not mentioned aloud. And Darling, himself, was in town.

Thus a moving element of drama entered into the expected gun duel between Wayne and Barry. Suspense was in the air. Most of those in Rainbow were acquainted with Barry's prowess with his weapons—he always drew both guns, but few knew the left gun was never fired first. Wayne's ability was a matter for conjecture and wild rumor. The majority felt sorry for him. And with a bunch of WP men in town, what would happen if he were killed?

That there would be scant opportunity for an indoor meeting became apparent before sunset. The crowds surged out upon the main street and congregated where it joined the short street that led to the road that turned off southward, away from the butte. This was the one principal corner and it was here that The Three Colors resort was located. The big resort was right at the head of Main Street. It might be said that its front doors looked down upon the town.

It was in the vicinity of The Three Colors that the crowd was densest. When the flaming crimson banners over the western peaks blazoned the sunset, the upper end of Main Street was lined on both sides. And it was a restless crowd, ready on instant's notice to part and scramble out of the line of fire. There was little talk, but an electrical wave of expectation pulsed through the throng.

The WP men were divided on both sides of the street. The supporters of Barry were equally divided but greater in numbers. The latter were given to growls and sneering remarks, and called to each other in open derision of the men from the Whippoorwill and Wayne. But McCurdy's orders had been strict and the Barry crowd got little satisfaction out of their word play.

It was a setting for a stage, rather than a small town street.

When Hunter and Wayne were nearly down the stairs at the hotel, Hunter touched Wayne on the arm. The latter looked up and Hunter motioned around the foot of the stairway toward the rear. Wayne nodded, and, after a few remaining steps, they turned abruptly and walked along the narrow hallway to a rear door.

Hunter paused with his hand on the knob. "Your gun in good shape?" he asked.

"I've seen to that," Wayne snapped. He wasn't thinking of his gun, or even of the impending meeting with Barry, but of Polly Arnold and the look he had last seen in her eyes. Every vestige of cheerfulness had left his face, voice, and manner. Within, he felt a burning resentment, a growing anger toward Hunter and the others—even toward Polly herself.

"Keep close to me," said Hunter as he opened the door.

They passed out quickly, turned sharply to the right past the livery, which was set well back from the street, and were soon behind the row of buildings that faced the street. They walked in the rear of these until they had nearly reached the upper end of the street when Hunter stopped at a door, rapped twice, and waited. Wayne had swung around and was keeping an eye out to the sides and rear. The door opened and it was Green, the gambler, who admitted them.

Wayne saw at once that they were in the rear of a resort. They turned into a room on the left of the short corridor that led to the main room. The front of the place was strangely quiet. There were no sounds of voices, of glasses clinking, of poker checks clicking.

Wayne looked from one to the other of the two men with a frown. "What's next?" he asked curtly.

"Both sides of the street outside are crowded," said Hunter slowly, cutting his words distinctly. "There's a crowd over in front of The Three Colors, too. Barry is in there. He's got to come out in the open. We've seen to that. We'll go out front and wait, and when he shows. . . ."

"Wait?" said Wayne hoarsely. "Wait! Let him do the waiting and I'll be the bait!"

In a moment he had flung himself out the door and was running into the deserted big room of the resort. He plunged through the swinging doors and elbowed his way roughly through the throng in the street that parted instantly. Then he calmly walked out into the dust of the street, his lightning glance darting in every direction, but returning constantly toward The Three Colors.

There was a breathless silence, then a general movement of the crowd. Which way would the bullets fly? Men crowded against each other, and the throngs swayed. A shout and a fight had started. As if at a signal, every WP cowpuncher was attacked. Men surged into the street from either side, WP men fighting their assailants and Barry men—perhaps Darling men—milling and shouting.

Wayne stopped short. The significance of what was taking place before his eyes struck him in a second. This was Jake Barry's trick.

He began to back down the street. More men rushed in and he was caught in the mêlée. Spectators were on the run, fleeing down the street, into the spaces between buildings, crowding through doorways, seeking points of safety. The shouting was deafening and the dust rose in a stifling cloud. But no man made an attempt to attack Wayne. Barry's orders, no doubt. No one could prove who started the trouble and in the turmoil Barry would seek his advantage.

And Wayne was right. In some fashion the milling, struggling mob ahead of him parted and Wayne saw Barry running from the front of The Three Colors. On the instant Wayne caught a glimpse of the single spectator who remained before the resort—a tall man in corduroy with a great black hat about which was a silver-studded band. He only needed that glance at the eyes. Darling!

The fighting ceased like magic. Barry was close, leaping from side to side. His hands darted to his guns and the shots came sharp and close—uncannily close—from Wayne's right hip.

Barry stopped, his mouth open and twisted, his right hand hanging loosely, clutching a gun, his left hand resting on the weapon in his other holster that he had not had time to draw. A red froth bubbled on his lips as he pitched forward on his face in the dust of the street.

A hoarse roar went up from the crowd and Wayne felt a grip of iron on his left arm, jerking him forward.

"Run for it!" It was Hunter's voice. "Straight ahead!"

The mob was closing in and Wayne and Hunter dashed for the entrance to The Three Colors. Bullets sang in their ears as they plunged through the doors.

"Right on through!" came Hunter's crisp command. Wayne saw he had his gun in his hand. He still held his own weapon with three empty shells in his hand. He had lost his hat.

The whole length of the room they sped and behind the partition at the rear to the door behind. Hunter jerked the door open, slammed it behind them, and turned a key. Two horses were in the space behind the resort and Wayne recognized his own mount as one of them.

"Let's go!" cried Hunter, running for the other horse.

"Wait!" shouted Wayne. "The boys . . . Polly . . . !"

Hunter whirled on him. "Think of yourself! They're out to get you and me, too. There'll be time to talk later, you fool!"

He flung himself into the saddle as a crash came from the door. The hostile mob was smashing its way out. Wayne hesitated no longer. He made a flying mount and they cut out from behind the building to the trail leading to the north road. Bullets spent themselves behind them as they raced over the bridge and headed for the purple bulk of Rainbow Butte, swimming in the twilight.

Chapter Nineteen

When Polly Arnold heard the key turn in the lock, and Wayne had gone with Hunter, she stood still, trembling, staring unseeing at the door. Ted Wayne gone with an outlaw—forsaking her for the danger trail that led into the shadows—gone bad!

She looked down at the riding crop. She had no heart to pound on the door to attract attention and be liberated. Her senses seemed numbed, and the swift heat of her anger fled, leaving her listless and limp. She moved to the window and sank into the chair beside it.

Her concern over anything her father might have to say about her adventure waned. The Bar A seemed far away; the Whippoorwill had vanished; the rest of the world was swept aside and her mind was in chaos. Slowly her disordered thoughts knitted into the realization that the one thing in life she wanted most was Ted Wayne. Outlaw or not, he rightfully belonged to her. They had known each other from childhood. They had ridden wild and free under the blazing summer suns, in the blinding blizzards, in the dust and the rain and the hail, in the breathless dawns and the long, soft evenings. He had told her he loved her and she had seen it in his eyes. She had told him she would marry him and then within the hour had said the promise had been actuated by pity. She had lied!

Polly Arnold had wept few times in recent years, but now the tears came, and they were not tears of self-pity. It was merely a woman's outlet for suppressed emotions.

The tears were short-lived. She dried her eyes with a dainty handkerchief and rose from the chair. She had sat and thought too long. As she picked up the riding crop, she tensed and listened. From somewhere in the street came the sounds of tumult. She ran to the window, removed the sliding screen, and leaned out to look up the street. She saw the milling crowd with the dust rising and the throngs on the sides running. The dust cloud obscured her view, but she knew a fight was in progress. Then came the shots, one, two, three, almost as one long-drawn report. Guns.

She ran to the door, shouting and striking it with the butt of her riding crop. But no one was upstairs and those in the lobby hurried into the street. Polly Arnold was not a weakling and the door was a flimsy affair. She spurned calling out the window for help. She grasped a straight-back chair and swung it against the thin, left upper panel of the door. The rear legs of the chair smashed through the panel as if it were made of cardboard. She reached through, turned the key that Hunter had left in the lock, and opened the door.

She could still hear the shouting as she ran down the stairs and through the empty lobby. On the porch the pale-faced clerk turned to glance at her, his eyes shining with excitement.

"Wayne got him!" he exclaimed.

"Got who?" Polly asked breathlessly.

"Jake Barry! Outdrew him clean as daylight. The dust just cleared so I could see it from up here. Look at 'em run!"

The crowd was running up the street. The girl was down the steps and hurrying in the wake of the throng before the clerk could say anything more. So this explained it. Ted Wayne had come to Rainbow to shoot it out with Jake Barry and had killed him. The first act of his new career. Sobs choked in Polly Arnold's throat and then an insatiable hatred of Hunter was born in her heart. She blamed him alone for what had happened.

In the deepening dusk men took little notice of her as she pushed her way into the big crowd that had gathered at the upper end of Main Street in front of The Three Colors. Here the throng was so closely packed that she couldn't get through.

She grasped a man by the arm in her anxiety. "Is he there?" she asked, almost hysterical.

"He's dead," said the man, staring at her in amazement.

"Dead? Oh, but Wayne . . . where is Wayne?"

"He beat it while the beatin' was good, or they'd have got him sure. He's on his way, that boy. Who're you, miss?"

But Polly didn't answer. She turned away sick at heart and started down the street toward the hotel just as Jack McCurdy came running up. "All right, back to the hotel, Miss Polly," he said sternly. "I was tipped off you were down there and you've got to get out of this *pronto.*"

"Is this why you came here?" the girl asked heatedly. "To protect Ted while he killed that Jake? You might better have got him away from that man, Hunter, Jack McCurdy, and you know it."

"Ted can take care of himself," said McCurdy firmly. "Don't worry about him. But you can't take care of yourself, not in this town. You're going to stay hid till morning."

"I'm going back tonight," she flared.

"You are not, Miss Polly, and there's no use arguing. I've had to send the men home because I won't risk a gun battle with these cut-throats. They may be chased and have to fight it out yet, for all I know. It wouldn't be safe for you to start back alone and you know it. I've got to stay here tonight to try and get some word of Ted. In the morning I'll ride back with you and we'll frame the proper story for your dad. Now, you're range stock, Miss Polly. Please be sensible."

They had reached the hotel and McCurdy hurried her upstairs. He led her into a vacant room in the front near the parlor and lighted the lamp, for it was fast growing dark.

She sat down on the bed and looked at him. Her face was pale. "If I'd known this, I wouldn't have come," she said in a faint voice. "I thought . . . I . . . oh, I don't know what I thought or why I came. I'm a fool!"

"No, you're not a fool, Miss Polly," McCurdy soothed. "I know a thing or two about you and Ted. You thought you could help him some way and so you came in. How did you know what was coming off?"

"I didn't know," replied the girl stoutly. "It was that outlaw, Hunter, who started Ted out on this . . . this wild rampage. Dad'll say he's gone bad, just as he always said he would. If he has, it's that Hunter's fault."

"What makes you think that?" McCurdy asked.

"Didn't I see them ride in toward the Whippoorwill day before yesterday? And didn't I see them ride back yesterday? I could tell by the way Ted talked and acted that Hunter had him under his thumb. Ted told me himself he'd had trouble at home over that Barry fight in town. So Hunter must have urged him to shoot it out with Barry. He came up here and got Ted tonight when Ted was talking to me. Now they say Ted's gone. Well, you can bet he went with Hunter and Dad says Hunter is an outlaw, a thief, and a killer. It seems to me"—there was scorn in her voice—"that you would try to do something." She flung him a look of contempt. "You claim to be his friend," she taunted.

McCurdy hardly heard her. He was thinking rapidly. For she had told him some things he didn't know. Naturally he knew nothing of the arrangement between Hunter and old Ed Wayne. But Hunter had told him he was Ted's friend. Was the man double-crossing him? The WP foreman's eyes hardened.

"Don't take too much for granted, Miss Polly," he said

soberly. "And don't think for a minute that I'm not Ted's friend. I'm as much in the dark in this as you are. I think there may be a way, through folks I know in this town, to find out where Ted is and to see him or get word to him, or from him. That's what I'm going to try to do. You shouldn't say the things you do." His frown was genuine.

"Oh . . . I'm upset," said Polly. "But, Jack, how did this thing come about?"

"Ted and his dad had some words and Ted came to town. Barry met him and gave him till sundown tonight to get out. And you know Ted well enough to know he wouldn't run. The word got to me and I came in with some of the boys to see that Ted got a square deal. I knew he could drop Barry, or I'd have roped him and drug him back to the ranch. Now you have the story. I don't know anything about this Hunter."

"Well, he's the man you want to find out about," said Polly. "Find him and you'll find Ted."

"Have you had your supper?" McCurdy demanded.

"No, and I don't want any," was the answer.

"I'm going to have some sent up," said McCurdy firmly. "And I want you to promise me you'll stay here, Miss Polly. Honestly it wouldn't be safe for you to go out. Barry's friends probably have a line on you by now and there's a bunch of Darling's men in town. I want to go out and try to get word of Ted, but I won't move a step unless you promise me that you'll stay right here."

"If that's the case, you bet I promise," she said simply.

"Good girl," said McCurdy, rising. "Now you eat a good supper and don't worry. Ted's all right and he can't get into trouble over this. Barry had it coming to him and he didn't have any too many friends, outside of those that ran with him. And I'd stake my life that Ted isn't going bad."

After McCurdy left, Polly pulled down the window shade

and bathed her hands and face in the cold water on the washstand. She had brought nothing with her. When she had finished, there was a light knock on the door and a girl entered with her supper on a tray. The girl kept staring at her and Polly surmised that women visitors at the hotel were few. She had a mind to ask some questions but refrained.

Despite her mental agitation her healthy youth asserted itself and she ate heartily. It was a good supper and she felt in better spirits when she had finished. After all, this might be Ted Wayne's last wild adventure. She turned the light low, raised the shade, and sat at the window, looking out at the stars over the shadows of the trees.

There was a light tapping on the door and thinking it was the girl returning for the supper dishes, Polly called: "Come in!"

When the door opened partly, she saw, not the waitress, but a man who put a finger to his lips as a signal for silence. She started to her feet.

"Don't be alarmed," said the stranger in a low voice. "I come with a message from Wayne and I have to be careful." He stepped quickly inside and closed the door. He was middle-aged, smooth-shaven, with a not unkindly eye, and dressed after the fashion of the range. Polly saw nothing particularly suspicious in his appearance and his voice was reassuring.

"What . . . what is the message?" she asked.

"I have to be careful," the man repeated. "If certain people knew I was here and what I was doing, it would be bad medicine for me. Wayne wants to see you. You're Miss Arnold, are you not?"

"Yes. How did you know I was here?"

"A friend in the kitchen told me the number of your room, but Wayne himself told me you were at the hotel. He wants to see you and sent me to take you to him right away. We must be careful, and go at once."

"How do I know what you say is true?" asked Polly doubtfully.

"He had nothing to send but this," said the man, drawing a hat from under his coat. "He sent his hat so you would know. There is a mark inside. He said I could bring it back to him with you."

Polly didn't have to look inside for the mark Ed Wayne had put there, and which had, of course, been seen by those who had inspected the hat. She knew Ted Wayne's hat the moment she saw it. She had held it in her hands, as she did now, many times. He had sent it so she would know the message was authentic and the messenger to be relied upon.

"Where is he?" she asked eagerly.

"He's outside of town, miss. It wouldn't be safe for him to come in just now, as you probably know. I will take you to him, but we will have to be careful that we're not followed."

There it was again: careful! Possibly, yes probably, Wayne was in danger. And he had sent for her. Polly flushed and thrilled, and then made up her mind.

"All right, I'll go," she said. "I believe I can trust you."

"You can," the man assured her. "Now, please do just as I say and follow me."

He blew out the light in the lamp, after she had donned her hat, and beckoned to her. They went out into the hall and he closed the door silently. "On your toes," he warned her. Then he stole down the length of the hall and they went down a rear stairway to the rear door. They hurried across the space to the livery and around behind it. Two horses were there and to her surprise Polly found her own mount, saddled and bridled. Fred Hastings had not returned to town that day after his furious ride through the dark hours of the early morning. In a few moments they were in their saddles and her guide led the way through the trees by a dim trail to an open space that reached to the bridge. They crossed this at a walk, and then spurred their horses to a gallop over the shadowy plain northward.

After two miles Polly checked her mount and called to her guide. He reined in his horse at once. "What's the matter?" he demanded. His tone was not as modulated as that he had used before.

"How far do we have to go?" Polly demanded. "We're just riding north across the prairie toward the butte."

"We'll come to a cross trail leading to the right shortly," replied the other. "And we can't be making stops and losing time. This isn't any fun for me."

"And it isn't any fun for me, either," the girl retorted sharply. She was nettled by the man's tone. "Surely you know, and I've a perfect right to ask, how far we have to go."

The man pointed off to the northeast where the dark shadow of timber showed. "We have to go as far as the trees along that creek. Now I've told you and done all I could. If you want to turn back, you can. I'm on my way." He put the spurs to his horse again and rode on.

Polly bit her lip. The first seed of suspicion had been sown in her mind by the man's manner, but his willingness to go on and leave her convinced her that he was carrying out a disagreeable errand.

She galloped after him and soon they came to the cross trail. This was in reality the trail to the badlands that branched off from the main trail some distance north of the bridge. They rode along this trail at a fast pace with the guide in the lead. Just as they reached the shadow of the trees, a number of horsemen burst from the cover.

Polly sensed the truth instantly and tried to whirl her horse, but too late. She was surrounded by a dozen riders—hemmed in. The message from Wayne had been false. Her heart fluttered and then she steadied. What harm did she, daughter of one of the most important stockmen on the range, have to fear? Her courage returned and she felt the hot glow of anger.

"What kind of a trick is this and who is responsible?" she demanded.

"This is a winning trick, ma'am, and I'm responsible." The speaker was a tall man, dressed in corduroy, mounted on a magnificent black horse. His eyes sparkled in the light of the stars.

"What is the meaning of it and who are you?" asked Polly angrily.

"It means that you're to be my guest for a time and you had better make the best of it." The voice was cold and convincing. "It won't do you any good to cut up. If you don't ride along with us lady-like, I'll tie you up and put you on a horse with one of my men. If you behave yourself, you'll be treated like the lady you are. My word is good."

Polly was startled. The man smiled and a gold front tooth flashed. She drew a quick breath and her left hand flew to her breast. "I know who you are!" she exclaimed tremulously. "You're . . . you're. . . ."

"Darling!" the leader supplied. "Now you'll understand it'll be best to take it easy." He twisted in the saddle. "Fall in!" he called sharply. Then to the girl: "Ride along ahead of me, ma'am, and later you can talk all you want to. I'll treat you right, but you'll take my orders."

The other riders were in motion, some ahead, some behind; there was nothing for it but to do as she was told. She rode on into the beginning of the wilderness, her heart pounding, tears of fear and chagrin in her eyes, conscious that she was utterly helpless and in the power of a notorious outlaw, the mention of whose name gave men pause. And Wayne? Thought of him steadied her. Was he, too, a captive? Or killed? Perhaps she could find out when they got to where they were going. And she knew in her heart they were going to the impregnable stronghold of the outlaws in the badlands east of the butte.

Chapter Twenty

Polly Arnold might have been an automaton in so far as being cognizant of her surroundings or the route taken on that night ride into the heart of the Rainbow Butte wilderness was concerned. Her brain was numb from futile conjectures, wild schemes, questions that would not answer themselves, and a growing fear for her own safety. About her were only dark shadows of trees, an occasional glimpse of wide expanse of sky as they topped a high ridge, the occasional ghostly white soap holes where the quicksands lurked. She seemed in a stupor when they finally halted and the stir about her brought her into her full senses.

They were in what appeared to be a small basin with sheer rock walls rising on every side. There was a stream and trees and horses and a number of cabins from some of which yellow rays of lamplight streamed through the windows. Men were moving about and someone was lighting a lamp in the small cabin before which they had stopped.

"All right, ma'am, get down." It was Darling's voice and he was standing on the left side of her horse. Polly thought she would faint when he grasped her arm to steady her as she dismounted. "Right in here," he said, putting as cheerful a note as possible into his voice.

He led the way into the cabin and Polly followed mechanically and sat down immediately on one of the two chairs by the small table upon which was the lamp. The cabin was small with but one window, scantily furnished with a bunk, the table, and two chairs, a cupboard, and a small stand. The floor was bare. There was nothing in the bunk save a straw mattress. This, then, was her prison.

"Your horse will be well looked after," the outlaw told her. "I'm sending a man along with some things, and later I'll look in myself to see that you're all right. There are two foolish things you can do . . . try to get away, which is impossible unless you can wade through quicksand, and worry. I'm not even going to lock the door on the outside. You can bolt it on the inside if you want. But I won't be responsible for my men if you are outside this cabin."

She didn't look at him, but she knew with what he had said last he had virtually surrounded her with a stone wall. He went out, closing the door after him.

It cannot be said that Polly entertained any great fear. She was nervous and frightened, as any girl of her age would be in similar circumstances, but Darling, for all of his formidable reputation, was conceded to be the smartest, as well as the boldest and most inexorable, outlaw ever to operate on the north range. He certainly would be too wise to harm the daughter of Pete Arnold and thus arouse the entire range, west and east, north and south, as well as the range across the line in Canada against him. Sheriffs' posses were one thing, but he had been careful that the attacks upon him came only from one quarter. Polly suspected his object in abducting her, and the more convinced she became as to his purpose, the safer she felt. Gradually, sitting there alone in the lamplight, her courage grew and a cold, white heat of anger suffused her. Then there was a single rap at the door and it was thrown open. She started to her feet but resumed her chair at once.

A man came in loaded down with bed coverings. He

deposited his burden on the bunk and stood across the table from her.

"Reckon you'll want to fix your bunk up yourself." He leered.

Polly shuddered. Evidently Darling had sent one of his most evil-appearing followers to impress her. For this thick-set man, unkempt, with close-set beady eyes, a stubble of reddish beard, and a huge, protruding jaw was the most horrible individual she had ever seen. She turned her gaze aside. "Go away," she said with disgust.

"Oh, sure. I ain't supposed to stay here. I'll get you some water." She could feel his eyes upon her and drew a long breath of relief when he went out.

She shuddered again as she looked at the pile of bedding. There would be no sleep for her here, and, if she did lie down, it would be on the mattress. She wondered as to the time. It was past midnight, of course.

In ten minutes or so the man returned. His grin, showing his wide, yellow teeth, enraged the girl. "Put what you have on the table and get out of here!" she commanded. "And you can tell that Darling that you're not to come here again!"

"Now don't get mad, lady." The ruffian smirked. "I'm just tryin' to make you feel comfortable. Here's a basin and water, and soap and a towel, sort of, and a drinkin' glass." He put the articles on the small stand. "You see?" He grinned that fiendish grin again. "Now is there anything else? I'm just tryin' to make you comfortable, and. . . ."

He stopped short as there was a footfall behind him. Over his shoulder, Polly saw Darling. The outlaw's eyes were narrowed and shooting fire. The look on his face was terrible. He reached for the man's collar, swung him about as if he were made of straw, and drove his right fist fully into the bloated, leering face.

The man went down on his back, but Darling, showing amazing strength against the other's size, grasped him again by the collar and jerked him to his feet.

"Who told you to talk?" the outlaw chief demanded.

The other's voice gurgled in his throat, and once again that powerful right shot out, crashing on the man's jaw and knocking him through the door into the blackness of the night.

Darling closed the door. Then, to Polly's astonishment, he took off his hat. "If there is anything more you want," he said in a moderate voice, "tell me. Or call one of the men from the door and send for me. They have their orders and my orders are obeyed."

"Why did you send such a man as that here?" Polly asked. She felt that Darling had done so purposely and had followed by beating the man for her benefit. But why? To intimidate her? He didn't have to stage such a scene to do that.

"To show you the kind of beasts I have to control," said Darling frankly. "Mine isn't an easy job. I hold it with my fists and my gun, as well as my head. I want you to know that I'm the only one here you can depend upon and behave yourself. I'm responsible for your safety and no one else." His tone was icy as he finished and Polly knew he spoke the truth.

"Well, Mister Darling. . . ."

"Leave off the mister, just call me Darling," the outlaw broke in. "We're none too polite here."

"But you were polite enough to take your hat off," Polly pointed out.

Darling frowned. "I take my hat off when talking to a woman of the dance halls," he said, "so I'm not showing you any favors."

Polly flushed. Here was no ignorant bandit—which made him all the more dangerous. "What are you going to do with me?" she asked curiously, although her pulse was racing.

"That'll depend. Just for now I'm going to hold you here. I could hold you here till winter if I wanted to, but I don't think I'll have to do that."

Polly had experienced a chill. "I suppose you know this is a serious offence," she managed to get out in a steady voice.

"I'm used to serious offences." Darling scowled.

"No doubt. Robbery, rustling, even killing isn't unusual in your line, I hear, and it wouldn't bother you to have a sheriff on your trail. But kidnapping is different, Darling . . . especially in the case of a girl. It has never been done on the range yet, and every stockman in half the state would be willing to send his outfit after you. I suppose you've thought of that."

"I have," said Darling calmly. "Just because a thing hasn't been done doesn't stop me from trying it. It takes time to get a lot of outfits on the move. It would take more time to corner me, if it could be done. Your old man wouldn't want you held by me any length of time, would he? I reckon you've thought of that."

Polly's lips tightened. "So you propose to hold me for a ransom?"

"It will be the easiest money I ever made," said Darling.

"And afterward . . . then what?"

"I have plenty of uses for money," said the outlaw dryly. "I'll find places to put it."

"I mean what about yourself?" the girl persisted.

Darling smiled. His smile was grim and disagreeable and the look that went with it was cold. "I've always been able to take care of myself. You needn't lose any sleep over what I'll do. The thing for you to do is think about yourself and behave until your old man has fixed this thing up. He'll be tickled stiff to fork over a cool fifty thousand to put you back in the Bar A parlor."

"Fifty thousand!" Polly exclaimed. "Father hasn't got that much cash . . . and you'd want it in cash." A feeling of genuine misgiving assailed her.

"He can get it." Darling nodded. "His name on a note is

good for it in any bank in the state. I'm going to give him seventy-two hours, just to show him I'm not afraid of a chase. He won't need more than twenty-four."

Polly clenched her fists. "And you'll want me to write him a note telling him to do it," she said angrily. "Well, you might as well know here and now that I won't do any such a thing."

"I haven't asked you to write any note and I'm not going to ask you to write any," said Darling with an edge to his voice. "Your old man will take my word without any notes. He knows better than to think I'm playing a trick when I tell him I've got you and the price is fifty thousand."

"You weren't above tricking me," said Polly with a catch in her voice. "Sending word that Ted Wayne wanted to see me and that the man would take me to him." Her tone had changed to one of scorn.

"Don't you suppose Wayne wants to see you?" asked Darling calmly. "As for the man taking you to him, you had a chance to back out. Those were my orders . . . to give you one chance. And now I'll tell you that you are goin' to see this Wayne." There was a momentary gleam in the outlaw's eyes that showed he was enjoying the situation keenly.

"Is . . . have you got him, too?" stammered Polly, unable to suppress the eagerness in her voice.

Darling shook his head. "He's coming here of his own accord," he said. "I don't even know where he is right now."

Polly rose impetuously. "Oh, this is mystery and trickery, yes, and lying. I don't believe you, Darling. You've captured Ted and goodness knows what you plan to do with him . . . just because he shot one of your men. It wasn't his fault." Her concern for Wayne overrode her own trouble. "You know Ted wouldn't come here of his own free will. He couldn't come unless you arranged it, anyway. You're everything I've heard say you are . . . a liar and thief and killer. But if you kill Ted Wayne. . . ." Her voice swelled in her throat and she ceased.

"You're the first person that ever called me a liar," said Darling smoothly. "But you're a girl, and excited, and a pampered young fool in the bargain. So I'll have to take it from you. But you'll find it best to get along with me while you're here, or wherever I take you. Think that over. Because I'm not going to give you up until your old man has come across. Talk to me just once again like you did then and I'll double the price."

Polly was speechless. She was just beginning to learn how hard and unrelenting this desperado could be. His calm talk was deceiving. Under the cool exterior this man's ruthless character could burst into flame, unseen, unsuspected. His present manner was a pose. Polly knew she was in danger. Her life, or worse, might hang in the balance. She sat down and folded her hands on the table. She must—she must keep her nerve.

"How are you going to get word to my father?" she asked dully.

"I'll manage it in my own way," was the answer. "If necessary, I'll take the word myself, although I don't like to leave you here."

Another feeling of panic gripped the girl. After all, this monster was her protection. If he should go away. . . .

"It won't be necessary," she said quickly. "I'll write the note."

Darling's eyes gleamed again. He rose from his chair and took up his hat. "We'll see about that. The man who took you out of town will bring you your breakfast in the morning. He's about the mildest-looking man in my outfit, and I've got plenty of men. You might as well get some rest. Those things on the bunk are pretty clean. They're the cook's extras. You can open the door in the daytime, even walk a little just outside. If any man speaks to you, send for me. Good night."

He strode to the door and was gone before Polly could reply, if she had wanted to reply. She hurried to shoot the bolt in the door. Then she sank on the bunk, facing the open window, and waited for the coming dawn.

Chapter Twenty-One

Wayne and Hunter rode like the wind as night fell, turning off into the trail that led northeast. Wayne sensed that his companion was making for the badlands district and he was minded to ask questions, but first it was essential that they outdistance any attempts at pursuit. Hunter was in a none too pleasant mood, and Wayne himself was experiencing a nervous reaction from the tension of his meeting with Barry.

Night closed in and the stars broke forth in clusters. They kept on until they reached the first clearing across the creek that formed the boundary of the breaks. There Hunter slowed his horse to a walk and they rode side-by-side.

"We'll go on to my place for the night," said Hunter. "That town outfit knows better than to come nosing around there. I reckon they'll cool off anyway when they're sure you sloped with me."

"I don't like the idea of running off and leaving Polly in town," said Wayne crossly. "She . . . well, at first she expected me to take her home."

"By the way she acted at the last, she didn't expect any such thing," Hunter remarked dryly. "But I take it she's mad at me."

"You can lay to that," Wayne affirmed.

"She thinks," said Hunter slowly, "that I'm leading you astray. Probably has the idea in her head that I framed the business tonight. As a matter of fact, if I'd thought you were too slow for Barry, I'd never have let the thing come off. At that he pulled a trick on us. The fight was a set-up. It's a wonder some of his gang didn't pot you in the back. I expected it."

"So did I," said Wayne. "But that's over. I'm worried about Polly. She's sore at me and all that, but. . . ." He bit his lip and ran his fingers through his hair. "I wonder who got my hat," he finished.

"McCurdy told me he would look after the girl," said Hunter. "Said he'd probably send his men back and take her to the ranch in the morning. He expected to see you after the fracas, if you came out all right. You don't need to worry about her and I can stake you to a hat."

"Humph." Wayne's tone was one of disgust. "I think a lot of that girl, Hunter," he confessed after a short silence.

"Don't blame you," said Hunter. "Reckon she thinks right smart of you. These differences have to come before two young people understand each other. What do you plan on doing?"

"I don't know," Wayne admitted.

"Well, suppose you trail with me a spell until things get settled and you make up your mind," the older man suggested.

Wayne could not make out the expression on the other's face in the dim light of the stars. "Where'll we trail to?" he asked.

"You've got me there. I don't plan much in advance and I haven't got anything in view just now. Anyway, you couldn't take a hand in my game very well."

"Why not?" Wayne demanded.

"Because a sheriff is liable to sit in on my play any time," was the slow answer. "I don't just thumb cards, Wayne."

"I had guessed that," said Wayne. "Well, I can't just thumb cards, either. I suppose I want excitement. Let's go see Darling."

This was a bold stroke and it told. Hunter looked at him quickly with a queer light in his eyes. "What do you want to see Darling for?" he asked.

"Just to see him," Wayne explained lamely. "Hunter, when

things were hottest tonight, there was one man stayed in front of The Three Colors. He was tall, dressed in corduroy, and had a sharp pair of eyes. That's all I had time to see. But he looked different from the rest of the crowd . . . a lot different. Was that him?"

Hunter was silent for some time. "Might've been," he said finally. "Don't know as I saw him. Might have been him, though, for he was in town. We'll have to hustle along again."

He took the lead as they entered a narrow stretch of trail through a clump of timber and up a ridge. He kept this lead until they had left the main trail for the dim path leading to his cabin. The dark outline of the butte loomed to the left. Off there was Devil's Hole and the clearing on the rim where Wayne had shot Boyd. He took stock of his feelings grimly. He had killed two men. He didn't like to think of it. He told himself he never would make a gunfighter. Did he wish to become one? Suddenly he began to feel a little sick of it all. But memory of his father's sharp words drove this feeling away. Fred Hastings had carried word of the impending encounter with Barry to the ranch. His father had merely sent word to McCurdy, leaving it up to him to act or not. Evidently he considered it his duty to do that much. For some reason he did not quite understand, Wayne felt hurt and angry. But what could he expect?

They reached Hunter's cabin before midnight and put their horses in the little corral. Hunter lighted the lamp and built a fire in the stove. "I can stand some grub," was his comment, "and I reckon you can take on a little yourself."

"Sure could," Wayne grunted. "What can I do to help?"

"Sit there and try to look cheerful," Hunter replied.

"That's a big order," snorted Wayne. "I've plenty to think about that's serious. For one thing, maybe I drew down too quick on Barry."

Hunter turned on him, his eyes wide with astonishment.

"You what?" he exclaimed. "Drew too quick? You didn't draw till you saw him going for his guns, did you? Not that I could see, you didn't."

"Well, they might think I didn't give him a chance," said Wayne with a shrug.

Hunter stared about the room vacantly for several moments. Then his gaze settled on Wayne. "Don't you worry about anybody thinking that," he said. "And remember that when a man's coming for you, after having given you your orders, don't stop to comb your hair before you begin operations. Beat him to it. And don't spill any more fool talk while I'm shaking up this grub."

He turned to the stove. Wayne drew his gun, broke it, and removed the empty shells. Hunter supplied him with a cleaning kit and he cleaned and oiled his weapon. Then he reloaded it, but, even as he did so, he could not repress the hope that he would never have to use it again after the fashion of that night.

After they had eaten and washed the dishes, both sat on the edge of the bunks and smoked.

"Hunter, I wish you'd take me along to see this man, Darling," said Wayne. "I'm curious, for one thing, and. . . ." He paused.

"Yes," prompted Hunter, "and what else?"

"Oh, I don't know exactly, but I'd like to see how he runs his outfit. I'm not looking for information and I'm not a spy. It wouldn't do me any good if I were. You can arrange it. Why not?" He looked steadily at the older man who didn't meet his gaze. Hunter had his own problem in trying to carry out the wish of Ed Wayne. How far did he dare to go? How far would it be safe to go?

"Hunter, I dare you to take me to Darling," Wayne said then.

Hunter looked up. "All right, I'll take the dare," he said quietly. "But remember, you're strictly on your own."

Wayne was jubilant, thrilled, uncertain. It was a long time before he could get to sleep. And while he was tossing in excited anticipation of what was in store, the outlaw he sought to meet passed on the trail to eastward, taking Polly Arnold to his rendezvous.

Jack McCurdy made his way to the little green house where he had first been directed by Miles Henseler at The Three Colors. There, as he expected, he found Green. The gambler had not been sure but that Hunter would come there accompanied by Wayne after the excitement of the shooting died down.

"Haven't seen either of them," he told McCurdy. "He went north with Hunter, I hear, and I suppose Hunter is hiding him out. These louts who trailed with Jake will be all over their revenge ideas as soon as they've had a few drinks and woke up to the fact that they haven't got a leader or any friends that amount to anything."

"Is Darling still in town?" asked McCurdy.

"I don't know," Green answered coldly. "He doesn't advertise his comings and goings. If you'll wait here, though, I'll go up to The Three Colors and nose around a bit. But it will finish my part in this business. I'm a gambler and don't pretend to be anything else. Just remember that. And I'm not going to get anybody down on me for old Ed Wayne or anybody else."

When he had left, Mrs. Trippett put out some supper for the WP foreman. "My Tom always said, when you'd had some trouble, to get away from where you had it as soon as you could," she told him. "That's what Hunter has done . . . taken this Wayne away. He would be wise enough to do that and there's no use of you tryin' to find them."

McCurdy realized there was much truth in what she said. Indeed, he would not know where to look for Hunter, granting Wayne was with him. If he had gone to the Rainbow Butte badlands, it would be foolish to try to find him. For McCurdy, like most cowmen west of the butte, knew nothing about the wilderness where Darling ruled.

He finished his supper and smoked several cigarettes before Green returned.

"Hunter and Wayne beat it," was the news the gambler brought. "And so far as I could learn, Darling and his outfit have beat it, too. That bunch of Barry fools have quieted down and are lapping up the happy water. If I was you, I'd call it a day and go to bed."

"Which isn't bad advice," McCurdy agreed. "Well, I'm much obliged, Green. I don't know as I did any good by bringin' the boys in, but I think it was wise to send 'em back. I'll take the Arnold girl home in the morning. I reckon it was a good thing I was here to look after her, anyway. So long."

They shook hands and McCurdy went to the hotel. He proceeded upstairs to the room Polly Arnold had occupied. No light showed under the door or through the keyhole. He tapped softly but got no answer. He hesitated about trying the door to venture inside, decided against it. The girl had been sensible enough to go to bed. He went back to his own room to get some sleep.

The first inkling McCurdy had of Polly's disappearance came in the early dawn when he went to the livery to see about the horses. The night man, who was still on duty, told him Hastings had returned but was asleep. Then McCurdy found that Polly's horse was gone.

"One of your men got the horse for her last night," the man in charge told him. "Said they were going back to the ranch."

McCurdy swore. "Are you sure it was one of my men?" he demanded.

"He knew the horse and the girl joined him out by the corral," was the reply. "When I saw 'em ride away together, I figured he knew what he was talking about."

McCurdy swore again. "There's one man that won't be with my outfit long," he said savagely. "Get my horse ready. I'll be starting back as soon as I can get a bite of breakfast in the kitchen."

He hurried back to the hotel and looked in Polly's room. The supper dishes were still on the table; otherwise everything was in order. The bed had not been slept in. "Just as stubborn and independent as old Pete Arnold," McCurdy grunted as he went down to eat. Half an hour later he had started back, intending to stop at the Bar A and make sure that Polly was safely home.

Chapter Twenty-Two

Pete Arnold was inspecting his herds on the north Bar A range. He had moved his beef stock north and planned to ship earlier this year than usual. Both shorthorns and Herefords were in excellent condition. Frank Payne, range boss, was with the Bar A owner.

Arnold had left the ranch house at dawn and had not seen or heard of the passing of Jack McCurdy and the WP cowpunchers. It was sunset before his inspection was finished and he stayed for supper with Payne and his men before starting the long ride back to the home ranch.

When Polly didn't appear for dinner or supper at the ranch house, her mother did not worry. The girl had often missed a meal, staying at one of the cow camps or at the house of one of the smaller ranchers within comparatively easy riding distance of the Bar A. Nor did her mother fret when she had not returned after sundown. Polly loved to ride in the twilight. But when the twilight deepened into night, Mrs. Arnold became anxious. True, Polly had many times come home late, but the fact that she hadn't been home for dinner or supper indicated she had taken a long ride. It was not like the girl to go to town without stating her intention. Indeed, her father had forbidden it. Still, Polly was self-willed and had been known to disobey. Her mother didn't worry so much about where she might be as she did over the possibility of an accident. For Polly rode a spirited thoroughbred and she rode hard.

By 10:00—an hour after dark in these semi-altitudes—Mrs. Arnold was out on the porch of the ranch house listening for the familiar sound of flying hoofs. Polly always came fast down the road from the bench. But another hour passed without sign of the girl and her mother became genuinely worried. It was not like Polly to remain away from the house all night without a previous arrangement, or without sending word. She had never done such a thing before.

Mrs. Arnold questioned the barn man, an old hand who was no longer fit for the hard work on the range, and he made light of it.

"Don't worry about Miss Polly," he told her. "She can take care of herself and no hoss is goin' to catch her sleepin' in the saddle. She's just ridden farther than usual and maybe it'll be midnight before she gets back."

This failed to reassure the woman and by the time Pete Arnold arrived at the ranch shortly before midnight she was in a serious state of mind. Arnold was tired. For a big man, physically, and not by any means young, he had done a strenuous day's riding. The news that Polly had not been home for dinner or supper, and still was missing, angered rather than worried him.

"She's probably met up with somebody goin' to town and gone on in with 'em," he said, frowning. "I've told her not to do it, and I'll tell her this time so she'll never do it again. Is there any coffee?"

His wife had seen to it that the housekeeper had coffee and some supper and Arnold went in to refresh himself. Shortly afterward hoof beats sounded in the courtyard and he stamped out with Mrs. Arnold following.

But the arrival was not Polly. It was a cowpuncher Payne had sent into town on an errand. He planned to stay in the bunkhouse and ride on up to the north range in the morning.

"Did you see anything of Polly in town?" Pete Arnold demanded.

"Why, no," replied the man. "Is she in town?"

"That's what I want to know," Arnold retorted angrily. "You didn't see her on the road or anywhere?"

"No. I didn't leave up north till late in the morning and I cut down through the Whippoorwill. But I'd likely have seen her if she'd been on the road goin' or comin' and I'd have spotted her hoss in the livery. There was only five hosses there and none of 'em was Miss Polly's. And there wasn't but two hosses tied to the hitchin' racks and none. . . ."

"All right," Arnold snapped out, his forehead furrowed. He turned to his wife with a look of perplexity. "I don't know of any place she would stay all night. Maybe she pulled up at some ranch where they're having a party or something." He took off his hat and scratched his head. He knew it wasn't like the girl to stay away, but he didn't want to cause his wife more worry.

"Peter, there's something wrong," said his wife stoutly.

"Now mother, you mustn't jump to any such conclusion," he said, taking her arm to lead her into the house. "It'll be daylight in three hours or so and I'm goin' to send that hand up with word to Payne to start the men out on a search, although I honestly don't think it's necessary. But it'll show her that this stayin' away late at night is serious business. It'll do more than my talk would do."

"It might be," said Mrs. Arnold, when they were in the living room, "that she visited over at the Whippoorwill and stayed there tonight."

Arnold's face darkened. "She knows better than to do that," he said grimly. "And what's more, after that young Ted ridin' around with that cut-throat of a Hunter I'm goin' to forbid her havin' anything more to do with him. That's first, last, and final!"

"Peter!" His wife spoke sharply, and, when she used that tone, the master of the Bar A listened. "You'll do no such thing. In the first place, Ted Wayne may be wild, but he's not as bad as you'd make out. And, in the second place, you ought to know that any such order from you would merely cause Polly to like him all the more. I don't believe she would stay at the Whippoorwill, but she isn't home and I'm ready to imagine anything."

"Well, that's just what it is," Arnold snorted. "Imagination. I don't think she'd go over there, for that matter."

He went out by way of the front door and his orders to the man who had just ridden in from town were short and explicit.

"Take a good horse, one of mine . . . and get up on the north range as fast as you can make it. Tell Payne that Polly isn't home and I want every man in the outfit in the saddle and out lookin' for her by daylight. Tell him to report to me here. Tell him I said she might have had an accident, although I don't believe it. Tell him to have the men keep a look-out for her horse. Now don't sleep on the way."

The stockman went to the barn himself to see that the hand got a good horse and an immediate start. Although he wouldn't have confessed it to his wife under any circumstances, Arnold was worried. Polly, incidentally, had not mentioned her second meeting with Wayne in the company of Hunter. For all Arnold knew Wayne was at the Whippoorwill. But was he? The rancher's eyes narrowed. Would Wayne have the audacity and nerve to run away with Polly, even if she were willing? It was this thought, and not any fear of accident, that troubled Pete Arnold. And he knew he would have to be at the WP ranch house at daybreak. First, he must make sure that Ted Wayne was home. If he wasn't. . . .

The stockman swore roundly as his messenger galloped away.

It was but natural that, under the circumstances, the last place Arnold would think of Polly going to would be Rainbow.

He knew nothing of what had happened there. Fred Hastings, on his way back, had not seen fit to stop at the Bar A ranch house and he had met none of the Arnold outfit. He had conveyed his message to Ed Wayne, had secured some rest, and had started back in the late afternoon. He had not ridden fast and had arrived in Rainbow long after the exciting events of the evening.

Arnold pondered deeply as he walked back to the house. He had no wish to tell his fears to his wife. For once in his life he was at a loss to decide what to do. He was stiff and sore from a full day and part of the night in the saddle and did not feel equal to riding out and searching the prairie until dawn. At the same time, inactivity irked him. Had Polly ridden in at this time he would have received her with a sigh of relief and his reprimand would not have been as fiery as she might have expected. But Polly was lying on the bunk in the cabin in Darling's rendezvous staring at Ted Wayne's hat on the table. She had thrust it within her blouse and brought it with her.

"We better get some rest, mother," said Arnold when he again met his wife in the living room.

It was the best way to reassure her, he felt. And his wife agreed that there was nothing to be done in any event until daybreak. Meanwhile, Polly might return. Though she would not think of telling her husband, the same troubling conjecture as to Ted Wayne and Polly had obsessed her. And she knew, too, that, if her fears were to prove well founded, she would stand by the daughter who was the sun, and the universe, and the life of their existence.

Thoroughly wearied, Pete Arnold slept until sunup. His wife had not slept and was up before him, preparing his breakfast herself. He bolted his food with a mild reproach at not having been awakened at dawn. His horse was ready when he had finished breakfast, and, after leaving orders that Payne was to wait for him when he arrived, he started for the Whippoorwill.

Ed Wayne had received the news. Acting on instructions from Jack McCurdy, one of the WP cowpunchers had conveyed the message. The stockman had listened complacently, but no emotion had showed on his face or in his eyes. He ordered the man back to the range. Then he went to his office in the front of the house and sat at his desk. He did not heed the sound of a horse as it came up the road. He was occupied with his thoughts, and they were not light thoughts. Would McCurdy bring Ted back? He had given his foreman no orders. And he felt that Ted wouldn't come back. Did he want him back already? Ed Wayne was perplexed, irritated, somewhat bewildered, and it was in this mood that Pete Arnold found him.

"Come out on the porch, Pete," the WP owner invited when his visitor appeared at the door of the office. "It's cooler out there."

"I don't figure on stayin' long, Ed," said Arnold nervously, "and I'm here on a sort of funny business."

"Yes?" Ed Wayne looked at him sharply as they sat down in chairs on the porch. "What's up?"

Arnold shifted uneasily. "Is Ted home?" he asked.

Ed Wayne frowned. "No. Ted left day before yesterday . . . on his own hook. Why do you ask?"

Arnold started. "He's . . . gone? Gone . . . for good?" he stammered.

"For good or not, he's gone until he can get some sense into his head and some of the fight out of it," replied Ed Wayne sternly. "What're you so worked up about? I can't see how it can interest you so much."

"Well, it does," said Arnold, regaining his composure and speaking rather harshly. "Polly has been missin' since yesterday morning. She wasn't home for dinner or supper and she didn't come home last night."

It was Ed Wayne's turn to stare. Gradually the force of Arnold's hidden meaning dawned on him. He ignored it. "Maybe she's in town," he said. "She hasn't been here . . . hasn't been here since spring, for that matter."

"I don't doubt that," said Arnold sharply. "You know what I'm drivin' at. I'm wonderin' if Polly and your boy have run off."

Ed Wayne's eyes hardened. "I see." He nodded. "You're afraid they've eloped. Well, Ted isn't that kind for one thing, and for another I happen to know that he was in Rainbow all day yesterday and the night before, and last evening. That Jake Barry called the turn on him for a gun play and Ted bored him for keeps. That doesn't sound much like an elopement, does it?"

"A shootin' match?" Arnold exclaimed. "Ted killed Barry? I was afraid . . . I was afraid. . . ."

"You was afraid he'd come to a bad end," Ed Wayne put in. "Spit it out . . . I know what you're thinking. But you let me do the worrying, Pete Arnold. I know Ted and Polly have been sweet on each other for a long time. We couldn't expect anything else. You might say they were brought up together. They're young and all that, but I don't think Ted would run away with Polly, and I don't think Polly would run away even if he wanted her to. That's how much respect I've got for our young people."

Arnold was angry and showed it. "If Polly did run away, you can lay to it that Ted talked her into it," he said hotly.

Trouble loomed between the two stockmen and always, when they had been at loggerheads, it had been Wayne who had kept his temper. Jack McCurdy, desirous of inventing a plausible story to explain Polly Arnold's presence in town, had not sent word to Ed Wayne that she was there lest the news get to Arnold before he could return the girl to the ranch. Thus the WP owner was unaware of the fact that Polly had gone to Rainbow.

"Wait a minute, Pete," said Ed Wayne coolly. "Don't fly off

the handle in this. I told you Ted was in Rainbow yesterday and last evening. Jake Barry gave him notice to leave town by sunset last night. Fred Hastings, who has the livery over there, brought me the word. I sent word to McCurdy and he went in with some of my 'punchers to see that Ted got a square deal."

"And maybe Polly went in, too!" exclaimed Arnold. "It would be just like her, if she heard about it and thought she could stop the gun play. When she gets an idea of a sudden, she works fast."

"Maybe she did." Ed Wayne nodded. "McCurdy sent the men back and stayed in town himself to try and see Ted after the shooting. He sent word to me of what had happened by one of the men. If your girl did go in, McCurdy certainly would look after her. And if she went in, she certainly didn't stop anything. Listen." He told Arnold in as few words as possible what had happened in town, but he knew nothing of Polly Arnold or of Ted's movements after the meeting with Barry.

Arnold rose, his face white. "That's just it," he said grimly. "Polly went to Rainbow. I think like you, that Mac would look after her, and I'll give Ted credit by sayin' that I feel he'd fight till the hills tumbled for her, but she rode straight into danger if she went. You know Darling and his outfit were probably in there. I wouldn't put anything past that blackguard. And what's more, Ed, I've missed cattle from my lower range." He paused and wiped beads of sweat from his forehead. "But that's nothing! It's Polly I'm thinkin' about. You don't suppose . . . ?" He looked at Ed Wayne helplessly.

Wayne rose. His face was set. "The thing to do is to get to Rainbow," he announced. "I'm going with you."

In a few minutes the two stockmen were riding at a swift lope across the Bar A range. They did no talking. They passed the road leading down to the Arnold ranch house and continued on to the lower spring. It was at the spring that they met Jack Mc-

Curdy who was taking the cut-off on his fast ride back.

McCurdy saw the question in Arnold's eyes before the rancher could put it in words.

"Isn't Polly home?" asked the WP foreman.

"No," replied Arnold, his face going white. "Have you seen her?"

"She was in town last night," McCurdy answered, staring from one to the other of the two stockmen. "The night man in the livery told me one of my men called for her and took her home . . . or was to take her home. Did you get my message?" He put the question to Ed Wayne.

"Yes," said Wayne, "but you didn't mention Polly Arnold. Did you send her home with one of our men?"

"Great guns, no!" McCurdy exploded. "I told her to stay in her room at the hotel until morning and I'd take her home myself!"

"Did Ted see her?" Wayne demanded. "Did he talk with her?"

"He saw her at the hotel and talked with her. But he lit out right after the trouble with Barry was over. I don't think he saw her after that."

"Go on to the ranch," thundered Ed Wayne, "and bring every man of the Whippoorwill outfit to Rainbow as quick as you can!"

Arnold suddenly remembered Payne. "Stop at my place," he said hoarsely. "Tell Payne to bring the Bar A outfit along . . . every last man of 'em!"

"And we'll go on to Rainbow," said Ed Wayne in a terrible voice.

Chapter Twenty-Three

Toward morning Polly Arnold fell asleep. When she woke, the sun was streaming through the window and someone was pounding on the door. It took her several moments to realize where she was and then the happenings of the previous night and the force of her predicament swept upon her. She had not undressed and now she rose and went to the door.

"Who's there?" she called before shooting back the bolt.

"Your breakfast . . . if you want it," came the sharp reply.

She opened the door and the man who had lured her away from the hotel in Rainbow entered with her breakfast on a wooden tray. In appearance the man did not seem as honest-looking as he had the night before. His voice had been different, too. But the girl wondered if this might not be a figment of the imagination.

"What time is it?" she asked pleasantly.

"I don't know," was the gruff answer. "You mustn't talk to me or anybody else, except the chief. I'll tip you off that nobody'll answer you if you do talk to 'em. It's orders."

"Nice cheerful crowd," said Polly sarcastically. "I couldn't believe anything you told me, anyway." She tossed him a look of scorn and turned to the stand where was the water, soap, and towel. "Get out!" she shot back over her shoulder.

The man had put the food down and now he hesitated a few moments. But if he had intended to say something, he thought better of it, for he went out the door, slamming it behind him.

Polly opened it immediately. There was one thing she had to do. She must show these men she wasn't afraid of them. For that matter, she did not feel afraid this morning, with the sunlight flooding the world, a cool breeze filtering down from the trees above the towering cliffs, and birds singing. When she had finished her ablutions, she looked out the door and was struck by the beauty of the place. The luscious grass was a deep green, sprinkled with wildflowers. There were tall, spreading cottonwoods, slim, trim alders, a few firs, and berry bushes laden with red raspberries. The cliffs were yellow and orange limestone and above them was a belt of green pines and firs that Polly suspected were on the lower slopes of the big butte.

She sat down to her breakfast at about the same time her father was eating at the Bar A before leaving for the Whippoorwill. Polly was young and healthy, and her appetite asserted itself. Whatever Darling might have in mind, he evidently had no intention of starving her. Nor did it appear that the outlaws fared badly. Her breakfast consisted of crisp bacon, fried eggs, hot cakes, jelly, a pot of excellent coffee, and three oranges. It was hot and well cooked, and the food was of good quality. Polly ate it all, save for two of the oranges that she put aside for later in the day. The thought uppermost in her mind was concerned with the length of time she would be held. $50,000! How could she ever forgive herself or feel the same at home again? The thought nearly spoiled her breakfast. Her father could afford to pay it, she knew, but what explanation could she make to him? What had seemed sensible when she had made her reckless decision to go to Rainbow the day before now appeared banal and silly. This realization irritated her almost to the point of anger. Then she remembered Hunter and her wrath was genuine. Darling had said Ted Wayne would come to see her. He had lied. But what could she expect of a man of his stamp?

After breakfast she sat in the doorway of the cabin. Men were moving about the other cabins that were some little distance away. Two were saddling horses near the bank of the little stream that flowed through the cañon, or bowl. She caught the sound of rough voices but could not distinguish what was being said. She was thankful that no one paid her any attention. Darling's orders. It was all very evident that the outlaw leader kept complete control over his followers.

The man came in for the dishes and took them away without even throwing a glance at her. She didn't speak to him. She wondered what had caused these men to take up such a life. Then it occurred to her that Hunter was most likely a member of the band. And Ted Wayne was traveling with him. This bothered her until she felt a growing resentment toward Wayne. After all, he was the indirect, no, the *direct* cause of what had happened. But she soon recognized this attitude as unfair. Then she saw Darling approaching.

The outlaw looked different in the clear light of day. Polly saw that the eyes were hard, the lips straight and firm, the chin rugged. He nodded as he came up and the girl noted that he carried pen, ink, and paper in his left hand. On his right a gun was strapped in a worn black holster to his thigh.

"Come inside, ma'am," he said in a voice that was nothing short of a command.

She followed him into the cabin as he stepped past her and put the paper, pen, and ink on the table. The note to her father. Polly's lips curled. He had said he didn't need any note. That, too, had been a lie.

"You don't have to write this unless you want to," he said slowly. She noted that he didn't take off his hat. "It's up to you," he continued. "I'm thinking a word might get you out of here quicker, that's all. I'm not hankering to be bothered with you any length of time, and I don't want my men to get to grumbling. They might get out of bounds."

"Oh, I'll write it," said the girl in resignation as she sat down at the table and drew the cork out of the ink bottle. "I don't know what to say, but. . . ."

"I'll tell you what to say," Darling interrupted. "Are you ready to write?"

"Yes, but I'm not promising to write what you say," flared Polly.

"You can do as you please," said Darling coldly. "Just say . . . 'I'm where Darling says I am.' That's all, and sign your full name so your old man will know the writing. Have you got it?"

"Is that all you want me to write?" asked Polly, surprised.

"That's all. Just . . . 'I'm where Darling says I am,' . . . and sign it."

The girl wrote *Dear Father,* and followed with the sentence Darling had dictated. Then she signed her name. She was glad she didn't have to make any plea in the brief note.

Darling took the paper, read what she had written, folded it, and thrust it in the pocket of his shirt. "I'll look around and see if there's anything in camp to read and maybe send you something," he said. "Take it easy and don't go more than twenty feet from this cabin. If you start to wander around, I'll not be responsible." He looked at her sharply, took up the pen and ink, and went out the door.

Polly sat at the table with her hands folded and wondered how the message was to be sent and what Darling's own message would be. She went out and sat on the doorstep again, thinking she might see the messenger leave. She had seen the men who had saddled their horses ride past the lower cabins and after a time she decided that the trail leading from the rendezvous was below the cabins. There was a cleft in the rock wall down there.

True to his word, Darling sent the man who had brought her

breakfast with some magazines. He put these down in the doorway and departed. This would indicate that the outlaw chief still was in camp. If there was anything that Polly did not want, it was the departure of Darling. She found herself relying on him for her safety.

She went inside and lay down on the bunk. It was warm and she dozed until her dinner arrived. She did not eat much this noon. In the afternoon it was hot. The sun poured into the bowl and the cliffs caught the rays and threw them off with dazzling brilliancy. She had tried to read but found it impossible. Anyway, the magazines were well-thumbed and dirty, and covers and pages torn. Finally she slept. She awoke to find her supper on the table. The water pail had been filled with fresh, cold water and she laved her face and hands after she had taken a long, cooling drink. The sun had set.

After supper she went outside. A cool breeze had sprung up. The cliffs were painted in all the colors of the rainbow and the sky was rose-tinted. She noted the camp was astir. Men were catching up their horses and saddling. Her spirits wavered. Were they going to move? Was she to be taken somewhere else? Or had arrangements for her release already been made? The latter seemed improbable. Then she saw Darling in front of the largest of the cabins, talking to one of the men who was mounted. Evidently he was giving orders. Shortly afterward the men rode away and disappeared in the timber below the cabins. Darling vanished.

A shadow drifted lazily over the trees and grass and Polly looked up quickly. A cloud was riding in the pink afterglow of the sunset. It was the first cloud she had seen that day. It might be the harbinger of a storm. She felt she wouldn't be surprised if a storm were to burst out of a clear sky. Nothing now could surprise her. Nothing. . . .

She caught her breath with sudden interest. Two riders had

emerged from the trees below the cabins. She recognized one of them at first sight, and then, as they came nearer, she recognized the other. She hurried into the cabin and stood leaning on the table, trembling with excitement. Ted Wayne—with Hunter!

"Remember what I told you," Hunter was saying to Wayne as they approached the large cabin. "You're here at your own risk, and I'm taking a long chance in bringing you."

"I know." Wayne nodded, his eyes sparkling.

"We'll unload here," said Hunter, indicating a spot near the big cabin.

They dismounted, loosened the saddle cinches, and left their horses with reins dangling. Hunter led the way to the cabin. They entered a large room, with a table in the center and chairs and benches about. It looked something like a clubroom. It was unoccupied and Hunter rapped on a door at the right end of the room. "Come in," a gruff voice invited.

The room they entered now was small and fitted as an office.

" 'Lo, Hunter," greeted the man at a flat-topped desk. But he didn't look at Hunter. He gazed steadily at Wayne out of cold eyes. Wayne needed no second glance to recognize Darling.

"This is Wayne of the Whippoorwill," said Hunter casually. "Wanted to come along and I took a chance. His dad let him out at the ranch and he's on a lone trail, looks like."

"Not as long as he's with you," said Darling, frowning. "But now he's here, he'll stay here." He looked searchingly at his visitor. "Why did you kill Boyd?" he demanded suddenly.

Wayne was taken aback by the abruptness of the unexpected question. "I had to, or get a slug myself," he said stoutly, scorning any evasion with this dangerous man.

"I saw it," said Hunter. "Barry was trying to shove Wayne off the rim into the Hole, and. . . ."

"Can't this man talk for himself?" Darling broke in with an oath.

"I reckon he can," drawled Hunter. "And I reckon you know all about it without asking him. I thought that white-livered Jake would whine. But I'll bet he didn't tell you that Wayne made a fool out of him up there with the odds about six to one against him."

Darling's eyes glittered and Wayne sensed the truth at once. Hunter was one man who wasn't afraid of the arch outlaw. And Hunter also was a man for whom Darling had a great deal of respect. It was apparent as their glances locked that Darling didn't wish to cross Hunter. Wayne remembered what he had heard about Hunter being sure death with his gun. Darling had the same reputation. Perhaps Darling was not sure that he could beat Hunter to it in a gun play.

"Jake didn't tell me anything," said Darling, his eyes narrowing, "but nothing goes on in here that I don't hear about. You ought to know that." He turned his attention to Wayne. "So your old man kicked you out," he sneered. "Maybe you're thinking of hooking up with me to rustle some soft money."

"I suppose you could call it being kicked out," said Wayne steadily. "But I'm not looking for any soft money."

"Then why did you come here?" Darling demanded sharply.

"I'll say curiosity, Darling," replied Wayne. "I wanted to meet you, and it's a fact that I don't know what I'm going to do."

Darling stared. Then he glanced at Hunter and swore softly. "Did you hear that?" he said. "He comes here out of curiosity, and you bring him."

Hunter nodded and blew a smoke ring. "He'll forget he's been here," he said. "I have his word and a Wayne's word is good. You didn't tell me you didn't want to see him."

This was the first inkling Wayne had that Darling might have been aware that he might visit him. Possibly the thing had been framed. For a moment his mind bristled with suspicion of

Hunter. But what would Hunter have to gain by any double-crossing?

Darling's queer, twisted smile was on his lips. "This is a new one," he said, his brow puckering. "Do you want to join up with my outfit?" he asked Wayne.

"That . . . would depend," said Wayne hesitantly. "I don't know as I would. But I'm not here as a spy or anything like that."

To his surprise, Darling laughed harshly. "Lot of good it would do you. A spy! If there's anybody welcome here, it's spies. If the soap holes around here could talk, they could tell a story. I'm not afraid of anybody on this range. Get every outfit together and let 'em try to get me. They'll grab a handful of free air and maybe a mouthful of dirt. Killin' a couple of men has gone to your head, fellow."

Wayne flushed with anger but kept back the hot words on his tongue. "I never coaxed any gun plays," he said, and was sorry as soon as he had said it.

"Well, you didn't side-step any, I'll give you credit for that," said Darling with a scowl. "You've done for a couple of good men and now you're here to make me like it, I gather. Go up to the end cabin." He waved his hand toward the cabin where Polly Arnold was confined. "There's a friend of yours up there." He bared his teeth in a vicious smile.

Wayne glanced at Hunter and thought he detected a glimmer of surprise in the man's eyes. Hunter signaled to him to go, and he left the room, closing the door behind him.

"Who is it?" Hunter asked sharply when Wayne had gone.

"It's Pete Arnold's girl," said Darling with a grin of triumph.

Hunter eyed him steadily and Darling frowned. "Kidnapped?" said Hunter. "I suppose you know what that means?"

"It's the softest play I ever had," said Darling angrily. "I'm asking fifty thousand to send her home . . . and I'll get it. That old fool isn't going to let his girl hang out with me any longer than it'll take him to get the money together, and you know it. I'm going to get more'n that, too. There's a bunch working on the north range tonight." He nodded, his eyes flashing fire.

Hunter was leaning forward in his chair. "It isn't going to be as soft as you think," he said. "The Bar A and Whippoorwill outfits will be on us with the sheriffs of two counties helping 'em. Stealing cattle is one thing, Darling, stealing a girl is another."

"You're gettin' blue behind the ears, Hunter," sneered Darling. "Don't you think I know? Arnold and Ed Wayne got into Rainbow this afternoon and half their outfits are there by now. I got the word straight. By this time Arnold's got the word from me. I told him he could find me and my men, maybe, but, if he started any rough stuff, he wouldn't find the girl."

Hunter stared at the cold cigarette butt between his fingers. "This means the end of this hang-out," he said quietly.

"Why not?" flared Darling. "This territory is played out anyway. After the clean-up, we cross the line. In Canada," he added with a significant nod, "we'll weed the trash out of our outfit. You and me have got a vacation coming."

Hunter met his gaze, tight-lipped, his eyes glistening. He knew what Darling meant. They would split the $50,000 between them and keep only enough men to handle the cattle Darling expected to run off from the north range while the two big cow outfits were away. And he knew, too, how Darling intended to weed out the men he didn't want. It showed in his cruel eyes. He had nothing to say.

"Now, can I trust you to take charge here tonight?" asked Darling.

"Why not?" Hunter asked shortly.

"All right," said Darling. "I'm going into town myself. Keep Wayne here. I let him see the girl because I may have to use him as a messenger yet . . . understand?" The dark eyes glowed with cunning. "He's telling her this very minute that he'll get her out." Again that twisted, sneering smile. "He can stay there talking to her all night so far's I'm concerned. But if he tries to get out of here, the look-outs will shoot him out of his saddle. I'm giving that order when I leave."

"I see," was all Hunter said.

Darling rose. The twilight had deepened until it was almost night. "If I shouldn't come back, Jim, it won't matter what you do," he said slowly. "There's just this. You went into this game with me, remember, and I expect you to play it. You're the only man I trust. I've played square with you."

He took down a slicker that was hanging behind the desk. The wind had freshened and there were more clouds. "So long," he said as he went out the door, leaving it open.

Hunter absently rolled a cigarette and lighted it. Then he went out to unsaddle his horse and Wayne's.

Chapter Twenty-Four

Wayne walked past the cabins toward the last one wondering what Darling had meant when he had said he would meet a friend. The meeting with Darling had been distasteful. Wayne knew he never could mingle with a band ruled by such a man. The glamour of outlawry, even of wild romance that had surrounded Darling in his imagination had been dissipated when the man had first spoken. Here was a cruel, rough bandit, who made his living, not by his wits, or through cleverness, but by dint of force, unscrupulous attack, bullying, and wanton use of his weapons, both guns and men. Wayne suspected that Darling trafficked considerably on his reputation. He could not understand how Jim Hunter had come to throw in with him. Perhaps there was a lot he didn't know—in which he suspected the truth.

It was just about dark when he came to the door of the far cabin. A figure was bending over the table, lighting the lamp. Wayne started back from the threshold with a little cry when he recognized Polly Arnold. He stood, looking at her as the lamplight framed her face against the shadows.

"Polly!" He stepped into the cabin. The girl looked at him steadily without speaking. "Polly, how did you get here?"

The girl pointed to his hat on the bunk. "A man brought me that at the hotel yesterday evening and told me you wanted to see me. I took his word and went with him. It was a scheme to get me here. That's easy to understand. But it's not so easy to understand how you come to be here . . . riding in of your own free will with one of Darling's outlaws. Is this what you've come to, Ted Wayne?" A rich scorn was in her voice; her eyes were cold.

"That hat?" said Wayne. "I lost it during the trouble. Darling kidnapped you?"

"You didn't know about it?" Polly inquired, raising her brows.

"What do you mean?" said Wayne sternly. "Of course I didn't know about it. Do you think I would have let this happen if I had known or suspected such a move by that cut-throat? Be sensible."

"But you're here, in his camp. He told me last night I would see you. He said you were coming here of your own accord. Those were his very words."

"He did?" Wayne was plainly mystified. His face froze in a frown. Hunter must have told the outlaw he was going to bring Wayne to the rendezvous, or else he had asked permission to do so. Then again, it might have been deliberately planned. Had Hunter known of the plan to kidnap Polly?

Wayne stepped to the door and looked out. No one was in sight. He turned back to the girl. "After the trouble with Jake Barry . . . I suppose you heard about it? I see. Well, I beat it with Hunter. I didn't think he was so bad for he befriended me. I didn't want to stay in town and have more gun play. I asked him to bring me here last night because I wanted to see this Darling out of pure curiosity and nothing else. I have no idea how Darling knew I was coming for we stayed at Hunter's cabin below here last night. So . . . it must have been arranged in advance." He paused and pressed his lips tightly. "That's how I come to be here and you know I don't lie. So put your mind to rest on that score. What did Darling say to you?"

"He wants my father to pay fifty thousand dollars to free me," said Polly slowly. "I wrote a short note saying I was where

Darling said I was . . . a note to Father. So he must have sent him word."

"Why the fool might know he can't get away with that!" Wayne exploded. He stared at her, thinking rapidly. "I'm going to get you out of here," he said in a low tone. "Do you know where you are?"

"In the bad country by the butte," replied the girl.

"You're in Devil's Hole," Wayne announced, "and nobody from our range except you and me has ever been in here. And what's more, Darling can stop anybody from getting in here. There's only one narrow entrance, a hard trail through quicksand."

He stepped again to the door and this time he saw Darling leaving the large cabin. He saw him beckon to a man and the man started off. Darling was carrying a slicker. He was going on a ride. When he had disappeared, Wayne saw Hunter come out of the cabin and go to their horses. As he started to unsaddle, Wayne again turned to the girl, standing on the other side of the table.

"I said I was going to get you out of here and I am," he said slowly. "I don't know just how I'm going to do it, but I'll make it if I have to shoot a way out. And it has to be done before Darling can get his hooks on that money. I just saw him go out with his slicker so he's riding somewhere, maybe to Rainbow."

"Ted!" the girl exclaimed. "I'm depending on him for my safety. He's the only one who can control the men. He said he hoped he wouldn't have to go for my sake."

"He's a liar to start with," said Wayne savagely. "Anyway, Hunter is unsaddling our horses so he must figure on staying here tonight, and I wouldn't leave you here under any circumstances. Polly, don't you believe me?" There was a pleading note in his voice, a pained look in his eyes.

"Yes, Ted," said the girl softly, "I believe you."

He took a step to go around the table and take her in his arms, but thought better of it. "Listen, Polly," he said in some excitement, "the clouds are bunching up and I reckon the heat we've had the last few days is bringing on a storm. I didn't see many men around and we did see a bunch leaving here before we came in. Hunter is practically the only man I have to reckon with. Put your light out early, and, if you hear two raps twice in succession, it'll be me. I'm going because I don't want Hunter to think we're framing anything. So long, girlie."

As he turned to the door, Polly hurried around the table, threw her arms about his neck impulsively, and kissed him. Then she held him off, breathless. "Don't do any more shooting, Ted," she said in a low voice. "I'd rather stay than. . . ."

"Leave it to me," he put in quickly. And then he was gone.

It now was dark. The gathering clouds were rapidly obscuring the stars. There was a wind, but it might be hours before the storm broke. There were flashing pale sheets of heat lightning.

Wayne met Hunter in front of the big cabin.

"We'll go over here," said Hunter, and he led the way to a smaller cabin. There was no one inside as they discovered when Hunter had lighted the lamp. There were four sets of bunks with two bunks to the set, one below and one above. A table and benches comprised the other furnishings.

Hunter closed the door. He sat on a bench by the table and Wayne sat on a lower bunk. Both rolled a cigarette.

"Do you know who's here?" Wayne asked, striking a match.

"Yes, Polly Arnold," replied Hunter coolly.

Wayne lighted his cigarette. He took a few puffs and put the question uppermost in his mind, looking Hunter straight in the eye. "Did you know Darling was going to kidnap Polly?"

"No," replied Hunter with a frown. "First I knew of her being here was when Darling told me a bit ago. How is she?"

"Oh, she's all right," said Wayne. "But it isn't a very pleasant situation for a girl to be in. It's a dangerous piece of work, Hunter. It'll make a hornets' nest out of this whole range. This is once when Darling will find things too hot for him."

"This isn't an easy place to get into," mused Hunter. "And there are guards on the outside with orders to shoot to kill."

Wayne wondered if this was said for his benefit. "Are we going to stay here tonight, then?" he asked.

"Yes," was the short answer.

"Has Darling gone away?"

"He's gone to Rainbow where your dad and Pete Arnold are this minute," said Hunter.

"Then the Bar A and Whippoorwill outfits will be following 'em," said Wayne. "Darling has nerve, at that."

"No one ever has accused him of not having it," Hunter remarked dryly. "He's safe enough, maybe, with the girl here."

Wayne wanted to ask him how Darling knew, or professed to know, that Wayne would be coming to the rendezvous, but he held back the question. Hunter pulled off his boots and took off some of his clothing. "Blow the light out when you turn in," he said with a yawn as he lay down on one of the bunks and turned his face to the wall.

Wayne smoked another cigarette before he put out the light and lay down in the bunk fully clothed. The lightning was playing, but there was no thunder. Wayne watched the pale flashes light the window and slowly evolved his plan.

Ed Wayne and Pete Arnold did not ride fast, and before they reached Rainbow in the late afternoon some members of the Bar A and WP outfits had caught up with them. The WP owner gave the order to stay out of the resorts and avoid any trouble.

When they had put up their horses, the two stockmen sought Fred Hastings. But Hastings knew nothing of what had happened the night before save for what his night man had told him. And this was substantially what he had told Jack McCurdy.

Ed Wayne and Arnold then went to The Three Colors. Miles Henseler invited them at once into his private office.

First they heard the resortkeeper's account of the meeting between Ted Wayne and Jake Barry. Henseler was careful to absolve Ted of all blame. He appeared nervous and his glances roved.

"Where did Ted go afterward?" Ed Wayne asked.

"He rode away with Hunter. He had to get out because that crowd of Barry's was set to get him any way they could."

"Have you any idea where he went with Hunter?" Ed Wayne demanded.

"No," replied Henseler. Replying to further questions he said he knew Polly Arnold had been in town, but thought she had gone home. He was genuinely astonished and puzzled when he learned she had disappeared.

"I don't know anything about it," he declared. "If . . . if Darling grabbed her, she's safe enough. He's wise enough not to harm her. I . . . well, I don't know anything about it and that's the straight truth. I wouldn't lie to either of you, anyway. But I have to be careful here and keep on the outside. I've got a peculiar trade."

He had hardly finished when there was a knock on the door. A bartender handed him an envelope. He closed the door and looked at it. "Why, it's for you, Pete," he said, handing the envelope to the stockman.

Arnold tore it open and found two notes. He read them and his face went gray. Without a word he passed them to Ed Wayne. Wayne read Polly Arnold's brief message first, and then one from Darling.

Your girl is safe with me at present. I want $50,000 cash, delivered to me by you in person and alone. Go to Rainbow when you get this *and wait for word which will come from me. If you raise a fuss things won't be too good.*

Darling

Pete Arnold was wiping beads of sweat from his forehead and hands. Ed Wayne's eyes had narrowed. He handed the notes to Henseler and turned to Arnold. "You're here," he said. "The only thing to do is to wait for the word from that cut-throat."

Henseler was staring at the notes, wetting his lips with his tongue. Arnold spoke to him in a low voice. "Henseler, have you got fifty thousand in cash?" he asked.

"Why . . . yes," replied the resortkeeper. "It'll cut me short, but you can have it if you want it."

"I'll give you a three-day note," said Arnold grimly. "Now Ed and me are goin' to the hotel. I suppose the word'll come through here." He took the two notes and pocketed them.

"Now understand, I've got nothing to do with this," said Henseler earnestly. "If Darling wants to leave word here for somebody, I can't very well help it. I'll try to find out who brought this in."

"Never mind," said Ed Wayne sharply. "Just remember where we are, although Darling's spies will find out quick enough."

As the two stockmen went out, Wayne told Arnold the wording of the note from Darling, instructing him to come to Rainbow, showed that the outlaw had expected the note to be delivered at the Bar A. Such being the case, the notes had been sent in the morning. "It won't be long before he knows we're here," he finished.

By midnight most of the Bar A and WP outfits were in town. And it was then that a messenger came with word for Arnold to go to The Three Colors.

"I've a good notion to throw the men around that place,"

said Ed Wayne. "We might. . . ."

"No," said Arnold. "I can't take any risks or make any hostile moves until Polly is safe at home. When I have her back, we'll wipe Darling and his gang out clean, and without botherin' any sheriffs. You stay here. I'll go up there alone."

Ten minutes later the visibly shaken Henseler led him to a rear room in the resort and Arnold found himself facing Darling.

"Don't try any tricks," warned the outlaw, his eyes gleaming, cold and hard. "If we don't come to terms at this meeting, we may never meet again. I know about the men you and old Wayne have got in town. Are you going to shell out?"

"Where's Polly?" asked Arnold, struggling to control his voice.

"I didn't come here to answer questions, but to ask 'em," said Darling in a sinister voice. "Are you going to come across? I'm telling you I haven't got much time."

With a great effort Arnold kept a grip on himself. "Take me to Polly and turn her over to me and I'll pay the money," he said. He knew it would be futile to threaten the man before him. And his whole concern was for his daughter.

"You've arranged for the money?" Darling asked sternly.

"Yes," said Arnold after hesitating several moments.

"All right," said Darling in a satisfied tone. "Stay here in town. And see that old Wayne stays in town. And keep all your men right here in town. I'll turn the girl over to you within twenty-four hours in my own way. That's giving myself plenty of time and that's the way I want it. And you can't make a move without me knowing it."

The skies had been muttering faintly, and now, as if to stress the outlaw's words, there was a distinct peal of thunder.

"You hear?" said Darling. "That may slow me up." He stepped to the door and whirled. "If there ever was a time in your life to watch out and not make a false move, it's now," he said slowly. His eyes burned into Arnold's.

"Take good care of Polly," said Arnold, his voice coming strong and stern. "You know why I'm payin' over this money, Darling. It's to get her back as quick as possible. I'm not afraid of you and I don't care a rap about the gang of desperadoes that trail with you. After this thing is settled this country will be too hot to hold you. I reckon that will be worth the money, too."

Darling laughed insolently in his face. "Brave talk," he sneered. "How about me? I'm in town with the two biggest outfits on the range here. Some of your men are out front now. That's how much I think of you making it hot for me! Keep your mouth shut and follow the orders I send you or you'll need more men than you can get to find your . . . Polly." The twisted, vicious smile showed below the narrowed eyes.

Before Arnold could reply, the outlaw had slipped out the door and was gone. A deafening crash of thunder was the signal of his going.

Chapter Twenty-Five

The wind lashed the trees in Devil's Hole. It roared above in a wild frenzy as the lightning flashes multiplied and streaked vivid and blue-white across the inky sky. Ted Wayne assumed it was midnight when he got up from the bunk. The lightning showed him Hunter in his bunk, to all appearances sound asleep. Wayne had made up his mind that to stop him Hunter would have to draw down on him and shoot. He took Hunter's gun from the holster on the table and spilled the cartridges into the bunk, covering them with the blanket. He replaced the empty gun. It did not strike him until later that it was strange Hunter should leave his gun on the table like that. He let himself silently out the door.

It was the work of minutes to get his saddle and bridle from the lean-to shed he had noted when entering the rendezvous. It was not so easy to catch up his horse, but in a short time he had done so and had saddled and bridled the animal. He did not attempt to catch Polly Arnold's horse. Time counted. He tied his horse just below the cabins and hurried back to the cabin occupied by the girl.

The thunder was rumbling and the wind shrieking down from the shoulders of the butte. Polly answered his raps on the door almost instantly. She handed him his own hat, which he exchanged for the one he wore as they ran from the cabin. A foolish detail he thought as he mounted behind the girl on his horse. "No time to get yours," he told her and rode down into the trail that led through the trees to the narrow entrance to the Hole.

A mighty crash of thunder rocked the world as they reached the opening and saw ahead a great soap hole with a ghastly covering of white over its treacherous, sucking sands. Instantly the skies opened and the rain drove into their faces in a solid sheet. All was obliterated save when the lightning brought out the trees, the ragged ridges, and the white sheet of the soap hole in clear relief. The velocity of the wind increased. Branches were torn from trees and hurled into others or sent flying over the tops. The lightning flashes followed each other at such short intervals that they seemed like a winking light in the universe. Thunder crashed with a violence that seemed to shake the very earth.

Wayne had heard of the terrific storms that centered about the butte. Never had he seen one like this. He got off the horse and helped Polly down, the onslaught of wind and blinding rain taking away their breath.

"I'll go ahead," he shouted in her ear, "and lead the horse! Follow right behind the horse and don't take a step to one side or the other! We go around the edge of the quicksand, but there's a place where we have to cross it!" He grasped her hand for a moment, and then started, leading his mount.

The water ran in streams down their faces and they had to shake their eyes free of it continuously. The lightning now seemed one long, lasting flash. Above, the detonations of the thunder were like a series of mighty explosions. Wayne had no fear of being shot by a look-out in that upheaval of the elements. No man could shoot accurately in the blinding lightning and the stinging rain. He had noted carefully the route by which they had come in and Hunter had been careful to warn him at the more dangerous spots in the narrow trail. He went slowly, feeling his way, making sure that each foot, as he put it forward, was on solid ground before he put his weight upon it. The horse seemed to sense the danger and was led willingly and easily enough. They came to the short stretch of hard trail that led straight across the quicksand. Wayne had taken bearings ahead and behind when he had crossed this with Hunter who had warned him. The lightning showed him the dead, leaning tree ahead that was his mark. He kept his eyes upon it and proceeded step by step, taking a step only when the lightning flashed. The crossing seemed to take hours. Once the horse stepped off the hard trail and lunged ahead to draw its leg out of the grasping morass. Wayne was knocked to his knees and got to his feet in a panic that sent a cold chill up his spine. The next lightning flash showed him the horse and Polly behind. He went forward—two steps—three, four, five—and they were across. Just as they gained the wide, firm ground, the wind tore the dead tree free of its rotten roots and hurled it into the quivering bog.

Wayne helped Polly into the saddle and climbed up behind her. He held her firmly with his left arm as they moved into the trail that wound around a high ridge and turned south. They were drenched to the skin and the water ran in a steady stream from their riding boots. Not for an instant did the ferocity of the storm slacken. But now they had the wind at their backs most of the time. They did not know that ahead of them Darling was fighting his way back to the rendezvous, cursing the storm, but jubilant, nevertheless, at the ease with which he had brought Pete Arnold to time.

"Like finding it in the street!" he shouted to the wind. Even in the fury of the storm he found time to plan. Divide the fifty thousand with his men? Never! He would make them think the girl's capture was a ruse to draw the Bar A and WP outfits off the range, leaving the cattle unprotected. The raids, even then being started, would net them a thousand head. He had seen to it that the outfits would stay in town all next day. It would take them all night to get back to their herds. But would they go back? Darling bowed his head against the driving rain and wind. He believed he knew old Wayne. As soon as the girl was returned, they would start to comb the badlands. It might be three days before they returned to their home range. Thus Darling's warped imagination betrayed him. And Hunter and Wayne. A deadly thought came into the outlaw's brain. Why bother with them? Why bother with the cattle? Why not take the money and go—alone. If he had to do it, two shots would rid him of dangerous pursuit. His thoughts were in keeping with the wild ferocity of the raging storm.

Wayne and Polly Arnold rode on. Wayne had taken note of every intersection on the trail and he followed his course unerringly. The storm reached its highest pitch, lashing the trees and strewing the trail with broken branches and débris so that they had to ride slowly. A thunderbolt crashed and a blazing ball of fire leaped at them. The next instant the world seemed torn apart about their heads. The horse stopped and they sat stunned as a tall tree, its trunk ripped to ribbons, plunged into the trail with a thread of flame running its length. The rain licked up the flame and smoke took its place.

Wayne looked about and caught sight of an overhanging shelf of rock. He dismounted and led the horse into its shelter. Here Polly slipped from the saddle and Wayne took her in his arms and held her close as the storm raced and roared past them. While they were here, Darling picked his way carefully around the fallen tree and rode on toward the rendezvous, his nefarious plan burning in his brain.

With the thunderbolt that struck the tree, it appeared that the storm spent its fury. The rain lessened and the wind began to abate. The intervals between the lightning flashes lengthened and the artillery in the skies rolled off into the southeast.

When Wayne and the girl again gained the trail beyond the

point where it was blocked, the stars were breaking out and the rain had ceased. Soon they were on ground that Wayne had traversed more than once. They finally emerged upon the plain south of the butte and turned toward Rainbow.

"Your dad is in town," Wayne told Polly. "And mine is there with him. Hunter told me so."

The girl didn't answer. She leaned back against his shoulder, a great weariness upon her. Now that she was safe, the reaction was taking its toll.

At dawn they rode into Rainbow, and Wayne turned down behind the buildings on the north side of Main Street to the livery. There they dismounted and Wayne helped the girl into the warm kitchen of the hotel. Already preparations for breakfast were under way and soon Polly was reviving under the stimulus of hot, strong coffee. Wayne drank a cup himself, and then shot a question at the clerk who came in for his early breakfast.

Wayne hurried upstairs and rapped sharply on the door of Pete Arnold's room. The stockman was up in a minute, calling out in an excited tone. He had the $50,000 in his coat pocket. Was Darling sending the word so soon?

He opened the door and stepped back with a startled exclamation.

"I just brought Polly back," said Wayne crisply. "She's down in the kitchen, getting dry and taking some coffee. Are any men here?"

Arnold's eyes shone. "Your outfit and ours are in town," he answered. "Is Polly all right? Is she . . . ?"

"She's wet and tired, that's all," Wayne snapped out. "Go down and see her. I'm taking the Whippoorwill outfit into the Rainbow breaks after Darling. Does your outfit go along?"

Ed Wayne, whose room was next to Arnold's, had heard and now he came out into the hall, looking keenly at Ted.

"Sure," said Arnold. "Do you know where to go?"

"I just brought Polly from there," Wayne answered grimly. He saw his father and now Jim McCurdy came into the hall.

"McCurdy is here," said Ed Wayne. "He'll get the men together."

"All right, Mac," said Ted. "But I'm taking charge. Get the men out. Here's Payne. Get your crowd together, Payne. It's Arnold's orders." The Bar A owner was nodding vigorously. Ed Wayne was staring at Ted.

"Did Darling's gang come into town last night?" Ted asked McCurdy.

"Not as I know of, and I reckon I'd have heard," was the answer.

"Then they're raiding the cattle while you're gone!" Ted exclaimed, his mind leaping to a swift and sure conclusion. "Let's get going. We want Darling, but tell the men not to bother Hunter. And we haven't got all day!"

Half an hour later the Bar A and Whippoorwill outfits rode swiftly out of town with Ted Wayne, mounted on a fresh horse, at their head.

Chapter Twenty-Six

It still was dark when Darling, who knew the trail well, rode into the rendezvous. There was a light burning in the cook shack off the large cabin and he saw a horse, saddled and bridled, which he recognized as Hunter's. What . . . ? He spurred his horse and rode up to the cook shack at a thundering gallop. He flung himself from the saddle and stood in the doorway. The cook was up and Hunter was there.

Hunter regarded him coldly.

"Was you going out?" asked Darling, his words knife-edged.

"I expected you any minute," was Hunter's reply.

"Oh." There was relief in Darling's voice and eyes. He beckoned to Hunter to come outside, and, when they were beyond earshot of the cook, Darling spoke hurriedly. "I saw Arnold in town. He gave in without a struggle. I've got to take the girl down and turn her over to him and he said he'd have the cash ready. I guess he got it from Henseler. Yes, that's about the size of it." He wiped his face with a big bandanna.

"The girl's gone," said Hunter in a flat voice.

The hand holding the handkerchief came down. Darling stared, jaw sagging, as if he couldn't believe his ears. "Gone?" he said, looking incredulous. "Gone, you say? Where?" He looked about vacantly.

"I don't know," said Hunter. "Wayne's gone, too. You said the guards had orders to shoot to kill and I told him that. If he tried to get the girl away, the chances are he's shot, or else the two of them are in the soap hole. I reckon we better get going and see."

"Wayne, too!" Darling's voice was as hard as flint and sibilant. "You let 'em get away, eh?"

"Listen to me," said Hunter sternly. "Did you expect me to sit up all night after you boasting about how well the place was protected and how nobody could get out? Maybe that was meant for me as well as Wayne, for all I know. I went to sleep. The storm woke me up and there was a lump in the bunk I thought was Wayne. I could only get a glimpse when the lightning broke. The storm got rough and I got up and lit the lamp. Then I learned things."

Darling's face was purple with rage. For a wild moment he thought of drawing down on Hunter and dropping him in his tracks. But there was a certain logic in what Hunter had said, and Darling was nervous and not in his best form after the hard ride through the storm.

"They didn't pass me," he fumed. "How'd they get the horses? And all this without waking you up!" His eyes were dark with suspicion and Hunter never for an instant took his gaze from his face.

"They only took one horse," he said. "That was Wayne's. If they didn't pass you, why. . . ." He paused, puzzled. It would seem but natural that Wayne would make for Rainbow. Hunter had told him his father and Arnold were there, and he had surmised at once that the ranch outfits would follow.

"Maybe they got off the trail," said Darling. "I didn't see a guard or any signs of shootin' when I rode in. Maybe they got lost. And now that it's getting daylight, they'll find the trail again. I'll catch up a fresh horse and we'll hit the trail. There's fifty thousand cold waiting in Rainbow and I've got their outfits sewed up there. Arnold listened hard. Tell that cook I'll want a cup of coffee before we start."

He was unsaddling before he finished speaking.

"Go in and get your coffee," said Hunter. "I'll take care of the horse and get you a fresh one."

Darling took him at his word and went into the cook shack. Hunter took the saddle off the spent horse, removed the bridle, and turned the animal loose. Then he caught up a fresh horse and saddled it. It was Polly Arnold's mount.

Darling came out shortly and swung into the saddle without a word. He led the way down the trail until they came to where the trees opened at the edge of the soap hole. The cold light of dawn was spreading from the east. Darling whistled, sending the peculiar signal splitting through the still air.

A man appeared from the trees on the right. "All right!" he called, hurrying toward them.

"What's all right?" Darling blurted. "Where's Bill?"

"That's what I'm wonderin'," was the answer. "Haven't seen him since before the storm. Maybe. . . ."

"Have you seen anybody else tonight?" Darling demanded savagely.

"Only you when you rode in," came the sullen reply.

"Where were you during the storm?" Darling asked smoothly.

"I was back in the timber a ways. It was a terror, wasn't it? Why, is something wrong?"

Darling swore horribly. "Yes, there's something wrong!" he shouted. "You're wrong, see, you . . . you . . . !" His hand flashed at his hip and his gun cracked sharply. The look-out flung up a hand and toppled over backward.

Hunter's eyes were narrowed to slits when Darling looked quickly at him, his lower lip drawn back against his teeth.

"You'll ride ahead," said Hunter sharply, and Darling started as he saw that Hunter had drawn his gun in a flash.

"He had it coming . . . the rat," said Darling as he sheathed his weapon. Then he started on in the lead.

When they had crossed the treacherous bit of trail across the quicksand, Darling reined in suddenly, pointing to the hard ground. "Look at that sign!" he ejaculated.

Hunter leaned from the saddle and saw the imprints of a horse's hoofs that the rain had failed to wash entirely away. "They got across," he decided.

"And they got lost!" thundered Darling. "Now they're looking for the trail, that's about the size of it. Come on!"

He led the way at a swift pace, continually leaning from the saddle to scan the trail. "Still on the trail here!" he called back several times when the tracks left by Wayne's horse showed in favorable spots on the trail.

The sun was up when they came to the tree blocking the trail. They circled it through the timber and had been on the trail but a short time when Darling's lips streamed curses. "Still on it!" he called back to Hunter with a horrible oath. His rage began to center on the man riding behind him. If Wayne hadn't lost his way, he had made town long before this. And he had gotten away from Hunter! And Hunter had commanded Darling to ride ahead! He was suspicious, then. Suspicion in any form, in so far as it concerned himself, was something Darling never had countenanced in his band. He had been a fool to tell Hunter to bring Wayne to the rendezvous if he killed Barry. He had made the biggest mistake of his doubtful career. Why had he done it? Sheer bravado? Curiosity? Did he think he could get Wayne mixed up with his crowd just because Wayne had had trouble with his father? He had had an idea that by getting Wayne involved with the band, it would help him in his rustling. But he hadn't then known Polly Arnold was in town or received the inspiration that led to her abduction. He cursed freely as they rode down the trail.

When they reached the lower stretch, which, as Darling well knew, Wayne had covered before, the outlaw gave up hope of overtaking the fugitives before they made town.

He slowed his pace and called back to Hunter. "We'll take a look in the open, but I guess he made it!" Then he drove in his spurs and they raced down the trail at breakneck speed. Darling knew he was not riding one of his own horses. He knew of none of his men who possessed as good a mount as the one he was on. Then he suspected the truth. He was riding the girl's horse. It was another mark against Hunter, although he had to admit that Hunter had picked the best horse available for him. But if he was seen on it, Arnold would swear he had stolen it. His brain was aflame. The world was whirling red. He raked the horse with the spurs again and dashed down the little valley that was the entrance to the badlands. At the lower end, his caution thrown to the wide winds, he plunged through the creek, still sinking the steel in the horse's flanks. As the tortured animal lunged up the bank and burst through the trees, it stumbled, throwing its rider over his head.

Even as he was hurtling through the air, he saw the horsemen. The Whippoorwill and Bar A outfits! He struck the ground with a curse exploding on his lips. A yell went up from the riders and in a few moments Darling and Hunter were surrounded. Hunter had flung himself from the saddle. He seemed to know what was coming as Darling scrambled to his feet and looked about, his eyes blazing. He saw Hunter as through a veil of blood.

"You're first!" he yelled. "You double-crossing . . . !"

His gun spoke too late. Hunter had drawn with the speed of lightning when Darling's right hand had winked at his side. The report of guns seemed to fill the air like a crash of thunder in the imagination of Wayne and the men with him. Darling sank to the ground and a single bullet sped wildly from his gun.

In the upstairs parlor of the hotel at Rainbow a small group was gathered. Pete Arnold and Ed Wayne were there. Ted was present, and Hunter.

"There isn't any use of you folks talking to me," Hunter was saying in a cold voice. "You've sent your men to the north range and what they find, they'll find. I'm not a rustler. The only thing I'll tell you is that I knew nothing of this kidnapping business until after it had been carried out. Darling is dead. I'm sorry I had to do it, but I had the idea all along that someday it . . . would come. I'm leaving town."

He rose and turned to the door.

"I want to see you a minute," said Ed Wayne, and he followed him out into the hall. There he pressed a roll of bills into his hand. "It's the ten thousand I promised you," he said. "You've turned the trick."

"I'll take the ten thousand, but no credit," said Hunter.

Wayne felt slightly embarrassed. "I was wondering if you would take a good job on my ranch, Jim," he said slowly.

"I'm too old to mess around with cows," said Hunter grimly. "But I'm much obliged. So long."

Ed Wayne watched him walk rapidly down the hall and turn down the stairs. As he opened the door into the parlor, he saw Arnold and Ted standing close to each other and Arnold was extending his hand.

"Well, I'm glad to see you don't hate each other," grunted the WP owner.

"I was congratulatin' Ted, not for rescuin' Polly . . . he doesn't have to be congratulated for that . . . but for, well . . . for something else," said Arnold. "I reckon we live too close together for any misunderstandings, Ed."

"I've never thought anything else," said Ed Wayne. He looked straight into Ted's eyes. "Hunter told me about Boyd," he said slowly, "and what happened up there on the rim of the Hole. I wish you'd have told me yourself. We'll . . . we will ride home after dinner."

"I think you and me being old-timers better ride back together," said Pete Arnold. "We'll let Ted take Polly home."

The prairie flowed like gold under the crimson banners of the sunset. On the north range a band of riders was fleeing for the line and the cattle they had tried to steal were scattered behind another group of riders in fast pursuit. But in the south, all was calm.

Ted Wayne and Polly Arnold had stopped at the spring. They were standing hand in hand, looking at the glory in the west as their horses nibbled the grass behind them.

"Polly," said Wayne in a soft voice, "I've had enough of it. I never knew till . . . till in the hotel in Rainbow how much I love you. Is your promise still good?"

She looked up with a glad light in her eyes. "It was always good, Ted, boy," she murmured. "I lied to you that day."

He took her in his arms. "If you always tell lies like that, sweetheart, we'll be happy for ever." Then he kissed her.

They rode slowly homeward in the sunset's afterglow, with a silvery blue sky above them, and a soft, sweet wind in their faces.

ABOUT THE AUTHOR

Robert J. Horton was born in Coudersport, Pennsylvania in 1889. As a very young man he traveled extensively in the American West, working for newspapers. For several years he was sports editor for the Great Falls *Tribune* in Great Falls, Montana. He began writing Western fiction for Munsey's *All-Story Weekly* magazine before becoming a regular contributor to Street & Smith's *Western Story Magazine*. By the mid-1920s Horton was one of three authors to whom Street & Smith paid 5¢ a word—the other two being Frederick Faust, perhaps better known as Max Brand, and Robert Ormond Case. Some of Horton's serials for Street & Smith's *Western Story Magazine* were subsequently brought out as books by Chelsea House, Street & Smith's book publishing company. Although all of Horton's stories appeared under his byline in the magazine, for their book editions Chelsea House published them either as by Robert J. Horton or by James Roberts. Sometimes, as was the case with *Rovin' Redden* (Chelsea House, 1925) by James Roberts, a book would consist of three short novels that were editorially joined to form a "novel" and seriously abridged in the process. Other times the stories were magazine serials, also abridged to appear in book form, such as *Unwelcome Settlers* (Chelsea House, 1925) by James Roberts or *The Prairie Shrine* (Chelsea House, 1924) by Robert J. Horton. It may be obvious that Chelsea House, doing a number of books a year by the same author, thought it a prudent marketing strategy to give the author more than one name. Horton's Western stories are concerned most of all with character, and it is the characters that drive the plots rather than the other way around. Attended by his personal physician, he died of bronchial pneumonia in his Manhattan hotel room in 1934 at the relatively early age of forty-four. Several of his novels, after Street & Smith abandoned Chelsea House, were published only in British editions, and Robert J. Horton was not to appear at all in paperback books until quite recently. *Raiders of Blue Dome* will be his next Five Star Western.